# AUPRÈS DE MA BLONDE

# Auprès
# de ma Blonde

## NICOLAS
## FREELING

VINTAGE BOOKS
*A Division of Random House*
*New York*

Library of Congress Cataloging in Publication Data
Freeling, Nicolas.
Auprès de ma blonde.

In English.
I. Title.
PZ4.F854Au     1979     [PR6056.R4]     823'.9'14
ISBN 0-394-74550-7     79-10783

Manufactured in the United States of America

Dans le jardin de mon père les lauriers sont fleuris:
Tous les oiseaux du ciel y viennent faire leur nid—
La caille, la tourterelle, et la jolie perdrix,
Et ma jolie colombe qui chante jour et nuit.
Auprès de ma blonde, qu'il fait bon, fait bon, fait bon
—Auprès de ma blonde, qu'il fait bon dormir!

Et ma jolie colombe, qui chante jour et nuit,
Qui chante pour les filles qui n'ont pas de mari—
Ne chante pas pour elle: elle en a un joli!
Il est dans la Hollande, les Hollandais l'ont pris.
Auprès de ma blonde, qu'il fait bon, fait bon, fait bon
—Auprès de ma blonde qu'il fait bon dormir!

Que donnerez-vous, belle, pour revoir votre ami?
Je donnerai Versailles, Paris et Saint-Denis,
Les tours de Notre-Dame, le clocher de mon pays,
Et ma jolie colombe qui chante jour et nuit . . .
Auprès de ma blonde, qu'il fait bon, fait bon, fait bon
—Auprès de ma blonde, qu'il fait bon dormir!


In my father's garden the bay trees have bloomed.
All the birds of the sky are come to make their nest:
the amorous quail, the loving turtledove, the pretty
partridge, and my sweet bird of peace. . . .

Sweet bird of peace sings night and day. Sings for the
girls who have no man—but not for her; she has a man
and a lovely one he is! He is in Holland. The Dutch
have taken him. . . .

v

What will you give, then, pretty girl, to have your lover back again? I would give all of Versailles, Paris and Saint-Denis. I would give the towers of Notre-Dame, and my village steeple. And I would give, too, my sweet bird of peace, who sings to me all day and all night. . . .

It is, of course, a military march and not a children's rhyme at all. The chorus is the *perpetuum mobile* of a route march, exactly like Kipling's

> Boots—boots—boots—boots—
> movin' up and down again!
> There's no discharge in the war!

It would be possible to say that the first strophe was an allegro vivace, the second an andante, and the last a maestoso; for to this day the ski troops, the chasseurs alpins, march to an unusually rapid tempo, whereas the Foreign Legion have an unusually slow time, that of the Roman legionaries.

"Saint-Denis"—a bitter little reference. In the parish church of this village outside the walls of Paris, the kings and queens of France were by tradition buried.

Atqui sciebat quae sibi Barbarus
Tortor pararet. Non aliter tamen
    Dimovit obstantes propinquos,
        Et populum reditus morantem,
Quam si clientum longa negotia
Dijudicata lite relinqueret,
    Tendens Venafranos in agros,
        Aut Lacedaemonium Tarentum.


—Horace, *Odes,* Book III, No. V.


He knew perfectly what torment his barbarous
enemies held destined for him. Nevertheless he gently
pushed aside his family who sought to prevent his passing: he made a way through the crowd that tried to
delay his departure, and embarked for Carthage with
mien as contented as if, having finished the affairs of his
clients, he were leaving to unburden himself of painful
labors in the fields of Venafrum or the smiling countryside of Tarentum.

—Translation in the eighteenth-century French
of Father Sanadon (Amsterdam: Wetstein &
Smith, 1735). English version by N.F.

PART ONE:

# In the Way
# to Study a Long Silence

WHEN DICK STOPPED to look into the jeweler's window, it was for no good reason, or even for a bad one. The little ends of thread leading nowhere that govern our lives, and can suddenly plait themselves together into a cord strong enough to hang a dog by.

Dick wanted to eat his sandwich. He hadn't really wanted the sandwich, and certainly not in that smelly snack bar, but he had some kind of nervous hunger which was making his stomach rumble. Nor did he want to eat it in the crowded street, and this was a good place, a privileged position, for the jeweler's sat back in a sort of bay where the pavement was broader, where the window-gazer was not bumped by the restless eddy of passers; privileged because most of Amsterdam's shopping streets are narrow and noisy, but this was not a place for zircon engagement rings and little plated charms, where you go for an alarm clock. A sanctum all dim light and ash-gray velvet; and when you go inside valuable but useless antiques like sedan chairs or inlaid chess tables are scattered casually about.

There was not really much to see: the shop was deep

3

but narrow, and had thick armor glass masked by baroque wrought-iron grilles, themselves masking sophisticated alarm systems. But the door pleased him: also very thick and heavy, a sort of glass box, or perhaps a glass coffin, thought Dick, standing up on end. It was divided into many shallow glass shelves, and these were filled with the little items of bric-à-brac which are good publicity because they are eye-catching —snuffboxes, scent bottles, uncut semiprecious stones, tortoise-shell whatnots studded with brilliants, and little figurines of amber or soapstone.

Dick chewed leisurely at his sandwich—a Dutch sandwich, a roll sliced lengthwise and overflowing with tough roast beef—and admired a little silver coach harnessed to six tiny silver horses, and became aware of a fish, a fish which swims up to the glass of an aquarium and goggles at the goggling spectator. He was being observed, probably with disapproval because he was blocking the entrance, or worse still, because he might be a hippie who would break something, or take something, not even to steal but just for the hell of it: no, he was neat, clean, and wearing a carefully pressed suit; he looked like what he was, a quiet, well-brought-up boy. He didn't care, anyway; he was doing no harm. Then the door opened slightly, and he still didn't care but chewed on stolidly. No law against eating in the street. If he had a lot of money, and wanted a snuffbox badly, maybe to keep pills in—then perhaps he would fancy that little enamel one, were it not that he took no pills, didn't want a snuffbox, and hadn't any money. He paid no attention to the silent figure watching him until the voice spoke, and then he was surprised at the voice not being hostile but friendly, and perhaps a thought amused.

"Good appetite."

Dick swallowed and, being a neat boy, found a paper tissue in his pocket and wiped his mouth carefully and then his hands, grinning back at the man, because anyway he was not being picked up with distaste like a scrap of fluff and deposited in a nice clean ashtray.

"Just killing time," he said easily. "Got a business date but a bit early. Doesn't do to be too early." It was not the prissy elderly stick in a black coat he would have expected, but a young man not much older than himself—well, not over thirty anyhow. Casual fair hair, casual tweed suit. Wearing more money; that was the only real difference. He was leaning against the door pillar, hands in pockets, smiling a bit, not patronizing or supercilious, considering Dick with alert amused brown eyes.

"You don't bother me at all. Relax all you please."

"Like you?"

"Oh, me . . . we're Oriental in this business. People come, go, buy nothing; it doesn't bother us. We've time for everything—and everyone. Looking, like yourself." He offered a cigarette case, plain silver, hammered, a nice one.

"Thanks," said Dick, taking a cigarette happily. "First today."

"Cutting down?"

"Just rationed."

"Ah—money tight," with sympathy, as though he knew all about that despite the case, the very good watch, the gold signet on the hand.

"Money nonexistent," as the lighter clicked. "Thanks."

"What's your business date?" Not in a prying way, just easily interested.

"Oh—job—possibly."

"Good one?"

"No, lousy. Selling some junk."

"Want it badly?"

"Yes, but not that one!" And both smiles blossomed into laughs. Suddenly the door opened wider and the man said, "Come in," politely.

"Why?" asked Dick, surprised.

"You've got a bit of time? Good: maybe I can offer you something more interesting," loosely, making a loose gesture with the hand, which was small and thin but tanned. "I've time, too."

Why not? thought Dick, said "Why not?" and stepped inside with a show of negligence. Nice, inside. Lights were dim but would suddenly glitter on things. The velvet was a faded apricot, and went back a long long way. At the front were modern showcases, and further back a jumble of ancient objects, but all in all, thought Dick vaguely, a hell of a lot of fancy things, complete quiet a meter away from the street, and most pleasurable quantities of money. Gave one an illusion of wealth, nice even if only an illusion.

"Like this," said the man reasonably. "Everything happens together. There should be a manager and an assistant here. The one was old and due to retire. So he retires, his right, and I take his place provisionally. And the assistant goes off for something—to bury a relative, I do believe—and probably has one too many, because what does he do but fall downstairs and break a shoulder. Which leaves me with the short straw."

"You're the owner?" asked Dick a bit dubiously: the man seemed too young, somehow.

"I'm Mr. Prinz's nephew, Larry Saint—at your service. Mr. Prinz's the owner. But he's away most of the while—valuations; he's a leading expert."

"I see—or I don't really see. You mean you're offering me a job as sort of assistant? But I know nothing

6

about a business like this. Anyway, you don't know me from Adam. And doesn't one have to be bonded or whatever they call it? I mean, hell—it's sort of sudden, isn't it?"

"My dear man," patiently. "If you're not interested, then say no more. Maybe your other offer's better. As you justly remark, there isn't a great deal of money for an untrained man."

"I didn't mean that—I only meant I'm standing there eating a sandwich and you just throw the idea at me. Thought you'd have advertised or something."

"Quite so," equable, "and what is advertising but taking people off the street? This is a high-class business and, as I remarked, Oriental. We want an untrained young man to learn this individual job. Even if we wanted a trained man, we wouldn't bother advertising—we'd work by word of mouth. I saw you, and I used my eyes. You're personable and obviously intelligent. And you're looking for a job, you tell me. What more do we need? You speak politely, with an educated manner. You know nothing, and that has no importance. We get maybe ten serious customers a day. Those you hand on to me, or stall politely if I happen to be absent. For the rest, you murmur polite phrases and butter up the idlers who haven't the remotest intention of buying anything. For this, we'll pay you. Not perhaps terribly much, but if you stay, and learn, and pick up the jargon, more. All we really need is for someone who is always there; if I'm called away, I dislike putting a notice on the door saying 'Back Soon,' or 'Closed on Account of Yom Kippur,' or some such pawnbroker's phrase. As for being bonded," with a shrug at this notion, "there's nothing to pinch here. Too easy to identify," and the hand flicked casually at an ivory figure with pieces of jade grouped around it. "This isn't the

7

Prisunic. If it doesn't appeal, of course—no harm done."

"Of course it appeals," said Dick, almost crossly. The man said nothing, stood leaning against the counter, legs crossed, arms folded, head a little on one side, expression of a dealer not hurrying a customer who is seduced but not quite sure if he can afford it.

"Just like that," muttered Dick, irresolute.

"Didn't I say we were Oriental? In this kind of high-class business, we work on trust. And believe me, one develops an eye."

"Very well," said Dick at last, almost despite himself: it seemed an Arabian Nights sort of situation, somewhat daft. "In that case, I suppose, you're on."

There was no show of pleasure or displeasure. Saint uncrossed his arms, leaned his fingertips on the counter behind him.

"Excellent. Now do you want to go and see this other fellow—is he counting on you?"

"Hell, no. Probably twenty people after two lousy jobs."

"I wouldn't want you to let anyone down."

"No question of that."

"Good. So you could begin by just staying here?"

"Well, I suppose—I don't see why not."

"It would be a weight off my mind; I've quite a few things to see to. We'll call this a full day, then, and if you're short I'll advance you something this evening."

Dick grinned. "Was it that obvious?"

"My dear man—standing there so careful with your shoes shined, looking, if you'll forgive the remark, so exactly the type on his way to an interview. Now let's put you wise. There's nothing to it, really. If anyone asks you something you don't know, just be open—be honest—it pays off the best. Say I'll be back in an hour,

8

hour and a half. My uncle will be in later. He's an old man, very quiet; he won't worry you. I'll show you where to wash, and so forth. The things in the door are for sale; they're labeled and priced—that price; you're sorry but you don't accept near offers. That will be all tourists take, anyhow, but let them walk about and look, and they'll be quite happy. All the other cases are locked and protected. Time enough to show you later; you wouldn't want any of that the first day, and how to deal with people who ask to handle a fragile object and then drop it."

"Suppose a bandit comes in with a gun?"

"Let him. He can only get the petty cash, anyhow. There's no big money here. The windows and cases alarm automatically if interfered with. Well—it's a deal?"

They shook hands, and then with perfect simplicity Saint said, "See you in a little while," walked to the door, closed it behind him, and was gone. . . .

Dick was left alone. He felt breathless.

There was plenty to explore in this Aladdin's cave, but he felt too nervous and restless to do more than fidget for twenty minutes, when customers came in, when he gulped and then became easy, because it was two American women tourists, not troublesome, and he was surprised to find how easy it was.

"Is it genuine? I mean . . ."

"Everything is genuine here, Madame."

"I mean it's not a reproduction?"

"Certainly not, Madame."

"The price seems very high."

"It is as marked, Madame."

"What period is it?"

"I'm afraid I couldn't say—I have only just started here."

9

"Well, I know enough not to be had, and at that price if it isn't eighteenth it's a fake."

"Then I feel sure it will be, but if you care to come back in an hour Mr. Saint will be able to tell you exactly."

"No—well—what do you think, Sadie?" They took it.

Then there was an old dear in a fur coat. Had her ring, her diamond ring, come back from the cleaners? He couldn't say? Hmm, tiresome: she snorted a bit before going off. Then there was a haggard man in a dirty polo-necked sweater with draggly hair who put his nose in, twitched, and said, "Louis here? No? Tell him I got them sapphires in—Jackie Baur, he'll know," twitched again, and vanished. A middle-aged, drably dressed, very conventional woman wanted to know where that miniature had come from, because it reminded her so much of her mother. Dick felt encouraged: one could bring a book, or the paper; there was an arrangement for making tea; it would be easy to organize a few comforts.

When time hung, there were explorations. The jewelry, the antiques, the yellowed picture on an easel with a dim sub-Caravaggio look did not tell him much. Some silky old Persian rugs—looked old, anyhow, and might, he supposed, be silk. In a range of little drawers were small objects wrapped in tissue—replacements, as he guessed, for the tourist showcase. A drawer of cleaning materials, a cupboard of old sale and auction catalogues, a drawer of small tools for precise measurements and calibrations, packets of stick-on and tie-on labels, a couple of loupes which he tried in his eye and got on poorly with. Some very yellowed stuff about what to do in case of fire. He gazed at some modern table silver and was bored by it: the really good stuff was all out of sight somewhere, he guessed. Before

Saint came back, he had made another sale: a child's christening mug.

"What did I tell you?" said Saint calmly. "Earned your keep, and with no trouble at all."

It was just before lunch when an elderly man came in, a big smooth face with a Roman nose, a lot of wiry gray hair behind a high brown forehead, a mustache, a cigar. He wore baggy gray trousers and a wide jacket of coarse tweed with huge pockets, all apparently full of junk. He looked at Dick incuriously, with benignity.

"Hallo, Louis," said Saint easily. "This is Richard—we've acquired him or he's acquired us, we're not sure yet. Everything okay?"

"Everything okay." Unmannered, unaffected, very relaxed—Dick felt that his Arabian Nights adventure was turning out with no problems, even if disappointingly prosaic. . . .

Van der Valk, sitting in his new office, looked at his neat desk with mixed feelings, and as was his habit when things got mixed, was writing them down in a notebook. He had several notebooks, ranging from the small one which lived in his pocket to the thick "desk diary" bound in artificial leather in which he was writing his thesis, but most of them were school exercise books. He looked at the small one with curiosity, as though it were a clue to something—a pocket diary for the year 1963, full of useful hints for electrical engineers, with "Technische Bureau Zijlstra, Dordrechtsekade 81, Alphen a.d. Rijn" printed on the cover. Where could he have acquired that? The smeary pages were stained with rain from being consulted in the street, grease from being written up while eating a sandwich, and, alarmingly frequently, beer as a result of telephone

11

calls made in cafés. They were full of phone numbers whose purpose had been forgotten, lines of shorthand made up on the spot, indecipherable even to himself a fortnight later, and chores like "A. sweater, pick up cleaner's."

And those exercise books . . . virulent plastic covers like kitchen tablecloths or shower curtains in the Campbell tartan; they'd got arty lately in a jazzy style, he had noticed. Surrealist butterflies all over everything were a recent Dutch craze. These exercise books, as with children, started by being neat and orderly, each for its own carefully defined purpose, but after a week the right one had invariably been left at home, or wasn't under his hand just as he was in a frenzy, and then loose ends from current inquiries appeared upside down in "Office Administration," or an orderly exposition to be written up as a formal report this coming weekend had disconcerting interruptions (paraphrase of undoubtedly interesting, if turgid, remarks by Professor Grimmeisen concerning infantile behavior, in which certain conclusions by Dr. Summers of Baltimore had been thought ill-judged).

Altogether a sorry collection, belonging in the satchel of a poorly disciplined twelve-year-old, and out of place in this proper building annexed to the Ministry of Social Affairs in The Hague. So was he; he took one of the notebooks, turned to a clean page, and wrote down "Pride." He was a disreputable person, and he had come by devious ways, but he had reached a summit that ten years ago would have appeared as unlikely as his going to the South Pole, he thought, writing down "South Pole."

It was the South Pole, which he had imagined in childhood as a rough pillar tapering to a point, like the war memorial in the Damrak in Amsterdam, and, like this deplorable object, much shit on by sea gulls. It was a new and shoddy building in a scrambling noisy quarter, a long white oblong like an upright flower box with some ungainly stilts splayed out at the base to give a fictitious stability. Twenty-eight stories of odd fragments from several Ministries, acquired to "house the overspill." That was him!—along with the effect of exhaust gases upon commuters stuck in traffic jams, and the seepage of industrial effluent into the subsoil. The Commission for Inquiry into Law Reform (subcommittee criminal code, studying the replacement of repressive elements by educative mechanisms), one of whose cogs was Commissaris van der Valk. He was sufficiently wary and experienced a public servant to be skeptical about committees, but he was a Principal Commissaire, and that is an animal high in police hierarchies, a thing to be proud about. He'd never thought of getting that far.

For a few years now, hampered by a crippling physical injury, and a built-in reputation for being both indiscreet and irresponsible, he had been at a dead end. True, as chief of a mobile criminal brigade in South Holland's metroland, he had been kept busy, but was aware of moving sideways—"voie de garage," as Arlette called it, the sensation of being on a shelf. No further promotional prospect and precious little of real interest. Everything in such jobs was cut and dried, dependent upon decisions taken thirty years before. Except in minor details, he had no power to innovate, to "fluctuate a bit" from time to time. It seemed a disappointing finish for a senior police officer with over twenty-five years' service. Especially in the last five years, in a society breaking up and becoming continually more fluid under the pressure of fermentations not understood yet, and least of all by government func-

13

tionaries, his work had come to appear increasingly trivial and irrelevant. Not much interest or pride to be found in the identification and sequestration of criminals in ever-growing numbers, most of them either not really criminals at all or defined as such for the wrong reason. But all had to be presented to the Officer of Justice, the instructing and prosecuting magistrate, who might sometimes agree with him that the reams of paper, the monstrously involved and detailed dossiers, were a shocking waste of everyone's time.

Even when summoned, as happened perhaps twice a year, to attend upon the Procureur-General, the chief legal authority in the province, he was bored. Once or twice in the past, it had meant an inquiry of an inquiry of too delicate or embarrassing a sort to come through legal channels, occasionally productive of amusing or hair-raising episodes, but such things were more trouble than they were worth. Senior officials whose wives had taken to shoplifting, ticklish behavior by Japanese or Bulgarian purchasing agents—such things no longer interested him. And mostly, anyway, such a summons had meant no more than a telling-off.

This time he had been surprised. The high official had been blunt, almost brief.

"Sit down. This is unofficial, and in confidence. Recent governmental conciliabule has tended to become increasingly preoccupied with social questions. The blurring or obliteration of traditional values—however, I waste no time on this with you; it's stale cake to both of us. Very well—most European countries, as you know, are studying these problems, and groups exist all over the place, many over-fragmented and isolated. Much work is purely empirical patching-over of holes, and more is over-theoretical. Now it is proposed that a commission be set up to coordinate some proposals on

14

a European scale, and to draw up further recommendations. I have myself been asked to submit my own notions, and also to assist in the nomination of some members of this commission. Much of that work concerns the reform of the magistrature, and some purely juristic points—let that pass. It was agreed that a voice from the police would be beneficial, particularly as concerns the relations of the public to legal codes. Your name was mentioned in this context, eventually put forward for serving upon this commission, and subsequently approved—subject, of course, to your acceptance. I have called you to offer you this position, and to explain a few of the conditions attached.

"It is not a paid post, but would in your case and a few others involve full-time work, so that the proposal is to withdraw you for this period, which might amount to two or even three years, from your administrative duties, and transfer you to The Hague, where evidently you would be continued in your rank and at full pay. A civil-service flat and of course an office would be found for you there. You have doubtless further questions; put them."

He had accepted on the spot. The Procureur-General had, he thought, been pleased by this alacrity.

"By the way, Van der Valk," as he was on the verge of leaving, "it is felt that the members of this commission should, where appropriate, possess titles," dryly, "of a certain weight and substance. I will therefore mention to you that I have implemented a recommendation that you should have the rank and emoluments of a Principal Commissaire, and add that I think this not inappropriate in an officer of your seniority and experience. That is all, I think."

"My wife will be very pleased," said Van der Valk with a small smile.

15

The Procureur-General, who was not without humor at odd moments, responded to this smile and tapped his fountain pen upon the virgin blotter before pointing it at him.

"Yes. You might give thought, too, to the idea that it is possibly the first time a police officer has been given his step for—aha—literary reasons. Well, goodbye, Van der Valk. Offer your wife my congratulations, would you?"

So now he felt pride. He had his name upon a door instead of his rank. He had an office smaller, to be sure, than the last, and probably even more dismal. But quieter, and definitely more private. And more luxurious, as befitted the higher pay. He no longer had policemen in shirt sleeves clattering in and out, or the public with its incoherent rambling tales of persecution and victimization. To tell the truth, he missed both these elements. But he didn't miss the wire baskets, piled with paper of unbearable crassness, the phone ringing all the time, and the floor dirty no matter how often it got mopped.

No linoleum here! A modern office, with moquette wall-to-wall! An austere desk, slab of so-called teak on a complicated metal undercarriage, and a black leather chair. A window which wouldn't open, for reasons of dust, noise, vertigo, possible suicides, and upsetting the air conditioning. The phones were throttled to a civil-service purr. And next door, with some chaste filing cabinets, he had a secretary, a rather wearisome female called Wattermann, a name whose associations of fountain pens, venereal disease, and French tram drivers confused him, so that he sometimes called her Miss Hasselblad or Miss Valentine, and she was convinced he did this on purpose, and tended to bridle—or was it bristle? Down in the basement was an I.B.M.

16

computer which he was waiting to catch out in some exceptionally childish error, and which supplied him with a great many more statistics than he really wanted to know (amazing the number of persons convicted of indictable offenses in Pittsburgh one or both of whose parents, when known, suffered from tuberculosis). Next door was a professor of something or other behavioral from Utrecht who was rather nice, quite human except first thing in the morning, and smoked Three Nuns in an English pipe, just what you would expect.

The desk was bare but for the notebooks and a jam jar full of ball-point pens and paper clips, but there were a few things put away in drawers: the small, bland Swiss cigars he smoked nowadays, eau de Cologne, and a terribly secret bottle of brandy, in case Wassermann came all over queasy and had to be revived. There was nothing else in the office but shelves holding his lawbooks, a growing collection of paperback thrillers, and a vase of flowers: he had thrown out—to Wattman's consternation—all the climbing plants. The corners were silting up inexorably with deposits of learning about criminal law; there was an awful lot of it. Under "Pride" in the notebook he wrote "Claustrophobia," because every now and then he found himself wishing that the mayor would suddenly ring him up with a tale about embezzlement in municipal parking lots: just the kind of thing that used to make him swear so. He looked at the notebook, scratched, and suddenly wondered what some bright young Ph.D. from Besançon or Berkhamsted would make of all this if he were to drop dead suddenly. These paleontological speculations were interrupted by his secretary. Not that you could call those discreet sliding movements an interruption, or even an irruption. Arlette called her Miss

17

Typhoo Tea: when asked why, said because she appeared like the tiny tip of the tender leaf.

"There's a young man asking to see you," she said.

"Has he filled in all the proper forms?"

"He says his business is personal and unofficial."

"Does he seem agitated?"

"No, quite reasonable and relaxed."

"So he's safe, in your opinion?"

"He doesn't seem to be on a trip or anything."

"Then, I think, frisk him for concealed weapons and send him in."

Van der Valk had learned a long time ago that to stand up and be polite, no matter who it was, never did any harm. The young man seemed "reasonable and relaxed" enough, but had a balky look Van der Valk knew well, that of someone who is already regretting an impulse.

"No, no, you don't disturb me; I'm accessible. You're quite wet; I suggest you hang your raincoat up over there, and there's a chair in that corner."

The young man had a student look, but was dressed in a suit and a white shirt, giving him a formal air. Dark hair, fairly long and very clean; pale skin and a washed appearance, or was that the effect of rain? The sober suit was that of a bank clerk. Neat hands; clean nails. Polished shoes, too, instead of those huge suède boots. Intelligent face; manner neither aggressive nor dotty. The usual difficulty in starting.

"Visitors are always pleasant," said Van der Valk. "You'd like a cigarette?"

"Yes—no—yes, after all, I will. Thanks."

"What have you got, a story for me?"

"I suppose—it's bound to sound silly."

"They mostly do"—rattling a matchbox to see whether there was anything inside—"at first. Which

18

you bring to me to make it sound less silly, why? Because I'm a policeman?"

"I suppose so; I don't know. Wanted your opinion, I suppose."

"Because I'm no longer an actively employed policeman, was that it? Seemed less compromising, somehow?"

The boy seemed relieved: yes, that was it. "It was because of the television, really."

"I understand. And you knew where to find me?"

"Well, I asked at the Ministry. They sent me on here."

"Bit of detective work?"

The boy grinned. "That's right."

Rather rewarding and encouraging, thought Van der Valk. Somebody had been looking at him—somebody had even listened.

It had been decided, nobody knew by whom, that the active members of the Commission should be introduced to the public, as a first step in the education campaign. Result, they were presented on television, safely late at night, with a bland young man to interview them.

"This evening, we have Professor Dr. Bandaid of the Institute of Industrial Psychology in Nijmegen, who has been studying some of the odder ways you and I behave, and he is going to tell us some startling things, which we believe will be having a lot of impact on this world of ours. I ask him to begin by defining some of the basic attitudes he believes we will have to adopt if we are going to be able to control our environment, a word we've heard a lot of lately."

With just the same patronizingly apologetic patter, Van der Valk had been given his turn at "speaking the Epilogue"; Tuesday nights after the variety show, when

19

one could feel comfortably assured that 95 percent of the sets had been switched off at the first syllable. Still, they had all gone through it, shrugging and muttering that after all it wasn't a bad idea, they supposed: secret Star Chambers were always a bad thing.

"With us tonight we have Commissaris van der Valk whose thirty years' experience with the Criminal Brigade has given him we believe an unusual insight into the traumatic perhaps I can use the word 'contacts' of the public with the criminal code of law. An increasing number of us perhaps feel frustrated by what we find an excessive rigidity perhaps in the application of what we might perhaps call a rather anachronistic and um . . . antiquated apparatus." The fellow is pleased with his phrase, thought Van der Valk. And he on his cue, bothered by sweating too much, hoping he did not sound condescending, nervous in a gray suit a little too heavy for the overheated studio and an expensive silk tie with little marguerites bought by Arlette.

"Most policemen," he began a little hesitantly, "are polite, clean, patient, and willing to take trouble. These are not the characteristics of pigs. Plainly this is not enough, since many people are convinced that we are pigs. It is also fair to remark that if one treats people—and policemen are people—as pigs, then they begin to behave like pigs. We have therefore two basic proposals from which we must start examining our problem: to educate ourselves, and to educate the public." The interviewer was leaning forward with an eager, expectant look, lips slightly parted and eyes shiny, so that Van der Valk feared he was sounding dull, and hurried on.

"Holland is a very law-abiding country. Our rate of serious crime is negligible, our gangsters are simple-minded and pathetic oafs, and we tend to congratulate ourselves that crime belongs in countries like England,

20

France, or America. This extreme complacency and self-satisfaction is, simply, catastrophic. . . ."

"Was I very bad?" he asked Arlette anxiously.

"Not at all, I think. Quite a future as a reforming popularizer." It wasn't quite the answer he would have liked; her remarks seldom were.

"I didn't make a fool of myself?"

"Pas trop." Not too much: faint praise.

And now this boy coming bumbling into the office with a silly story . . . But wasn't that what he had meant—a renewal of trust between the police and the public, a renewal of communication. He should be grateful!

"Well," he said, "suppose you tell me your silly story."

When it came to the point, the boy squirmed a bit; they always did. He'd done something stupid, and then invented a whole drama to cover it up, which was boring. It was a job for kind-hearted Harry from Ham Common, the rustic cop on English television. Boy worked in this jeweler's, and there were all sorts of odd occurrences—yes, to be sure, and . . . Van der Valk had avoided the bleak act of give your name, place, and date of birth, and the rest which was so discouraging, but one could overdo the kindly paternalism.

"You pinched something," he said.

"Well—yes and no—the thing is, I'm sure it was meant."

Yes, of course! "What was it?"

"This." It was a plain, square, severely expensive wristwatch, a solid-gold Patek Philippe; yes, indeed, seductive thing. Banal affair.

Van der Valk shrugged; still, he would be full of forgiveness and make no fuss. "Simple enough—put it back."

"But I'm telling you—I'm sure it was meant—that I was meant to take it."

"That's catch twenty-two, I'm afraid; being meant to take it is no defense in law."

"Yes, but look, I mean, when I tell you I'm sure you'd agree. There are these drawers, see, full of junk, and Larry—that's the boss, so to speak—said very casually to clear one out and throw it all away. A lot of packing stuff, you know, little cardboard boxes, foam plastic, and crap that little leather cases come wrapped in, you know, so I took an armful to the dustbin, and then this box seemed a bit heavy, you know, and this was just thrown inside, no label on it or case, and it's not marked on the stock sheet—I looked—and, well, he said to sling all that junk, but then after I thought, Hey, there must have been an invoice; but there wasn't and how could I put it back, and where?"

"Simpler still—give it back. When in doubt, tell the truth."

"But why isn't there a record of it?"

And now he thought of it, yes, why wasn't there? And come to that, he had known firms do things of astonishing stupidity. Even big firms sometimes just went home forgetting to lock the door after them. As a policeman, he had known human error of staggering magnitude. But jewelers—those notoriously careful stocktakers who counted everything every day—no, it was true; they did not do such things.

"And Larry Saint—he's a nice guy, but there's no denying he's a bit—I mean he's so easygoing, it just isn't for real. About getting this job, now, I mean, I'll tell you."

"Yes," said Van der Valk slowly, "you'd better let me have some facts." He reached for a notebook. A third full of some legal guff: to punish the legal guff, he turned it upside down and smoothed out a virgin page.

Richard Oddinga, age twenty-two. Father dead. Had been businessman up in backwoods of Friesland; boy been sent to Amsterdam to read law at the university. Failed some courses, been dropped; had been leading the happy-go-lucky loafer's existence of the phony student which is so common. Had been suddenly offered this job in, of all places, a jeweler's and it did sound a bit persuasive. Could there be something in this? Hmm, to plant a watch and acquire a hold on the boy was perfectly classic and laughably easy—but what would that be aimed at? Though it still sounded like an episode for Mac of Mockturtle, the understanding bobby.

"I think it might be a kind of bribe," said the boy. "And I don't know—I think they've got rid of anyone who really knows anything about the business, on some kind of pretext."

"Where is this shop?" Van der Valk picked his pen up to note the address.

"Prinz."

Astonished, he put the pen down again. "Prinz?— you mean there on the Spui?"

"That's right."

"But that's dead fancy—Cartier, Van Cleef and—all that stuff, and dressy antiques, Fabergé easter egg or whatnot in the window."

"Just try and find anything that genuinely is by Cartier. Some boxes, maybe."

Van der Valk, by now amused, pushed his glasses up and rubbed his eyes. "Do you have some conclusion about all this?"

"I don't know—I thought of some insurance fraud— they would stage a fire or a burglary or something, but I suppose that's too crude."

"A little," smiling. "Insurance companies aren't

23

quite that soft a touch. Perhaps something that, if you'll forgive me, would look innocent enough to a more experienced eye. Has even an innocent explanation."

"I guessed you'd say that," downcast. "And yet—I know I couldn't prove it or anything, but I do have a feeling something funny's going on. That's why I thought of you, I mean coming to say—but I might have known, you've got no use for that, so I've wasted my time. Sorry."

"No. Not mine or yours. Funny feelings are sometimes better than facts. They have, occasionally, more resonance. But it would still be more sensible to put the watch back. On the other hand," with regrettable frivolity, "suppose you were right and it was a sort of bribe—it might be interesting to know what it was and why. If you get into trouble on account of this, come and tell me. All right?"

The boy looked relieved. "As long as I'm covered. I mean, that's what I came to see you for."

"Quite," said Van der Valk dispassionately. "You pinch a watch and see whether you can't arrange for me to be an accessory. No, don't worry, I'm joking. Put it back or not, exactly as you please. You've made no formal deposition, and I'm making no record. All informal—I haven't even written anything down."

"Such a cheap business," said Larry Saint with distaste, putting a tray of little boxes back and resetting the alarm. "Rings . . . watches . . . one might be selling lucky charms. We only do it, fortunately, for a few people as a favor, Dick, remember that. Watches simply aren't worth the trouble. By the way, I was reminded of a stupid incident I'd totally forgotten. You recall that drawer full of old rubbish. Extraordinary mentality, old Bosboom—one of those people who

24

keep crooked nails and little twists of string, because you never know, 'it might come in handy.' You did clear it all out, didn't you?"

"Yes," briefly.

"Oh, good. That's all right, then. One slightly comic detail—do you remember those incredible people a few years ago who kept all their savings in the dustbin?"

"Yes, now that you mention it." And indeed it had been exactly the right newspaper story to keep all Holland in an ecstasy for a fortnight, and was a favorite of Van der Valk's. Some worthy people with a nest egg of a few thousand pounds in bank notes had had the brilliant notion of foxing burglars by keeping it in the dustbin. In an unhappy moment, the dustbin had been put out for emptying. . . . From the municipal garbage truck to a collective dump, to the "garbage train"—a tidy Dutch phenomenon—to a dump on wasteland far far away in the wilds of Friesland, these unfortunate people had engaged in a dogged pursuit worthy of a film by Erich von Stroheim. For day after day the whole family had haunted the enormous dump, which had since been tidied and leveled by neurotic bulldozers . . . helped by many eager amateur treasure hunters. Van der Valk, a great believer in "getting to know a man by his garbage," had made sociological observations about the habits of Amsterdamers which had staggered even him, and written a witty report on the subject which had not been appreciated by his superiors, or Arlette, who had sent all his clothes to the cleaner's because "I'd never get the smell out."

"Lovely," pursued Saint with enjoyment. "I've only just rumbled that, all unwitting, I'd contributed something rather nice to the same worthy cause. But of course you hadn't noticed—how could you? No, of course you don't understand. You see, Dick, I had one of these tiresome people—this is rather a good lesson for you in customer psychology—who always feel that they must be cleverer than the dealer. They have an obscure need to score points. In fact, he's quite sane about his subject, which is Chinese pottery; that T'ang horse went to him, which Louis bought specially from Spink's in London. Well, to oblige him I sold him a watch from Patek Philippe, rather nice. And of course he comes back and says it's not right, and I sent it to the workshop, who had it on the electronic counter for a fortnight, and of course it's perfect, but knowing this old loony, I'm perfectly aware that this is just an act, because he and people like him do these tricks with a vague notion of putting us in our place. I fixed him up with a Perregaux model he was perfectly happy with, and as I now recall"—there was enjoyment in Saint's voice—"I slipped the other, which was perfect, into an old box, and heaven knows why—all my fault—I dropped it absent-mindedly into that drawer. And now," in accents of classical tragedy, "it's been flung out and has been swept away by the bulldozer. Louis would be most upset; we mustn't tell him. A pity—it was a pretty one."

"You don't think there'd still be a chance of finding it?" asked Dick.

"No, no, alas, not a hope. I'd be ready to give a handsome reward to some honest dustbin man who turned it in—but there's no chance of that. If you'd found it, I'd have given it you, actually—no good to us any more; I wrote it off as a trading loss. Didn't matter because, just between us, Louis did rather well with the horse."

"Well, as a matter of fact—"

"Don't tell me you found it," said Saint, clasping his hands in a dramatic attitude of prayer.

"I thought it was junk, slung like that—I mean, I felt sure you'd never tell me to throw it away when it was of any good."

"So you slung it?" sadly.

"Well, actually, I thought the strap might be worth keeping—it seemed good still."

"But, my dear Dick—don't keep me in suspense— you've got it?"

"Well, yes, actually I don't know why I never mentioned it; I suppose I thought it was just not possible it could be any good."

"But isn't that wonderful? You keep it, my dear Dick, and bloody good luck, the thing's perfect."

"But don't you want it back?"

"No, no, no. As I told you, I wrote it off in the books. Couldn't resuscitate it now, ha-ha; the tax man would wonder what was going on."

"I mean you don't think I stole it or something."

"Come, now, Dick, don't be absurd: you know perfectly well that's impossible. No, no; no false feelings, I beg. I'm only too glad it wasn't wasted."

"You see, I wasn't feeling very happy about it. I mean—now of course I understand. But I couldn't quite make it out."

Saint burst out laughing. "Dick, Dick, I do enjoy you. No, no, don't be offended; I don't mean that as sarcasm or to be patronizing—just that at your age one is so touchy and suspicious, and at the same time so innocent and transparent. I knew perfectly well you had that watch—no, don't stare like that. I'd been wondering where the hell I put it, and realized it must have got in with those junky boxes. I was ready to write it off, and then I noticed how guilty you were looking each time we were handling watches—not exactly blushing but embarrassed and fidgety."

27

"You mean you could see that?" asked Dick, startled.

"But of course—I'm a dealer, my lad, I've learned to use my eyes. What are the things I tell you—never be tactless, never show impatience, never sarcasms or personalities. Making personal remarks thought to be funny—rather a national thing, that—terrible. Not too much servility, not smiling overmuch; well, you're learning all that. And of course you're picking up technical stuff; recognition of china, silver, glass. But learn to use your eyes on art and you'll learn to use them on people. Study the artist: why did he do it that way? To please? To follow a fashion? Or more than that? No, no, I could see you there, bothered about that watch, wondering whether you'd stolen it, worrying whether to give it back and what I'd say. I did wonder for a moment whether if I mentioned it you'd make an act of pretending not to know what I was talking about. I'm very pleased to see I wasn't wrong. Come on, my lad, to work. Work and then play. You haven't any idea yet how to play, either—you'll learn something about that, too, one of these days."

Van der Valk, coming across a couple of scribbled lines in a notebook, wondered what they were, read them with a bit of difficulty, and meditated a moment.

"Tale about stolen watch supposed planted," it read. "Why come to me? R. Oddinga, Lindengracht, job peculiar hazard, nothing tangible but sensation atmos. not quite right. Seeks reassurance, comes all this distance, power of television, energy impulse sudden imaginative flare boys this age, it struck me." As quite often happened, he was not sure at first what all this meant. He recalled the episode, but the note had been meant to link his mind to another idea altogether. Yes,

28

of course. He reached out for another notebook, the one holding notes for his thesis, ruffled his hair, lit a cigarette, polished his glasses, and wrote rapidly.

"The relearning of sensitivity. The professional police detective has none because he is (a) overworked; (b) overspecialized, i.e., deals only with fragments of an inquiry; (c) blunted by repetition; (d) same as (b), he is part of a clumsy machine, a cog, with no interest or understanding of other cogs.

"Contrast now the attitude of the classical fictional 'private detective'—he is one man, with all the elements in his possession. Invariably his time and leisure are used in contemplative and imaginative work, aided by pipes, violins, dope, as S. Holmes, or chess and whisky, as P. Marlowe. Quite unreal, because such type does not/cannot possess all elements. Consequently author cheats—imputes far more knowledge and skill than one man possesses. Hence mechanical introduction of brain waves, produced by opium or whisky, and series of handy coincidences: he always happens to be 'on the spot' instead of in bed or sitting in the lavatory when something exciting happens, which is legitimate and necessary in fiction, but in life . . .

"Nevertheless there is a valid lesson. The sensitivity, the skills at analysis and synthesis are indispensable and not easily acquired by police-school training. Conclusion: a criminal investigation unit should perhaps consist of no more than four or five men, each with specially sensitized skills. Cf. fictional Maigret. Lucas the elderly, careful, good at details, patience, perseverance; Janvier, young, ambitious, and imaginative; 'the little Lapointe,' sensitive and idealistic, innocent and kindly; Torrence, who is muscles; and Lognon, the indefatigable plodder—this is a clever formula, remaining workable for fifty books. Now postulate smallish

29

flexible computer unit, able mechanically to perform all that time-wasting checking. It can give mechanical evaluation, but cannot replace sensitive human understanding, can never replace Maigret! The 'private detective' element cannot be eliminated. Take for example this boy Richard, which is perfect fictional 'private' example. A Marlowe/Archer might be interested because he had nothing better at the time to do. Existing police structure would have no interest and no ability anyway. Since no complaint has been made, no administrative machinery has even been set in motion. Said ad/mach. hopelessly lumbering and cumbersome."

He closed the notebook, pushed it away, and took another, marked "Experimental Psychology."

"Suppose we conduct an experiment," he wrote. "Cf. notion of difficulty insertion private detective in crim. brig. unit. This boy Odd, odd-ball odd boy. I would be interested in knowing, assuming I chose to handle this individually, with no official aid or backing (a) how far I would get with it; and (b) whether there's anything in it! . . . Administrative note: since the hypothetic 'private detective' must be a highly trained and well-paid unit, how the devil do you justify this to the financial comptroller, who always has the last word? Whereabouts could he be inserted in a hierarchy? Experimentally irrelevant because my time is my own. Note consequently what time I spend on it and with what result!"

Lastly he took his little pocket diary, and wrote, "Richard, A'dam, Lindengracht, watch plant fiddle, what's in it?"

It would be interesting, he told himself. Suppose he tried a test case investigation on a purely personal basis of this boy's tale. There was nothing in it, so that it remained purely experimental. He wouldn't cheat, as fictional private detectives always did—when they got stuck on administrative detail, they always remembered they had a pal somewhere in an administration who "owed them a favor," and they rang him up to ask for information that could only be got by professional leg-work! He wouldn't do that. He would work on a strictly private basis, and only in his own time. He could start a notebook called "Experiment." He looked in his drawer—no more notebooks. He got up and opened the door to Miss Wattermann.

"What are you doing?" suspiciously eying a pile of paper.

"A précis for Professor de Hartog." Aha, his neighbor, who shared her. Nothing for him, thank heaven, in that alarming mass of print.

"Have you any more of those exercise books?"

"No, I'm afraid not. I can buy you some if you give me an order. I'll have to get it receipted by the shop and then send it in to the accountant."

"No, no, I'll buy them myself." He went back frustrated, took his notebook marked "English Criminal Precedents" (a very tiresome one, for not only did the English have no criminal code, so that their law depended on judicial decisions whose interpretations were very difficult to follow, but the English system was altogether different to the Scottish, and quite a few of their own experts thought the Scottish system better: long groans, and pity the poor policeman).

He turned it upside down, was aghast at finding several other notes on totally unconnected subjects because he had done this trick before, found a clean page, decided he didn't care even if it did cause muddle, and wrote a heading saying, "Experiment," and underneath, "At present no factual information—even the watch might have come from a different source." After biting his ball-point and lighting another cigarette, he produced the following.

"Sole fact—the boy came to see me. Whatever else there is in the tale, there is some truth. Starting points otherwise nonexistent. No factual notes taken, or even possible. Boy is 20/24, of intelligence and some training—i.e., secondary school and probably a couple of university years. Presents well—carefully dressed, neat, well-spoken. Has sensitivity, intelligence, and ability. Engagement by jeweler plausible. Origin Friesland, nothing known save father dead, and boy is largely independent following family conflict, but no money; job therefore imperative. That could only be checked by municipal inquiry but is plausible, thus so far acceptable. Nothing known of jeweler. Must have access to criminal file if only to confirm negative on this. Larry Saint—some personal observation: address, etc., easily obtainable. L. S.—is it a pseudonym?—cf. identical initials. Observation Spui unlikely to tell anyone much, obviously, but worth an effort. Possibility the retired manager who has been mentioned, and assistant said to have been drunk.

"Approach to old man—since we have no standing or conceivable pretext whatever, we must be very cautious—the slightest complaint would start a terrible hullabaloo: I am absolutely without any defense. All it comes down to is: the boy took the trouble to come and find me. It is therefore reasonable to take trouble with him. I have no earthly excuse for just letting it drop. The boy wanted reassurance, and in a sense advice, but he also wanted help. I cannot neglect possibility that he needs help. That is a very unprofessional remark, and an unprofessional attitude. Quite. Hence the experimental nature of this whole notion." That would give him the reference he needed, and he would buy a new notebook and use if for "case notes." And now, please, it is time to do some real work. . . .

Van der Valk's experiment in private detection might still never have come to anything had it not been for Inspector—now Commissaire—Kan and a rather awkward late-afternoon appointment given Van der Valk by his dentist. Kan, an infernally active, important, bald person, was now in charge of the Economics Squad. Van der Valk, who had been busy in the archives, met him in a corridor and was moved to ask a question.

"Do you know anything about a jeweler called Prinz?" Kan had always been fanatical about knowing absolutely everyone.

"Prinz, Prinz—aha, yes, I'm with you, jeweler, antiques."

"That's what I said."

"Anything known, mm . . . no, no, can't say there is; never been any trouble there—unless it was before my time."

"Archives have nothing; I already looked."

"Nice job you've got—with us just for the day? Nothing like a day in the city, old chap, to sharpen up that provincial mind of yours, ha-ha. Remember me to your wife, do." And was gone with bouncy footsteps. Always had been so tiresomely sure of himself; if Kan didn't know it, it didn't exist.

Been right in one thing; he did always feel sharpened when in Amsterdam. He had been away for several years now, but it was still his home town, different to anywhere else in Holland, and he was faithful to people and to places in an innocent way, saying things like "You'd never find a dentist that good in The Hague." The dentist was handy, too, to Police Headquarters,

33

five minutes down the road in the Keizersgracht; another devotedly loyal Amsterdamer, who moreover collected Chinese porcelain.

"Oh, that's lovely now; you can rinse that if you like. Two helpings of amalgam, Annie. Old Louis, let's see; about six months ago, he got me a celadon plate, Ch'ing, rather nice. He's genuine, you can rely on him."

"D'you know of a nephew?"

"One moment, we'll just polish that a bit. Nephew? No—nice old boy there called Bosboom; never seen anyone else there. Honest? Good heavens, yes, as the day. You people in The Hague suspect everybody, your professional deformation, ha; don't chew on that for an hour or two."

He walked back toward the station; he hated bringing the car here and it was rush hour, which made trams impossible. Floods of little typists, thousands of boys and girls piled onto bikes and scooters, running for their suburban trains, ruthless about pushing this elderly gentleman, with his hat and his stick and his briefcase: what's the matter with you, dad; if you want to stay still, buy a hammock.

Beating up laboriously across wind and tide toward the Lindengracht, Van der Valk felt sorry for all these fresh-faced country children who come down to Amsterdam because that's where it's at, and find themselves in those appalling lodging houses. Now that, he thought, really must be a potent factor in the antisocial tendencies. They may or may not be exploited at work by capitalists, but in furnished lodgings the last drop of juice is wrung from them by the pettiest and greediest of the bourgeois. A ghastly breed in general, lodging-house keepers: busybodies with lists of nasty rules and glorying in the power to make as many more rules as they liked, and extremely quick to put their victims on

34

the street at the least sign of anything but meek conformity to their bullying.

Squalid windowless minds, living in squalid windowless basements to screw ten extra gulden from four square feet of glassed pane in an attic. Extortionists, and blackmailers, too. Despite all his experience, he had always felt an oppressive emotion of contempt for those houses where children barely out of the shell were taught the facts of life in a capital. If those rats would show a scrap of charity or just humanity—the very smallest dose of something like home. The wretched children, getting the bleakest work, eating in the greasiest cafés, sleeping in the most threadbare shelter, trying to create warmth and happiness and the right to be an individual with the pathetic means they had . . . He had reached the Lindengracht.

At least this boy Richard was luckier than most. Richard's landlady let Van der Valk in without a sour complaint at being brought up the stairs. Even the smell, close and mean though it was, held a memory of air and light however narrow the passage.

"Sorry to disturb you," he said politely.

" 'S all right," she said. "Oddinga, 'm, dunno 'f he's in 'r not," clipping her ripe Amsterdam accent. "I s'pose y'can go on up, he's mostly back b'now." She wasn't going to face those stairs! He had to, hitching his leg behind him; it was these interminable ladders as much as anything that had made work here impossible to him, but he was going to manage in a good cause.

A startled voice said "Who is it?" to his tap, opened the door on his prudent silence, staring on the dim landing, recognizing him, becoming filled with confusion, glancing alarmed down the well to where the landlady had an ear of unrivaled sharpness cocked, muttering, "Oh, it's you," with embarrassment. The boy looked about as though trapped, and said finally, "Er—oh, hell—sorry, it's a bit of a mess, but come in anyhow."

The usual narrow room, where there is nowhere to put anything. The bed that contrives to sag and be a plank, the cretonne curtain behind which to hang one's clothes, the window sill holding an iron and a packet of detergent, the rickety basketwork table and chair, the suitcase holding clean shirts, the camping gas ring with the dirty saucepan and the jar of Nescafé, the tin ashtray, and the transistor radio. The boy wearing the cotton track suit, which is the uniform of students indoors, his good suit taken off and put on a hanger, the shirt anxiously inspected to see whether it will last a day more. The dim twenty-five-watt bulb, the antiquated and threadbare narrowness that would bend the stoutest heart, a smell of socks, and an old towel kept to masturbate on. Van der Valk had seen so many. He sat on the creaky chair, crossed his legs, lit a cigarette, and said mildly, "I'm not butting in?"

"No, no—I only just got back and hadn't time to tidy up yet."

"Doesn't bother me."

"Something the matter? I mean—you coming specially like this."

"No. I was in the quarter; just occurred to me you'd be home, thought I'd pass to see if you were okay. Job all right?"

"Oh, yes."

"No trouble with that watch of yours?"

"Oh, no."

"Mean you put it back?"

"That's right—well, actually—there was no need—I mean, I made a bit of a mistake, got in a bit of a panic, I don't know why. I mean, I shouldn't ever have

36

bothered you, mean to say, you're busy, and an important kind of person, there wasn't any real need. I mean I don't know how I got the idea in my head, it wasn't anything at all really. Really there's no need to worry, I wouldn't want you to make a fuss, I mean there's no sense in that, it'd just be wasting your time and—"

"That's all right," peaceably.

"No, I mean I don't want any more fuss," in agony.

Van der Valk took pity. "That's okay, I won't make any."

"I mean I'm sorry you're putting yourself out, but really there's nothing to do any more."

"Of course," blandly. "I'm glad to hear that. Putting it back was sensible," looking at his watch. "Good, I'll be off to my train; rush hour'll be quietened down by now. Bye-bye, then, Richard, glad to hear you're all right."

And he took himself off, bumping on the stairs but knowing the landlady would recognize the strange step and that her antennae would relax. He was happy: he hadn't wasted his time!

He walked as far as the café on the corner of the Noordermarkt, decided he was in no hurry, ordered a black-currant gin, and phoned Arlette to say he'd be a little late. The phone book told him Louis Prinz lived in a frumpy street over by the Jacob van Lennep, where— he knew those streets—the flats were full of nineteenth-century furniture with plush and mahogany carved scrollwork.

"Oh, Mr. Prinz. So sorry to trouble you. Fact is I was trying to find Mr. Saint, but he doesn't seem to be in the book; aunt of mine . . . Yes, recommended by a friend, little matter of business, thought I'd give him a ring. . . . Oh, I see, thank you so much; awfully sorry to have troubled you." How nice! Mr. Saint lived just next door—well, very close by, in the Leliegracht; obliging of him. Hmm, the neighborhood was what you called picturesque but there, these old houses were often flats where pleasant people lived at pleasantly low rents, having been ensconced therein for numerous years. He had no pretext, or even a reason, for calling on Mr. Saint. But Dicky-boy's behavior was of interest. It was so close by, be worth looking at.

Yes; picturesque. Picturesque—but very respectable neighbors: an Italian grocer with a windowful of lasagne and mortadella; a saddler with riding boots, bridles, and the front end of a realistic horse. Wasn't room for the back end, but a tasteful array of velvet jockey caps and the like. And, in between, Mr. Saint lived two floors above a sex shop. Dear, dear, but one made a joke of it to one's friends. Anyway, half the houses in central Amsterdam now had the same problem. Judging by the curtains, Mr. Saint was at home, but it wasn't what you'd call a thrill. The shop had a fancy name—The Golden Apples of the Hesperides; blimey. He had been a bit intrigued by that idiot boy, but not enough to make him want any golden apples. He went home and had supper, in the new and nasty flat in The Hague, and shortly after went to bed with a book about King Charles I, whom he had hitherto known only from the portraits on cigar boxes. He could not get very excited about this tiresome person, but Cromwell was always interesting, and the Marquis of Montrose was a discovery.

He woke up feeling forceful and energetic, and moved in on Miss Hufflebloom aggressively.

"Get me the Amsterdam fire brigade on the line, will you—Hell, I've got to go again this morning."

"Not finished with your dentist yet?"

38

"Committee meeting in the Overtoom, an awful bore. . . . Yes, hallo, Van der Valk here; tell me, fire alarms, when for example you had a jeweler holding valuable stock, and everything barred and bolted. . . . I see, yes—you'd notify, yes. . . . Can you tell me now, Prinz's there by the Spui. . . . No, Van der Valk, Commissaris of Police. . . . That's right, The Hague. . . . I see. Yes. . . . Aha, Bosboom, that's interesting; he's the manager there, but I've a notion he's retired and they haven't brought you up to date. Where is it he lives?—nearby, I take. . . . Max Planck Straat— oh lord, that's miles away. Thanks very much. . . . Yes, that's right, the Ministry. Goodbye, thanks. . . . Very worried they were, giving away information; thought maybe I was planning to set the place alight. Listen, Miss Wattermann, I'll likely be away all day. I've quite a few chores."

The conference of governmental powers awaiting him was due to take place—for reasons that escaped him—in a dreary building on the Overtoom, whose one advantage was that it was a direct tram ride from Amsterdam's Central Station. He was clanking along the Leidsestraat before he missed his new gloves and realized he'd left them on the train; he leapt off the tram to phone before the worst happened!

Waiting for the next tram, on the drafty corner of the Koningsplein, he glanced irritably at his watch and was exasperated to find it stopped. Misfortunes never come singly. He took it off to investigate, and his chilled fingers dropped it on the street, where it fell—it would—into the shiny groove of the tramline. As he stooped—how is it possible these things should happen to me?—the growl of the swift monster and the kling-kling-kling of its alarm made him lurch back, treading on somebody's toe, and see his shabby beloved watch, which he'd had for twenty years, chewed up under the pitying "Oh dear" of a middle-aged woman, the nervous ashamed grin of another, and the blank indifference of an elderly man with troubles of his own. Van der Valk arrived at the Overtoom in a very bad mood indeed.

He wasn't in the least consoled by the concierge coming to meet him with a tale about the station sous-chef running fast along the platform before the train pulled out and meeting halfway a dear good soul with a pair of gloves she'd just that minute found. He was tetchy at his meeting.

Still, when he left he was grinning, because he'd had an idea. Not in the slightest superstitious, he enjoyed it when something allowed him to pretend he was. Losing a watch on the Koningsplein was at least a sign from heaven telling him to go and buy another from Mr. Saint just across the road, and that was something to grin at: he told his colleague, a lawyer with whom he was having lunch.

"A lamentable thing happened to me, a purely personal and relatively trivial accident. It might change the whole shape of a theory I'm working on." The colleague was amused.

"But that's rather naughty, isn't it? I know from reading your reports, as well as from the way you speak, that you have a highly subjective way of going to work, but isn't this an exaggeration?"

"Yes, of course; I've been reproached with it before now. I know all the arguments—a lawyer considering a brief does not stop to worry about his client being guilty—or personally unappealing—or sadistic toward his wife. He couldn't. A negotiator—a civil servant, let's say, working on agricultural price supports—he doesn't stop to think how much he likes New Zealanders. First of all, I'd be inclined to answer that he's never truly objective however much he thinks he is, and secondly that the virtues of objectivity are greatly exaggerated. As far as police work is concerned, there is too much objectivity applied. Crime hasn't got much to do with absolutes like right and wrong—like some more coffee? A policeman is a good deal of an actor—a comedian, if you prefer. Is a doctor's job to cure disease or to alleviate suffering? Both, of course. It all sounds easy. But when he finds himself in conflict, when the objective good of the patient is not identical with his own moral standards, as in the classic instance of abortion? He follows the law, and the law is very often bad."

"These are student arguments," said the lawyer dryly. "Anybody of experience knows that crime or disease, or whatever it may be, calls for a remedy; the remedy must be applied, and if the patient dies—why, that's just too bad."

"I quite agree. Cardinal Richelieu condemned one of his own oldest friends and most faithful servants to death for reasons of state, and I approve. There's a deal too much sentimental cant spoken about compassion—in fact, in this world there's a great deal more cant than compassion."

"Alarmingly true."

"But there are moral issues where the good of the greatest number or the safeguards of society have no bearing and where only our own personal conscience can suffice. Objectivity isn't a virtue; it's an overrated dodge for evading responsibility."

"Your ethics are questionable and your logic deplorable," said the lawyer, smiling.

"Quite so," agreed Van der Valk. "Now if we split the lunch bill in half, is that objective? Or if we toss for

41

it—is that objective? And is either more ethical than my paying for it? Give me subjectivity every time." And a loud laugh made several Dutch lunchers look at the two of them, without any objectivity at all.

"Cant," said Van der Valk, feeling in his raincoat pocket to make sure his gloves were there, and remembering they weren't, "is our worst enemy. I hear more humbug . . ."

He passed the Spui on his way to catch a tram, and his nose twitched. No place to buy a watch—too dear! If he found any good reason for leaning on Mr. Saint a scrap, though, it might be in a good cause.

Mr. Bosboom was a great consolation to him. Wholeness, simplicity, honor—and an earthy Dutch choice of language: it pleased him no end.

A minuscule house in the suburbs, with a minuscule front garden full of roses which had used their available space to the last centimeter. Roses occupied the metal fence and leaned over the gate, rioted round pergolas and climbed up to the gutters of the roof, embowered the front door and framed the windows. Mr. Bosboom, when he appeared, was better still: a huge bowlegged frog with horn-rimmed glasses and a nose like a potato, a shambling walk, a rumbly voice, and a waistcoat with a watch chain across it. More like a man who has spent a life in trade unions than in jewelry. He glared at Van der Valk through roses and asked, "Who are you?" No finessing here.

"Police. Commissaire van der Valk. Need your advice."

"My advice, is it now? What can I advise the police about?"

"Rose-growing, by the look of it. Not the police—me. In a private capacity. Rose by the name of Prinz."

42

Bosboom suddenly looked shrewder, though no less rustic. Shaggy eyebrows came down over the rim of his glasses.

"Satisfy me."

"A young boy of twenty has been employed there. He came to me with a childish tale. I'm not municipal police; I have a special job. I'm not investigating anything. I'm seeking to satisfy my curiosity, and I have a sensation that this boy was asking me for help, although he denies it. I'm looking for information. That leads me to you."

Bosboom stared, searchingly. "Didn't I see you on television?"

"Yes."

"Come in." Inside was as honest, old-fashioned, and clear as champagne. Chintz, lavender polish, and walnut. On the walls hung flower prints framed by someone who knew his job: one of the few details hinting at a past in the antique business. The name was on the tip of his tongue; Bosboom saw him looking.

"Redouté," he said, nodding. "Valuable!" in a tone between sardonic humor and surprise that anyone like him could possibly possess anything valuable. "Tea?"

"Yes, please."

"Mother!" bawled Bosboom. "Tea!"

"Astonishing," looking out at the rosebushes. "If this were June, now."

"Yes," said Bosboom. "What can I do for you?"

Van der Valk explained. Mother appeared with tea, which had jasmine in it. A woman with a lot of character, who said absolutely nothing.

"Well," said Bosboom at last, putting down his cup. "You realize I'm retired. I owe them nothing. They owe me nothing. Louis I'll say nothing about, save that I've known him and worked with him for thirty years, and

43

that he's honest. You needn't look for anything there. He's a genuine expert, a good businessman—that shop wouldn't be there if he weren't—and a good human being. Has his share of human weaknesses—like most of us. Enough is enough—no, don't go reading anything into my words, and I'm not answering any questions. Loyalty still means something to me."

"A young man called Saint," suggested Van der Valk.

"A young man called Saint," mocked Bosboom. "Young dog."

"You know him well?"

"No, thank God. Larry Saint," in a mimicry of affectation. "Name's Leopold. Leopold! Leopold Neil, what a name. Old man's nephew—sister's son, I believe. I don't know anything about him—don't like what I see. One of these characters that go about psychoanalyzing Christ and His saints—an honest atheist I can respect. But a cynic. No self-respect. Undermining everything. Seeing evil in everything. A bad man," he said abruptly.

"You know that you interest me strangely?"

"That's all right. Conclude what you please. I don't know him. I don't want to know him."

"He worked there with you?"

"No!" contemptuously. "Knows nothing about antiques."

"He seems to be running the business."

"Then God help the business. I suppose you think that'd be just my jealousy saying the place couldn't run without me, but it's a business you can't know without feeling—no, stronger—without love. A man like Saint doesn't love anything. His own adored self."

"Did you know he'd got rid of the assistant as well, as it appears?"

Bosboom seemed surprised. "Really?"

44

"Some story of his falling down and breaking an arm, and being a drunk."

"Mm. I suppose there's some truth in that, but he was a decent chap. Kissinger—German chap—unreliable, certainly, but a good craftsman. Wonder why he hasn't been to see me."

"You've his address?"

"I can find it for you, if you like—out in Sloterdijk somewhere. Strange."

"What d'you make of this business of hiring a boy?"

"I can't see the point of it at all. What use is that? Might as well have a typist-girl. What can he do? Stick on stamps, answer the phone, make the tea. What do you make of it?" with a suddenly shrewd, heavy stare.

"I don't know at all."

"There's something, and you feel it—or you wouldn't be here. The boy came to see you—a tale of finding a watch, you say . . ."

"Which he thought was impossible."

"So it is," with a snort.

"This story of stock being run down—one can't attach anything to that, because what could the boy know about it?"

A shrug. "Some modern stuff—it's of no importance. I know roughly; I mean that Saint was always in and out, sniffing and peering, and went on at Louis about modernizing. That's all tripe: what does a good antique business need with modern silver?"

"You saw no virtue in it?"

"Och, it's well in its way; I've every respect for good French craftsmanship, but those Scandinavian things—flibbertigibbety. No real balance, no real taste. Might as well open a hairdressing saloon."

Van der Valk laughed. "Good word."

The old man snorted. "Good word for Saint. I

45

dunno—perhaps not. If you were to take him seriously, you might find more gibbet than flibbet."

"What makes you say that?"

"Can't say, really—nasty crooked way of looking at things. I don't like the chap, never did—that's no good to you. Give you another good word—means the same in French. 'Patibulaire.' I shouldn't say things like that," he added with a grunt. "Not fair. Not evidential. Just backbiting, anyhow. Benefit of the doubt, and all that. Must be accurate: I've nothing against him."

"What can he possibly want with the boy?" wondering aloud.

"No, no, not that; he's not that way. Or I'd be most surprised."

"Would you say," suddenly, "that he has something on Louis?"

Bosboom looked extremely disconcerted, and barked once or twice gruffly to get himself under control. "Nonsense, nonsense. Anyway—I'm not going to discuss Louis, I've told you that. Gave me his confidence for many years, not going to abuse it. Sorry and all that, no wish to appear offensive to yourself. But nosing around like this—why not just walk in and say what *is* all this? Do the boy no harm. Fellow's got anything to conceal—why, then, you've more chance of finding out than all this conjecture."

Van der Valk nodded. "I even thought of walking in as a bona-fide customer and putting on an act. I want to see this Saint."

A big grunt. "Want to buy some antiques? My advice would be don't unless you know what you're after."

"No, I broke my watch this morning. For good, alas."

"Ach—man," went Bosboom impatiently, "if you really want a watch, I'll tell you—why, I've even— Here, I don't know whether it's any good to you, but

46

it's virtually new." He lumbered up and over to a secré-taire, fumbled in the little drawers. "I've had this some time. Old-fashioned but nice. Proper gold, not plated; movement's an Omega. Not automatic, no quartz vibrator. It might vary a minute or two in a month; don't know how important that is to you." Van der Valk took it in his hand and liked it at once: a slim gold circle with a white face and roman numerals like an old hunter.

"No second hand," said Bosboom in his expert voice, which was gentler and with love, the way he might talk to his roses, "and won't tell you the date or the phase of the moon or that technological stuff. Not even phosphorescent. But if you press the winder it'll chime for you, very tiny; it's a repeater. Was made special. I'll show you." His fingers winding were stubby and earthy, but amazingly precise and delicate. "Quarter past three, see." He pressed the winder and the watch chimed minutely, a church twenty miles away across an Alpine valley. Van der Valk was delighted. "Isn't it a pretty thing?" said Bosboom, as though it were a new baby granddaughter. "I kept it for my son—he wanted something more modern," heavily. "Let you have it for an apple and an egg." The old-fashioned Dutch phrase completed the seduction.

"With much gratitude," said Van der Valk, taking out his checkbook. He would pay more than an apple and an egg, but he was not to know that. If he had gone that evening to get a watch from Saint . . . He would have accepted the defeat had he known, because he was accustomed to big events hanging, often, upon very trivial occasions.

He went out to Sloterdijk instead, a tiresome trip across the town, and, as it proved, a great waste of time and energy. It held, even, tragedy. He found a haggard, embittered, wretched woman in the worst kind of Dutch flat, where the economy in space and the meanness of material is not compensated by a gallant display of green plant and mopped floor but pulled down into utter squalor by neglect, smelling sour like an unaired dishcloth. The woman would not even open the door, but kept it on a chain and glared through the gap with a mad yellow eye, the eye of a captive sick parrot.

"He's not here. He's in hospital. Who wants him? Why? What good could that do him? It's too late to think about that now. He's in hospital, I tell you, and he's dying, I know he is. He's got cancer, and what will become of me then? You go and ask Mr. Spire that. I won't talk to you. Go away or I'll call the police. I've nothing to say. Get away and leave me solitude at least. It's all I've got left."

He trekked wearily back into the town. On the bus, he made his new watch chime two or three times in his ear, secretly. Time, it said to him, time. End of the round. One minute's rest to recuperate. Put stuff on the man's eyes, get the swellings down or he won't be able to carry the fight. Time again, and keep your left hand well up.


That afternoon's deceptive mild February sunshine, which had sent Bosboom out with string and sécateurs to see how his beloved roses had withstood the storms of winter, lifting and airing sodden earth around the boles with love, care, and compost—the sunshine had vanished, as it always did, and now the evening was coming down and bringing fog with it as the weather turned colder again. People shivered, tempers shrank and snapped; trams clanged monotonously and desolately in the open spaces of the Leidseplein, modern plague carts tolling to the population to bring out its

48

dead. Van der Valk sat heavily on a covered terrace and had two large glasses of brandy and a fresh-squeezed lemon. Saint had a hold on Louis Prinz. That much was obvious. Bosboom had stopped him, going out, by laying that big badger's paw of his upon Van der Valk's forearm, very gently.

"Uh—one thing. Should you find out anything, through my remarks or otherwise, that may seem discreditable to old Louis—why, I'd like to ask, knowing I've no right of course to interfere in your work, but I'd like just to ask—take it easy. He's an older man than me, and he's no children. Just not to let your judgments get too abrupt or too severe is all—you won't mind my asking you that?"

It was a temptation to go and see Larry Saint, and create a big drama about watches, and no doubt alarm that silly boy Richard, who was now in such an agony at any interference, and see what happened. Still time before the shop shut. It was a perfectly good tactic, to lean on the laddie a bit. Richard had probably been certain that Van der Valk had forgotten all about that flustered, impulsive visit. Or at least would shrug and do nothing about it: what was it after all but a piece of childishness, almost hysterical? The boy had made a fool of himself, had been humiliated—and now, instead of letting it slip, that bloody policeman comes bumbling officiously around Amsterdam, walking into his own private room, the one place where he can forget his extreme vulnerability. Tactless!

Van der Valk grinned. It might, too, provoke Saint in some way. The odds were that Saint had not witnessed his apotheosis on television, but if he was the man Van der Valk took him for he might have a sharp nose for plainclothes policemen, and the story of the watch dropped in tramlines had just the right fabricated sound to make him suspect something fishy while wondering what on earth it was. The chap must be up to something—but for the life of him, Van der Valk could not tell what it could be. What can you get up to in a jeweler's shop? Bosboom had discounted any financial fiddle very firmly.

"The professionals would be on to that in no time at all," he had said. "Too many people involved—all that business is by word of mouth."

He might be exaggerating, from self-respect and pride in a business where he himself had spent most of his life. But still—a good witness, a responsible person.

Why should Saint pretend to lose a valuable watch, let the boy find it in circumstances tempting him to put it in his pocket, and continue to pretend he had noticed nothing?

"What I don't like," he had said to Bosboom, with whom he had been frank about his errand, "is that it's such a classical maneuver with a young boy; I mean it's absolutely the three-card trick. It's a bribe, and as well a handle. I mean that technically the boy can be made out a thief, and threatened with that. Not much of a grip, because these boys nowadays don't take that kind of accusation too seriously. They know they won't go to any real prison, and couldn't care less about a night or two in the jug and a scolding from a police-tribunal magistrate. Nor does the social stigma bother them: petty pinching is now so widespead. Still, it's quite a valuable object—seven or eight hundred, surely, a gold Patek Philippe . . . So that it's a substantial hold, and also could be a fine bribe for a boy—not just a lousy underwater watch, huh. But what I don't see is how that could help Saint. Vice, presumably, but not just a banal bit of sodomy—comes too expensive and he can get that for free—anyway, you discount that idea."

50

The shops will be closing, thought Van der Valk, looking at his watch (and taking it off to put in his pocket: Louis Prinz might know it again). The rabbit-scurry in the wavering light reflections on the Leidseplein was thickening steadily, and next door the flower shop was putting up the shutters. Louis might not be going home, but the Jacob van Lennep was not far away; it cost nothing to go and find out. And on the whole this seemed the best line of approach. If Saint had something on the old man, it was quite probable that in return the old man knew something about nefarious activities, assuming there were any. It was even on the cards that he had a hand in them.

A shabby street, and at a foggy February nightfall intensely dreary. Gloomy dreary surroundings, a sense of heavy dusty hangings and curtains and old women peering out behind them. Van der Valk was well aware that he was being "subjective" again, and very unfair, and that all the arts of civilized living can flourish around the Wilhelmina Hospital as well as they can anywhere, but he had never been quite able to rid himself of an old suspicion: that around here the stock-exchange page of the newspaper gets very thoroughly read, but precious little else.

Van der Valk did not expect Mr. Prinz to be a great fan of late-night television, either, but was taking no chances. On the quayside, where fog was settling heavily upon the greasy black canal, he adopted a disguise. He had two sets of reading glasses, one with tinted lenses. The hat, the briefcase, the precise fussy manner as of Special Branch types, for whom he had always had a healthy dislike. He took his hat off and combed his damped hair down flat. Might be a risk, but not, he thought, much of one.

An old woman—there are always old women—let

51

him into a flat of such gray stillness and silence that the many objects of beauty seemed to have become dulled and stilled and to have lost all their sparkle. She made a great deal of fuss, and he had to be pompous. Mr. Prinz was not back yet, but was expected, yes—grudgingly—anytime. Van der Valk, as he always did, had a bloody good peek about. Such a contrast to the bright sunniness of the little villa where Bosboom grew roses and collected Redouté prints. The wallpaper was gray, the paint gray, the fat chairs and sofa covered in faded gray velvet. Carpet an ancient Turkey thing, hearthrug dirty white. Even the gilt picture frames had lost all their luster. Plenty of comfort for elderly widower—or was he a bachelor? Decanters with sherry, madeira, whisky (lifting the stoppers and sniffing all three). A cabinet with a complete set of Meissen monkey musicians, and some gilded stuff that looked ugly to him but was no doubt exceedingly good. Two gilded torchères going with a large ormolu mirror, an intricate round-bellied commode with fantastically elaborate marquetry in kingwood and tulipwood and lord-knew-what-wood, so that he wished his father, who had been a carpenter, were there to explain. Glass-fronted diamond-paned bookshelves, obstinately locked. And a great many pictures, all intensely dull to the untrained eye: he could recognize nothing but two Daumier etchings, which were signed anyway. And a key in the outer-door lock, and a shuffle of old woman's feet in carpet slippers, a whispered murmur. Noises of an elderly gentleman taking off his overcoat, hanging it up, and washing his hands at the little lavabo in the entrance. Door opened silently. Old gentleman with a severe, questioning face. Van der Valk had a stiff formal bow. He had no cards but his own, but was ready to gamble with one of them if called for.

"Police Commissaire van der Valk from The Hague. Just an informal call, Mr. Prinz. Just a friendly discussion. Documentary work as part of a large-scale survey." This was an easy role to play: pedantic governmental functionary worrying about his bits of paper; bothered about forms not being filled in properly.

Prinz looked solid enough, but left an impression of lassitude and fatigue. The eyes were ringed with pouched, discolored flesh, as though by chronic liver trouble. The movements were slack and dragging; a carpet-slipper walk. Ponderous expression with a listless quality, as though he did not much care what was said to him, and was not even really listening. That might be most deceptive, because the face was shrewd, sensitive, intelligent.

"Sit down." He gestured, and moved over toward the decanters. "Drink?"

"Thank you, thank you, but no."

"Sorry—I've had a busy day." He sat heavily in a big armchair, pushed his glasses up to rub his eyes. Big flat ears with bunches of dark hair growing on them, pale massive hands that were beautifully shaped, this beauty accented by two antique rings of pale massive gold. His hair needed cutting, but his gray mustache was neatly trimmed. He was wearing an old-fashioned waistcoat with two buttons undone, and a flannel shirt, but there was no egg spilt on them. The presence of a commissaire of police was giving him, possibly, a hunted look, but that might just as easily have been a wish to escape from boredom.

"We're not very happy about art," Van der Valk tittuped on. So might the president of a large chemical company address his board of directors—"I'm not very pleased with fertilizer, just at present." A prim cough. Prinz looked a little blearily at him; he might have had

53

a rough day, but that was nothing to this poisonous clown awaiting him at the end of it.

"What is all this about?" he muttered.

"We're not really content with existing income-tax and death-duty provisions," Van der Valk went on mercilessly. "And we have grave cause for concern in the impoverishment of the national heritage brought about by an increasing tendency toward the export, which is upon occasion quite illegal, of paintings and other objects of art for which licenses have not been granted." Did Prinz sit up slightly? Rock him back to sleep quick. "Now, the experience gained in Italy," he droned on hastily, "gave lacunae in juridical procedure . . . cases have been brought to our attention . . . we feel considerable cause for concern . . . a speculative approach to objects of art. . . . You've got some nice pictures here."

The simple phrase—it was actually comprehensible —aroused Prinz from apathy.

"You know something about pictures?"

"No, no, no, no," with perfect truth. Prinz seemed relieved; at least he was not going to get told about art.

"They're of no great value except to myself. Wouldn't do. The insurance, you know, too . . ."

"And the—er—ormolu?" looking at the chimney piece.

"After Caffiéri only," explained Prinz carefully.

"Quite so. Now, in your business?"

"I handle the technical side: my nephew, Mr. Saint, handles the finance and the administrative details. I'm sure you'd find everything in order. You'd need to produce authority for anything like examination of our books or anything like that."

"To be sure, to be sure," said Van der Valk, who did

54

not want to get wound up in this, especially as he knew there was a real person somewhere who worried about illegal export of works of art. He waved such indecent suggestions aside. "No, no—in view, er, of the breadth, er, of your experience—the respect in which you are held, er, we should like to feel that if you were cognizant of irregularities anywhere, er, you would be quick to cooperate, to assist, er, the authorities in any inquiries."

"I know of no irregularities," said Prinz politely. "I hope you will excuse me, Mr., er—a dinner appointment."

"Not at all," said Van der Valk and made a getaway before Prinz could think of asking "What was your name again?" or asking, even, for his card.

Van der Valk drew pictures in his notebook, because there was nothing to write. He hadn't learned anything, and yet he had seen a lot. A series of shaky aspects— his arabesques were building up into a shape a very long way indeed after Caffiéri. It was true that he knew little about art, but he had recognized the pictures for what they were, a dozen well-made affairs by minor but good seventeenth-century masters, people whose names caused no sensation in an auction-room catalogue but would make the nose of anyone who really knew his subject begin twitching. People like burglars, dealers, or restorers would have no clue at all; only a dozen or so people in the world really understood such things or knew what they were worth. He had this confirmed for him by Charles van Deijssel, an old acquaintance, a picture dealer whose brains he went to pick when it was anything to do with art, whom he asked out for a cognac, and who appeared, as usual, looking like a fashionable dress designer, in lilac linen with an orchid in his buttonhole.

"Of course," said Charles, "I wouldn't even know, probably, if I saw them except to say, yes, good—as you know, I don't pretend to be expert outside my period. I know how it's done, of course. They pick these things up in the bread-and-butter line, pay fifty, do a bit of work, get an identification, and sell for a few hundred; and every so often you think, That's interesting, and you do some detective work on it, maybe a great deal, trace it back to a catalogue maybe two hundred years ago. Getting the confirmation for that, really nailing the provenance and the author, might take years. Easy enough to point to some dusty old studio inventory saying *Diana and Actaeon* or whatever—proving it's another matter. And you've got to find proof; otherwise it'll never be worth more than a few hundred."

"Whereas if you did find proof?"

"Quite a difference," dryly. "In that case, might easily run to several thousand."

"You know anything at all about Prinz?"

"What would I know about him? Just because we're in the same business—we scarcely meet unless a general sale has stuff that attracts us both. Know him to nod to. He has enormous erudition, handles coins, ivories, miniatures, bronzes; he's not really a picture dealer except by accident. He probably does too much, and doesn't get anything really first-rate in that shop of his—the specialized competition's too fierce. But he does very well with the second-rate, and every now and then, probably, he'll find something really good and turn it over with no trouble at all."

"Not putting it through the books?"

"Well, you know"—Charles with a false smile—"books are there to be cooked. Not your line of country, though, is it?"

"No. Just sniffing privately. Nothing to go on, no

witness, no material evidence; just a person, who interests me somehow. No, no, not Prinz."

"He's perfectly honest, as far as I know."

"But possibilities of all sorts of little quiet fiddles."

"Yes, of course, but you'd have the devil's own job ever proving anything."

"That's what I guessed."

Yes, he thought, going back on his train, no good having feelings about things. Prinz loved beauty and beautiful objects, just like old Bosboom. In perhaps a darker way, more secret, more twisted. People left a stain upon the mind. Sometimes clear soft colors, tranquil patterns; and sometimes harsh clashing muddy reds and purples, jagged distorted shapes. He had got a somber feel in that somber flat. Bosboom had as good as told him straight out that there was something. Crooked corners in a character. He shrugged. What link or tie with Mr. Saint? Never mind. One could not press people; one never got any information that way. He had leaned on the old man ever so slightly; just brushed him, as it were, with police wings. He would do the same with Saint someday soon, next time he was in Amsterdam. And he looked at his new watch with pleasure. Yes, he would lean on Saint a little, just for fun. Private detectives did not learn much. But they had fun. What could that boy have meant with a phrase like "all being steadily cleaned out"? Were they realizing assets, gathering up all the liquid money they could find, perhaps for some really big deal? Could the old man have found some really major picture somewhere, running into the hundreds of thousands? Van der Valk shrugged. And suppose he had? What would they want that boy for? And was it any of his business, let alone police business? The train slowed. He hoped Arlette had something nice for supper.

* * *

57

Richard was beginning to feel confidence, and even beginning to taste that pleasant sensation, the growing certainty that one is on to a good thing. He was accustomed to the shop by now, had learned to move with some assurance in handling the bric-à-brac, and Larry Saint left him an amazing amount of freedom and responsibility, left him increasingly alone. Larry was, in fact, a hell of a cool card, and up to some sharpish tricks. But not small, thought Dick with a bit of half-reluctant admiration. Not just a squalid little fixer. He had laughed when Dick appeared finally, impudently— worried lest it might not be a bit too cheeky—wearing the watch.

"Quite right, Dick," he had said chuckling. "Shows you've got good taste. But it's small fry, you know, small fry. Stay with us—you'll get better opportunities than that." Dick no longer felt that slight fear of Larry he had had at the start. He went a bit hot and cold still, thinking of that policeman. He'd made a monumental fool of himself there. Still, the chap was retired now— no threat. Elderly, desk-bound, lazy, playing about in the university or whatnot with theses and a lot of sociological crap. Having in his day—only a few months back, but Dick felt he had become a great deal more adult since then—toyed a bit with sociology courses at the university, he could afford to feel disdainful. Anyway, he had choked the fellow off. No nosy policemen had come hanging about.

He no longer felt the awe he'd had for old Louis, either; in fact, he had said "Morning, Louis" in quite a casual way this morning, and the old boy hadn't got on a high horse but just said "Morning, Richard." True, those muttered conversations still went on at the back from which he felt excluded, since if he happened to be in that direction silence fell, and Larry had been inclined to refer to the old boy in respectfully hushed

58

tones; but he had noticed a thing or two these last days—Larry's way of talking had got a lot freer. He had that casual, throwaway style of speaking still, but his words were more to the point. It was as though Dick had passed a period of probation, had been sized up, as it were, and not found too stupid. Well, he wasn't too stupid, even if he said so himself. Normal that Larry, who was sharp as a bloody needle and missed nothing, should have understood that. He had worked hard, been willing, run all the errands, cleaned up a lot of dirty old junk in the cellar—a few of those old pictures had absolutely the filth of centuries on them. He hadn't complained once, not asked for more money or anything. He was still getting peanuts, but, well—look at that watch. A perk, Larry had said, laughing. Was worth a lump.

Only just this morning, Louis, too, had been freer in speaking in front of him than hitherto. Just showed he was being given more confidence. He'd pricked his ears up for a second, too!

"Had some policeman in to see me last night," Louis had said.

"Really?" said Larry indifferently. "What was his name?"

"How should I know? Van something. I didn't look at his damn card."

Dick had prickled for a second before reflecting that half Holland was called Van something, that nothing could be done officially—there had been no complaint made—and that it had nothing to do with old Louis, anyway, who didn't even know they stocked any watches, like as not: he was quite uninterested in the front of the shop.

"The usual, I suppose?" Larry was saying, reading the paper.

"No, they come here to the shop from time to time

with their little lists—we know them, usual burglary-detail types. This was some damn bureaucrat, customs and excise stuff, worrying away about export licenses. I've had the same kind of thing before once or twice. Just a warning, really, to lie low. What about that—you know, the French one?"

"Why worry?" Larry did not even look up from his paper. "Are we involved or something?"

"Well, but . . ."

"But what? It was in our cellar for over five years—no question of a speculation there. We made a perfectly fair deal with a third person. If he has dealt illegally, we don't even know."

"Oh, I'm aware how adept you are at invariably finding a third person. It will never be you, my boy, who carries the can, will it now?"

The paper rustled slightly, as though with irritation, but Saint did not allow his voice to rise. "I don't see you complaining when there's money to be made."

"If it was only in this business—if it was only pictures," said Louis angrily. Dick, embarrassed, was staying very still, but Prinz had perhaps forgotten all about him. "There's nothing wrong with this business and one should stick to it. I've said so a hundred times."

"You've said so a hundred times," repeated Saint, in a colorless tone that was somehow more insulting than mimicry.

Prinz was stung. "That girly stuff, and dirty books— I suppose that's trivial, but—"

"Not to you it isn't," and this time Saint's voice had an unmistakable edge.

"These other fishy deals . . ." Louis's voice trailed off.

"That's my business," slowly and coldly. "You're the picture expert. You stick to art."

60

But Prinz was not going to be snubbed. "Art," with a snort of real contempt, making for the door. "You talk about art as though it were groceries in a supermarket, and to you that's about all it is. You think yourself clever, my boy, and you take all your precautions—oh, yes, I realize—but you'll never know anything about art." He could not slam the shop door, because it could not be slammed, but he went through the movements.

Saint lowered his paper and smiled sidelong at Richard, as though inviting him to share a private joke.

"Dear old Louis; whenever he gets cranky—you must make allowances; he's no longer as young as he has been—he always thinks he can squash me by telling me I know nothing. The old invariably think that, as you'll have noticed."

"My god, yes." Dick was pleased at not having to be embarrassed any further. It had only been a little spat of words, a little family squabble. "And after all he really is a big expert, isn't he, and they can't bear being wrong."

"Very good," said Saint, laughing. "Well observed. Of course Louis is a first-class expert, but not on life, as you'll find out. Their trouble is their refusal—or their inability—to understand the limits of their expertise."

"What was all that about dirty books?" with immense casualness.

"Unimportant." Saint shrugged. "Forms a part of any antique business—erotic engravings, and all that— what booksellers call the 'curious' trade. Any dealer has a few dirty books; that and 'occult'—it's part of the business. There are always good customers for it— nothing for you, though; the customers like somebody older; they find him more 'understanding' of their special needs."

The morning was much as usual, with Saint absent for most of it. A little before lunchtime he reappeared,

61

pottered about aimlessly for a minute or two, and then said suddenly, "Come and have a drink, Dick."

"Lovely. Though I don't drink much. Can't afford it on my salary."

Saint grinned. "That's all right, I'm paying. We won't go to a bar—let's see, you've never been in my flat, have you?"

"I don't even know where it is. You live on the Leliegracht someplace, don't you?"

Richard was first surprised, and then impressed. The shabby, mean little entrance next door to the sex shop did not seem like Saint, nor did the narrow, fusty stairway. That the flat should be so big, so airy—and so rich . . . he opened his eyes. Persian rugs and some good antique furniture—well, Larry was in the right business to get hold of them. But he liked the creaky old parquet floor with an inlaid pattern in pale hardwood, beautifully lavender-waxed, the superb bathroom where he was taken to wash his hands, the ease and elegance of it all. When he thought of his own ghastly room . . .

"Is that really a Renoir?"

"No, it's a fake," said Larry negligently. "But people think it real when I want them to think it real, which is just as good. Now—Campari, Lillet, Chambéry? Or a Spanish Pernod, nearest thing to real absinthe nowadays."

"Campari, please," since it was the only one he'd ever heard of.

"What about a cigarette? Those are blonde, those are French, and those are reefers; take your pick."

"I don't get reefers as a rule," with a self-conscious giggle. "Too dear. I say—pretty good here."

"Yes," vaguely. "Ice? A dealer gets his hands on all sorts of things, as you are beginning to understand, and some of them can make plenty. That, now—no, you needn't bother; they aren't dirty books—the poems of Horace in the original binding, sixteenth century, right here in Amsterdam; you'd be surprised what it's worth."

"Nice."

"Yes, you've got taste. But it's only like your watch, you know; these material things are small fry. The moth corrupts and the rust spots—I say, that sounds Biblical, doesn't it? They get burgled or broken or lost in a fire, and where are you then? It's brains that make money, my lad."

"You've got to have them first, though, don't you?"

"Oh, one can acquire them," merrily. "I like you, Dick. Been watching you, as you know, and pretty happy with the promise you show. I'll let you into something—how would you like to come tonight? I've a bit of a party on; I don't want to sound patronizing, but I think it's time you learned something of the world."

"You bet—but I don't have anything much to wear."

"No strain—we don't go for dinner jackets any more. If you have money, spend it on clothes if that's what you enjoy; if not, a shirt and corduroy pants goes just as well. Gray matter is what counts. What was your comment again—that one didn't always have it? Very true, but other people have, or they have talent. One deals in that," shaking the ice blocks in his drink gently. "The best basic capital, Dicky, the most fruitful, the most adaptable. Doesn't get wet, warped, or broken. A clever impresario makes a little country girl into a singer—a star. And he refuses ten million dollars for her. Takes skill, I grant, and luck, too, but no more than the stock exchange, or any of those other nine-teenth-century ways of getting rich. Barney Barnato to

63

Bernie Cornfeld—how out of date it all does sound. Like politics, whether it's Perón or Papa Doc, they made plenty, I grant you, but how clumsy, how complicated, how restricted—and dangerous, too," as an afterthought, "always at the mercy of some imbecile with a gun. Things can get taken away from you. Finding a thing you understand and using it, like Charles Engelhard—pretty good—gold, wasn't it? Metals, anyway. But human beings are better. Find what the ruck wants, and give it them. When the small fry start getting into the act, then get out."

"The ruck?"

"The populace, my boy, the consumers. The ones with the money."

"But if it were that simple, everyone would be rich."

"A surprising number of people are," blandly. "They don't advertise it, that's all. No need to get the tax people in too much of a fluster."

He grinned suddenly. "Beginning to sound like a James Bond villain, am I? Dr. No or something?" Richard was a little shocked. Larry had that disconcerting way of putting things. "I'm just small fry, too. This place is nothing."

"Oh, I don't know. You've got some pretty nice things here."

"Toys," contemptuously. "Nothing. But I'm learning, too, Dicky, you see. This town is nothing much."

"What, Amsterdam!"

"Ach, it's fashionable. People think it's terrific. It's a springboard, I suppose. No, it took me a long while to learn, and I've hardly begun to move. I've got my arms free at last. I was stuck in that bog of a shop for too long."

"Hey!"

"Yes, quite—now it's you that is stuck there. And

64

there you'll have to stay for a while, my boy. But it's not a bad place to learn. You have to learn to be lucid, and how to control yourself. Handling people is surgery, that's all. Oh, yes, I did a few years' medicine at the university. I was bored stiff, but now I realize it was very good training; you learn to understand the human machine, that's all it is. You learn when to leave things alone altogether, when to let them ripen a while longer. When to make a little incision, and when to cut deep— you have to do that, too, sometimes, and it takes nerve. There is a flow of blood—and you learn to cut that off. Nobody need be frightened by a flow of blood, but it does take training. If you're interested in learning, I'll find an object lesson for you one of these days. Meanwhile you get on top of this piddling jewelry business— oh well, it's a milch cow. Like another? The ice bucket's there on your side. Time before lunch still. And about this evening—you'd like that? Right, then, fine; you trot along here around eight or nine—not a dinner, but cold things I get a place to send along for me, so there'll be plenty to eat. Nothing formal, nobody to be alarmed at, just a few people, imbeciles for the most part, make a good first lesson for you. That's understood, then. Pay no heed if old Louis gets a bit shirty with you; he might be humiliated at having let his hair down in front of you."

"A quiet evening," said Van der Valk, yawning. "I couldn't for the life of me say why, but I've had a hard day, I think it's Shufflebottom, she's so extraordinarily energetic." He looked at his wife with pleasure and surprise, both more underlined than was usual after a hard day.

"I've no wish to contradict," said Arlette, with a listlessness that was for her unusual, too, so that he felt quite agitated: what was wrong with them?

65

She wasn't getting younger. Discovering she had gray hair, she had become extremely unbalanced about it, and spoken dramatically of "un coup de vieux." In fact, it suited her so well that she was prettier than ever, and the gray streak was no more than just noticeable anyway in an ash blonde, unless one stared madly. But she was a lot thinner, and more energetic in a nervous way: she moved more, as well as more rapidly. She hadn't got over the "new flat" yet. It was, true enough, sadly poky. There hadn't been room for more than half the furniture even if they had wanted to bring it: the solution had been to send a lorry-load to France, to "the cottage" bought for retirement and now really home. It made the years to go till retirement shorter somehow to know that those things were already there. They had agreed that with his disability pension it would be worth it to retire early, even though he was not yet fifty. Good-looking woman, he thought.

At present she was nursing a grievance about the television. The place for it, she said with French logic, is in the kitchen, or at a pinch the dining room—they never had had a dining room, but since they ate in the kitchen this was a politeness. Dutch kitchens, alas, are very small, and living now for the first time in a modern building where space has been mercilessly economized, she had been hit by this lack. It really was a tiny flat by any standards, doled out with the utmost parsimony. "Well, since your children are grown up," said the housing official, "you don't need all those bedrooms," and everything else had been reduced in proportion. It was true that the boys were never home now, but the principal bedroom was too small even for their bed, so that it, too, had been sent to the cottage and they slept on narrow shelves. It was like being in the army. Ruth, their adopted daughter, the only child at home and now a silent, secretive teen-ager, hated her bedroom, too, as much as they did theirs. "Beastly little cupboard." She didn't think much of her new school, either. Altogether Van der Valk was not free of regret at having accepted his glamorous new job. "Think of the money we're saving, though," he'd said wistfully.

"Shit," Arlette had replied nastily. "What would we save money for?" The cottage was paid for. The boys were nearly through their studies and were already talking of the grandiose jobs they had lined up. "I see us as a really cranky pair of old biddies," she had remarked, "seeing our children about every six months, when they dump their brats into our laps before disappearing on another Caribbean cruise."

She hadn't been altogether happy about the cottage, either. "I'm sure it will rain all the time."

"Quite, and that is why the entire population is growing grapes. It's just right," said Van der Valk defensively, "just midway between," for he had been taken by Voltaire's distinction between countries where one thinks and those where one just sweats.

"If we always agreed," Arlette had said, resigned, "life would be very dull. But I am always bossed about."

"You like to be bossed about."

"But only after a considerable argument." She was a poor advertisement, she remarked gratefully, for women's lib.

The new life was very bourgeois. Arlette had found a new hospital to work in, and came and went on a bike, because there was "too much traffic for the deux-chevaux." Ruth, who had further to go to school, complained bitterly that she was not old enough to drive the deux-chevaux, and longed for a motorbike. He was nearest to his work, so he went on the tram and walked home.

"What's for supper?"

"Sort of tart, with leeks in, and cream sauce. Bouh, your raincoat's sopping, and where the hell does one spread it out to dry in this detergent packet of a place is what I'd like to know."

"Has anybody seen my German dictionary?" asked Ruth, coming in crossly.

It was all very humdrum, thought Van der Valk, picking up his book about Montrose. He liked history; it was one of the best ways of putting life into proportion, by distancing things. Arlette liked fiction, but wanted it to be an easy read; something that told a story. Unless Kai Lung unrolls his mat, she said, I'm not there at all. She was not interested in Montrose. Scotland in the seventeenth century, she said with elaborate shudders, what could be more barbaric? A great mistake, he told her austerely.

"Supper," kicking open the door from the kitchen because both arms were full.

Marvelous flat, thought Richard, taking off his jacket and selfconsciously displaying his splendid pale-green shirt with metallic silver stripes, bought just that afternoon. If everything was new, it would look lousy however much money had been spent: it is those faded dark blues in the worn carpet that make one realize. The big room had an exciting, theatrical smell, like grease paint.

"You've come a bit early; that's nice," said Larry with his curved smile. "You won't mind giving me a hand to get a few things cleared?"

"Of course not." The sensation of being behind the scenes added zest and gave a comforting familiarity which obliterated awe. Richard had no experience of parties except the student sort, with Algerian plonk and a treasured bottle of cut-price vermouth, and the excessively prim little "receptions" of his childhood: his mother's agonized fussing in the kitchen with tiny bits of cheese and bacon, limp shrimps and watery smoked eel, imploring the red-handed servant girl not to touch the good china on any account. He was surprised when Larry locked the drinks cupboard with a wink and put the key in his pocket, and more surprised still to find a depressed man in the kitchen unpacking large wooden boxes. There was a pompous big pâté cooked in a golden crust, a whole side of smoked salmon already sliced and cunningly reassembled—there were no less than two crates of champagne. Richard's dazzlement was completed when one of the coffins proved to have a zinc lining and to be filled with huge bars of ice. China, glass, silver, and napkins appeared magically; the caterer's man tapped at ice with a little silver hammer, put the first dozen bottles into buckets, bowed, produced an imposing inventory, said "Will that be all, sir, please sign here, thank you very much, sir," pocketed his tip too deftly for Richard to see how big it was, and vanished.

"Who's getting married?" asked Richard boorishly. Larry gave the bottles a turn to settle them in the ice, wiped his fingers fastidiously, smiled, and said, "You and Daisy."

"Who's Daisy?" in alarm, and too late because the doorbell was ringing.

There were so many lessons to learn, so many tests to pass, so many little traps, so many awkward moments in which he felt his provinciality, his adolescent lumpiness, and his crude student manners being brutally removed—as though with paint stripper—and painfully sandpapered down, that he certainly did not enjoy himself. He understood a few things he had wanted to ask but had had no time for, like "Suppose someone doesn't like champagne?" One of the men, a German with a noisy laugh, asked for whisky, and he heard—with admiration—Larry's silky voice saying easily, not offensively, "My word—we should have gone to the pub, shouldn't we, to stock up." And at one moment he heard the same voice, soft and silvery, whisper, "Don't drink so much," in his ear. It was already too late, and he had to disappear discreetly a little later to vomit in the bathroom, but by making an effort he brought himself back under control, and there were other moments when he felt he was not doing too badly, as when Daisy gave him her huge flashing smile and murmured, "You know, Larry, I like your protégé." Daisy had disconcerted him greatly, and he hadn't at all grasped the "marriage" joke, because she was very thin, not really pretty at all, and when he tried being flirtatious in a rather heavy provincial way he found her icily distant. Her dark sea-green frock fitted her too well, she wore too much jewelry, and her perfume was so harshly somber it had a choking quality, almost like ammonia. Anyway, she was nearer fifty than forty if he was any judge.

But everybody was—except for Larry, of course, himself, and a young girl of perhaps eighteen, called Thalia, who was ravishing, with a silver lamé frock and a black velvet scarf and magnificent breasts. Nobody had familiar solid Dutch names: there was a Winifred and a Maxine and a Franziska; they spoke Dutch when they weren't speaking English, and their accents sounded Dutch, but they weren't like any Dutch people Dick had ever met.

He thought Thalia had been invited a bit perhaps "for him," since she was the only one his age, but found her very arch and standoffish, and much more interested in Heinz, the burly athlete who had wanted whisky. A slight narrowing of Larry's eyes warned him, and he did his best to squire Daisy assiduously. There were several underground patterns he realized he didn't understand, little formal movements of conversation like some kind of old-fashioned dance which he hadn't learned. The men, he realized, were in an oblique way talking business, and he had sense enough not to interfere. The eating went on a very long time, but somehow he never did get an awful lot himself; he was kept too busy getting things for Daisy and Winifred, a big handsome woman with a deep soft voice who, he had at last realized, was married to the German. A long time later, it seemed, a professional waitress in a black frock and white apron was suddenly serving coffee, and Larry was standing in front of the ornate brass-inlaid cabinet drawling, "Calvados, Jean-Claude?" He himself wasn't asked, but suddenly he found a brandy glass in his hand, sipped at it wondering what it was—he had never tasted Calvados—and was greatly taken aback to find he had some kind of sugar syrup with no alcohol in it at all. Daisy was drinking framboise, and Winifred brandy.

Up to now there had been no music, only that intricate, difficult conversation that turned and dodged and doubled in and out of business; magic—an extraordinary conjurer Daisy had seen; sport—ski and tennis; New York geography; and restaurants in Holland and Germany. There were some subjects that were totally taboo. Art was one, oddly enough. Politics was another. "Oh, my dear," said Daisy, "that Minister who takes his shoes off at conferences; don't talk to me about such boring things." It was tricky sometimes. Money, naturally, was never mentioned; Richard had understood that nothing is more provincial than money. But neither, oddly, was anything remotely metaphysical, even where the magician was concerned. When, as occasionally it did, the conversation lapsed, Dick missed the comforting shout and thud of pop groups with ever more contrived names picked out for them by copywriters. It was a relief to him when, after the maid had cleared away the coffee cups and disappeared, Larry put on a series of French chansonniers who agonized in a low-keyed, illegible, but determinedly intellectual manner, and said gently. "Well, perhaps we might have a little entertainment. Thalia, my dear?"

Aha, that was the point of Thalia—she turned out to be a dancer. She did what seemed to Richard a rather brilliant imitation of a Balinese girl, a great deal of carefully finished work with the elbows and fingertips, the silver lamé melting and shivering, liquidly decomposed, and reforming into stylized flowers. She retired modestly to the bathroom, came back in a classic tulle skirt with a tight satin top, and did a Balanchine-Stravinsky parody which was really extremely clever. Slightly less modestly, she took this off, displaying much rippling muscle, and struck an attitude before saying in her childish, tinny voice, "In the style of Maurice Béjart." This was, athletically, extremely difficult and did not always come off, but was greeted with much warmth.

"A bronze drum," said Larry elegantly.

"My god," murmured Winifred to Daisy, just loud enough for Richard to hear, "her breasts really are superb; I could almost feel jealous."

The girl sat cross-legged on the carpet in something like a lotus position, with her head bowed, panting from her exertion. Her tan gleamed with sweat; she seemed unconscious of the remarks being made. She's magnificent, thought Richard with wholehearted admiration and fierce desire; he had drunk no more cham-

72

pagne, but a glass of water and the two cups of strong coffee had made him less woozy. He had had just enough to eat so that his stomach was stabilized. He radiated energy; he felt fine. The girl's body—she was very tanned, and was wearing nothing but white tights—charged him as though with electric current: he tingled with force.

When her breathing quietened, Larry said, "Now the Netherlands Dance Theatre," and put on a new record. This one was a percussion group, so intricate in texture that it became orchestral: the rhythms, at once stiff and liquid, both emphasized and parodied the primitive quality in urban, sophisticated embroideries. The girl stretched out on her back, lay still, began to tense and relax her muscles, trite rhythmic movements modulating gradually into plastic experiments which began with no more than a flutter of her fingers, spreading up her hands and arms to her torso and gradually to her whole body, dying away again and finishing in a kind of trance that had a catatonic quality, so that it was uneasy and frightening. Suddenly she planted her feet, threw her head back, arched her body, and peeled the tights off. Richard found his teeth clenched hard, and a nerve in a back tooth reminding him angrily that it needed filling.

She stretched her arms out above her head and, without moving her feet, began to follow the music with her body. Too tensed and angular to be serpentine or fluid, too painful to have any beauty, her movement still held and gripped attention; it was a possession, resembling those ritual performances in which the participants pierce and wound themselves without apparent effect: even the flow of blood is suspended. The percussion clashed and jarred angrily: her body became increasingly harsh and anguished. Was she doped? No,

73

Richard did not think so, but she had drunk a good deal. He felt soaked in sweat; his eyes blinked dizzily, slipping out of focus; he felt as taut and strung as she appeared; her muscles bunched and roped like a gymnast's. If she had a knife or anything, he feared, she would be doing herself an injury. She had no knife—the movements shuddered to a climax and she began to make love to herself in a way so harsh and cruel that he had to look away; it was unbearable. He saw Daisy's face a few inches away, as hard-set as the girl's body, a line of sweat along the stiff-curled upper lip. He looked uneasily, as though with relief, back to the girl. Everyone in the room had the same rigidly locked immobility. The girl's body collapsed to the carpet and she lay there as though guillotined, head turning from side to side, neck muscles twitching in violent involuntary jerks. The music stopped.

There was a harsh hot moment of silence. Larry's voice, as always soft and easy, sounded with a shrill edge to it.

"Who will add to the gaiety? Winifred?"

Her laugh was like a crystal chandelier tearing loose and falling on a parquet floor.

"I wish I could," she said.

Another woman got up suddenly, a youngish, colorless-seeming woman whom Richard had scarcely noticed. She was carrying a glass of brandy. She stooped, half knelt, put her arm behind the girl's head, pulled her roughly sitting upright, held the glass—shoved it—against the pale lips, and said, "Drink," abruptly.

The girl sipped, drank, shuddered violently, and sputtered half the glassful back on the woman's shoulder. The woman paid no attention; she threw the glass under a chair, where it rolled and lay and no one bothered about it. She put both hands under the girl's shoulder blades and with a violent effort heaved her upright. The girl was limp, the woman more than half drunk; they staggered about and wobbled uncertainly. The woman braced her feet, wrapped both arms around the girl's body, and clutched it with a sort of ferocity, so that the skin, gleaming with sweat, left smudges on the pale frock. She held it so tightly that the body arched over and the head stretched back, opening the lines of the jaw and neck down to the collarbones. The woman pressed her face into the girl's throat, kissed it, and bit her ear.

Dick found suddenly that there was a pain in his palate, and at the root of his tongue, keen and crippling. His eyes filled with tears; he leaned over without caring about manners, seized Daisy's half-full glass, and gulped what was in it. The alcohol took his breath away. When he wiped the moisture out of his eyes and could again see, the girl was holding herself up by her two hands clasped behind the woman's neck. As he watched, her fingers flickered, flexed, caught hold of the zipper running down the spine, and tugged at it. He could see that her eyes were shut, and her lower lip caught up in her teeth in concentration.

The tension was snapped by an abrupt movement of Larry's toward the wall. The lights in the room were all put out together. Richard felt Daisy make a sudden movement; he turned toward her with a despairing feeling that he knew what to do, but felt sure he was going to make a very poor job of it.

Van der Valk, lying in bed in The Hague, absorbed in reading all about that restless, slippery, crooked fellow the chief of the Clan Campbell, banged irritably at his pillow, which had slipped down, and said, "Have you any peanuts?"

"No," said Arlette. "An apple if you want, but no

75

peanuts. Do stop bouncing about like that. D'you want half my apple?"

"No," irritably. "I want something salty."

"Now come on, wake up," said Saint sharply. He himself was as fresh and unmarked as the fine morning. Richard made an effort.

"That auction stuff that Louis bought—a van-load of it. I'll try and get it unpacked and cleaned up, shall I, and then make some coffee?"

"Good," said Saint an hour later. "You're learning to make coffee, too. All part of the same thing," helping himself to a little more sugar, "a social exercise; whether it's in manners or coffee, you must keep to the rules. . . . You did well there, Dicky, and for a first time it was a bit rough, I had no idea that fool of a girl was going to go that far."

"What happened to her?"

"She got taken off by that man with the loud laugh, the waterski type. He's a cretin, that man—they make a well-matched pair. Now if I hadn't stopped you, you'd have been running after her. That might, I suppose, have been more fun."

"But isn't she—?"

"Not at all; does that because she thinks it's more fashionable and makes her appear more interesting. Give me some more coffee, would you?"

"Daisy . . ." hesitantly; was it a taboo subject?

"Daisy, yes, not easy; she likes her geese green and that's what you are, if you'll forgive me saying so, Dicky. But it will be very valuable for you. She'll tease you, persecute you, cut you off and on again, wait for you to lose your temper, make scenes—she enjoys that. That other calf is too stupid to be vicious, but Daisy is for real and that's what I want. Come through that for a week or two, and I'll give you a present. To help you—look at her as though she were a work of art. Her movements, her laugh, the way she eats—watch her when she's dressing, or putting on make-up, and you'll see her studying her art. You got that stuff cleaned up?"

"Lot of dusty old tat," distastefully

"I don't mind you saying that," said Saint in his driest voice, "as long as you don't start to think you know what you're talking about."

"Sorry."

"Yes. Let's get it straight. You've heard me make remarks about this place being a good old moo-cow, and you add that to other scraps of conversation you overhear, and you conclude that I'm milking this business for purposes of my own. That's one thing. Then I tell you an elementary fact or two about markets, and you realize that I'm interested in the young, and after adding that to the obvious fact that the young do not spend money in antique jewelers you think you can behave in an arrogant fashion. An exceptionally stupid attitude. Talking of youth, there's mayonnaise all over the window again—get that cleaned up, Dick-boy, and make sure while you're at it no dogs have been looking for lampposts." It was a continual grievance. The clientele of the snack bar strolled along the street refreshing themselves with things in paper bags. They stopped to look at shopwindows, and covered the glass with greasy finger marks. Richard, realizing this to be a rap on the knuckles, went obediently to get the little bucket and sponge. Larry and his goddam discipline. He hoped Daisy didn't take that moment to come strolling along the pavement. That would be humiliating.

Mr. Saint was also thinking of Daisy—along other lines—when the stupid boy came hurtling in as though

77

a bull were chasing him, and rushed through into the back of the shop.

"Forgot the shammy leather," he muttered confusedly. Mr. Saint was considering this uncontrolled behavior with raised eyebrows when the door swung open afresh and Van der Valk walked in with a pleasant imbecile smile tacked all over his face.

"Good morning, sir," said Saint with his invariable politeness.

"Good morning, good morning. A lamentable occurrence—I've broken my watch. Irreparably, I fear."

"We'll see what we can do. Perhaps you'd like to sit down."

Van der Valk had decided that his "personal investigation" was dragging a little and, having come from another of his boring meetings in the Overtoom, had thought of improving the hour. Leaning upon Mr. Saint a tiny bit was obviously the next stage.

"It was very sad," he burbled. "I dropped it in the tramline, of all things, right there in the Koningsplein; I never would have thought it possible, would you?"

"A very unhappy accident," agreed Saint gravely. "There is, of course, nothing we can do there. A new watch is the one solution to your problem, I'm afraid."

"I fear so, I fear so," shouted Van der Valk. "Something quite simple—er—classic."

He was amused. He had been studying a window full of shirts—blimey, King Charles I got up to dance the Lilac Fairy—when he had seen his idiot boy come trotting out with his bucket to clean the window. He stood grinning a dozen yards along the pavement, wondering what the reaction would be, and was delighted when the boy caught his eye suddenly while gawking about, stared in open-mouthed consternation, and bolted.

Saint came sliding over with a velvet-lined tray of expensive stuff in restrained good taste, hitched another of the little Empire chairs across, and sat down, the specialist at the patient's bedside. Van der Valk put his elbow on the little circular table and prepared to have his blood tested. An interesting face, that, a foot from his own. Character there, and determination. Very highly polished. A "bad man"? He had no idea. He had been many years a policeman, but had met few bad men. Plenty of silly men, and a great many stupid ones. This was neither. A man, quite certainly, in whom one could grow interested.

"The quartz crystal vibrator . . ." Saint was saying.

"No, no tuning forks. They sing at one all the time," explained Van der Valk vaguely.

"Then a classic movement. Now this Jaeger le Coultre . . ." The boy was still fumbling about, pretending to be busy in the back. What was more, Saint had noticed. He glanced at the door and the fine silky eyebrows drew together a little: a slight sidelong glance without turning the head; a flicker of the well-cut nostrils—no, he would say nothing in the presence of a customer.

"Perregaux . . . there are very few made, you understand, only a hundred or so a year. These are all really exclusive models."

"They're perhaps a little rich for my blood," with a loud self-conscious laugh.

"I do rather like this one," Van der Valk went on happily—it was a Patek Philippe, not so very dissimilar to the one the boy had had. Would there be any reaction to this extremely light touch, or should one lean a little harder? "I mean it's most distinctive. Not the kind of thing one sees every day."

"Quite so." No, no flicker. Could he really not have

79

known about that watch? Bosboom had pooh-poohed that as absurd. "Should I perhaps look up the prices for you?"

"I'm afraid they'll be alarming."

"Yes, well, they run at around a thousand, you know. Of course, that is solid gold—a real investment."

"Not plated?"

"We sell no plate," with delightfully simple hauteur.

"Oh dear. I'm quite perplexed. I do rather fancy this one." Van der Valk had a good stare round, with the vacant gaze of someone wondering whether he can afford it: tempted but frightened.

"Just so. You might, of course, wish to think it over." Mr. Saint was evidently well accustomed to people who went off to "think it over" and were seen no more. . . . That boy was still lurking in the shadows: locked in the lavatory, as likely as not. He wouldn't come out now, that was certain.

"I hardly feel able, alas. . . ."

"But, my dear sir, there is no obligation."

"But putting you to this trouble," said Van der Valk most earnestly.

Saint smiled. "There is no trouble."

The smile told him much. It was the smile of a man who makes a habit of contempt, and practices it frequently. Of a man who is clever, but his cleverness will never amount to much because of his vanity. When their vanity is that great, decided Van der Valk, they will bear watching.

"I think perhaps an Omega or a Longines . . ."

"We don't have them, I'm afraid. But of course you will have no difficulty—you see, we are jewelers, really, not strictly speaking watchmakers except as objects of decorative art."

"Something a bit more practical, I feel . . ."

"But I understand perfectly. Good morning, sir: thank you for your visit."

Van der Valk left the shop.

Saint stood a moment thinking. "Dicky . . . You're not still looking for that shammy leather, are you?"

"Sorry—er—I had to go to the lavatory."

"How sudden," said Saint dryly.

"Louis, you recall you told me of a visit by some bumbledom policeman the other day—can you tell me at all what he looked like?"

"Looked like? I don't know. Sort of between two ages. Biggish. Glasses—sort of hair which isn't fair and isn't really gray. Hell, I didn't look; I wasn't buying him."

"Did he have a walking stick?"

"Now I come to think, believe he did."

"Walk a bit funny, a little stiff?"

"Didn't see him walk, not to notice."

"Talk a lot—voluble, persuasive?"

"God, yes. Been on at you, has he?"

"I rather think so."

"Not going on about that French picture, I hope."

"No. In fact, I wonder whether he's really interested in art at all."

"What, then?"

"Snowing me with a ridiculous tale about a watch. Don't bother, Louis—perhaps if you run across him again, you might mention it."

"In pictures," Van der Valk wrote laboriously, spelling it all out, "there is plenty of opportunity. There are large sums—now what is he doing with large sums? There's no proof or even evidence of any large illegal deal, but it doesn't matter. The fact is that things and

81

people are being manipulated—why? Louis is obvious —he needs his technical expertise. But the boy—what can he need the boy for? Not for personal reasons, said B.—and he's pretty shrewd, he'd know. But—a 'bad man' . . ." It didn't add up to anything, except that by the trick with the watch—and some trick there was— he had a hold over the boy. And Bosboom had said as good as straight out that he had a hold over Louis. And people who liked to acquire holds over others were never altogether to be lost from sight.

Well, what could he do? He shrugged a bit at the silliness of it—the private-detective lark. He was still a working policeman; why not make an official memo, turn it over to the criminal bureau in Amsterdam— people whom he knew, after all—and ask them to spend a little time there, preferably working from the hypothesis of a tax fiddle on works of art? No, he wouldn't do that, because it wouldn't get anywhere. No complaint had been made, no evidence existed, there were no grounds whatever for any perquisitions or examinations—they simply would not act, and Amsterdam would not fail to point that out to him. What could they do anyway but warn Saint that they were interested in him; and then he would cover up anything not already well covered, and quietly go to ground.

Anyway, this would dash his private-detective experiment.

Did that make any difference? Was the experiment any use at all beyond a foolish whim? Hadn't he already proved that one couldn't do anything as a private detective except hang around and bother people, and even that only when someone was handing out large sums of money as a retainer? Nobody had handed him out any retainer. But that, he told himself, was the point. Nobody was his principal, nobody had any say in

82

his doings; he owed nobody secrecy, loyalty, or silence —except the state. Hadn't that been the basis of his experiment—the notion of a private detective who has no client to protect, no ax to grind, no vendettas to indulge or honesty to be compromised except his ordinary state oath, getting rid of all those fictitious private eyes with private codes of ethics?

Anyway, he had done all that a private man could do. Lean on Prinz a bit, lean on Saint a bit—unless Saint was a very stupid man, he would surely have realized that an eye had rested on him, and that it might be a police eye; not anyone inviting him to come to the station and insist on inquiries, but a very gentle, very discreet touch intended to provoke him into getting rattled and doing something silly.

Would Saint now react? Probably not. He would lie low to see whether the cat would come out of the tree—a good Dutch phrase, that. So for Van der Valk there was nothing to do yet awhile. Just think about it from time to time, and notice whether any other fact came to his notice, huh. And that is a very sensible conclusion, he told himself, as the train slowed to stop at The Hague. He had a briefcase full of work, and he didn't know when he would have the time to think of Mr. Saint again, let alone do anything about him.

That very evening, oddly enough. He was finishing his book about King Charles I, and got to the sad bit about how the Scots finally rounded up and chopped Montrose—as well they might, seeing as how he had put the fear of the very devil into them for a longish while. What a relief to see that fellow's head on a pike! And what a typical thing, to see this immensely gifted and noble partisan leader—moreover, an exceptionally skillful guerrilla general—sold to the government by a fellow he had trusted. It was nice to know that the said fellow, a petty local squire in the backwoods, called Macleod, had acquired undesired immortality as the prototype of a dirty bastard. The Scots were quite unconcerned about treachery, which was their historical bread and butter, so to speak (Charles I himself was an absolute past master at double-dealing), but they did draw the line at treachery for money; one didn't altogether blame them. They had written a poem about this fellow—probably, he thought, originally a popular song for the boys to sing in the street, full of down-to-earth insults. Not bad, either—there was a fine indignation in it, a splendid contempt, and even a spark of poetry: the "stripped tree of the false apples, Neil's son of woeful Assynt." The bitter phrase stayed with him, but it wasn't till next morning, going to work, that an assonance somewhere brought an idea to life. Saint! Leopold Neil Saint! Standing by his desk, before even taking his coat off, since otherwise it would be forgotten, he took a notebook, reached for a ball-point, and wrote, "Neil's son of woeful Assynt." And the fellow living on top of a shop called The Golden Apples of the Hesperides—a sex shop, bonne mère; if that isn't the tree of the rotten apples, I've never bitten into one. And with a grin across his face he scribbled in, "The stripped tree of the false apples, too." Had perhaps the boyo Saint an interest in the sex business, and was that an idea which might lead him further? Louis perhaps dealing in porn? Might that be the little disgrace Bosboom had hinted at? Really, next time he had a committee meeting in Amsterdam, he would go and have a look at those golden apples! He was interrupted by Miss Wattermann, who had heard him come in.

"Professor Sammels has been on the line."

"This early?" groaned Van der Valk. "What's that old pedant want?"

84

"He's most anxious to have your opinion on his abortion law."

"Oh, bonne mère," moaned Van der Valk. Professor Sammels was the most tenacious talker he knew, and on the subject of his proposed new abortion law notoriously inexhaustible. It would be a hard day.

It turned out, too, a hard day for young Richard Oddinga. Not that the morning had anything especially troublesome about it; just that Larry stayed unaccountably still and silent most of the morning.

Usually he came in first thing, to open the shop up and do the usual round of chores: checking the locks and shutters for any sign of interference, testing all the alarm circuits, keeping a severe eye on the cleaning women, going to the bank with the take and bringing back the petty cash "float," and then as a rule spending an hour with the mail, typing a few letters, signing a few checks, while Dick rearranged things, bringing out and cleaning up an acquisition of Louis's that would be left a few days casually in the front of the shop even if, as was often the case, it was already sold. After which Dick would make a cup of coffee, Larry would drink it while giving any memos or instructions he might have, and immediately after he would be gone, quite possibly for the whole day, though he did mostly drop in again either before lunch or after it. But only for five minutes. What had got into Larry that he stayed the whole damned morning in the little cubbyhole where he wrote letters, reading the paper and putting it down every two minutes, gazing into space—a rarity—and smoking a great deal—even more of a rarity? Dick brought him coffee and he drank it without looking. Jackie Baur the silversmith, who liked coffee—and a nice gossip—got short shrift this morning. Even "the Baron"—one of their best customers and a snip for anything even remotely Louis Quinze—was made to feel faintly unwelcome when he dropped in for advice about the specially made gilt nails for re-covering a footstool which he liked to believe had once supported Madame de Pompadour's active and artistic shoes. Richard felt somehow bothered. But it was nearly eleven before Larry suddenly called him, rubbing out a cigarette lengthily in the big bronze bowl which Louis had finally proved was not, as he had hoped, fourth-century Gallo-Roman but a pretty impudent Italian fake.

"Dicky."

"Hallo."

"Shut the shop."

That by itself was highly unusual, rather disturbing; slightly ominous. Even if there were no customers at all, Larry hated shutting the shop.

"Done. Here's the keys. Aye, aye, sir."

"Don't be funny. Sit down. Stay still. Listen attentively. Don't tell lies. Dicky, who is the man that came in with a big load of bullshit about dropping a watch in the tramline? Don't say 'What man?'—his voice was carrying from here to the Rozengracht. You were cleaning the window. You dropped everything and bunked. Afterward you claimed you had to go to the lavatory, which was manifestly untrue because I heard you prowling the whole time he was here. I conclude that this peculiar gentleman was not unknown to you. Don't interrupt. Now people don't drop their watches in tramlines; it's a ridiculous tale. The tale was meant to be ridiculous, and I was meant to notice that. It was a warning. You being an exceptionally downy chick would know nothing about that, so I'll explain. It's the thing the police do when they're looking at you but they've got no evidence. It so happens that the same man called on my uncle with an equally absurd tale about export licenses. It just happens that I know something of the man who works on that. I've checked up. He knows nothing about it and he knows nobody who corresponds to the description: *ergo* a phony policeman. That interested me. I worked for a while on that assumption. Until, considering your behavior, it struck me that it might not have been a phony policeman—simply one from another department trying on an act which I do not understand at present, but which I intend to understand. Now who among your acquaintances fits that description, Dicky?"

There was not an awful lot Richard could do. He twisted about in the net, but it closed on him. Saint was a handy cross-examiner, witty, wounding, sarcastic, joking, implacable. He let Dick develop complicated lies for as much as five minutes on end before puncturing them. He never lost his easy conversational voice. He never forgot a detail or an expression he had used a quarter of an hour before. He would have made a good prosecutor had it not been for a slight sadism, which a judge would not have permitted—an enjoyment at embarrassing, at confusing, at setting the boy floundering. By lunchtime Larry had found out everything.

"Well, Dick, go and eat your dinner. Good appetite." It was a very well-aimed Parthian shot.

When the kangaroo court sat again that afternoon, judgment was reached without any great delay: Larry Saint had spent his lunch break usefully.

"Well," very gently, "I have now a little more background. A commissaire of police who is not actually on the retired list, but who is now inactive—committee work for a Ministry in The Hague. Having weighed it all up rather carefully, I think it most unlikely that he has made, or even can make, any official move. His own words to you—please correct me if I am mis-

87

taken—were that no complaint had been registered, no official action could be envisaged, and that he himself was prepared to forget the whole thing. And yet he didn't. I wonder why. Could it be, Dicky, that this fellow is taking an interest in any of my business activities? And would that be on account of your childish indiscretions? No, Dicky-boy, I don't think we would be going very far wrong if we were to say that you've made a hole in the dike and that it's now up to you to mend it. Wouldn't you agree, Dicky?"

"Well—I don't know—I suppose that sounds logical—but I don't see—I mean I didn't know how I could—I mean I had no idea of giving you away in any sense. Anyway, I don't see what I could do. I mean it's too late now."

"Is it? I wonder. I rather think not. Not for a cyclone shot. Which might appear a bit radical applied to an elderly busybody with time on his hands, but that, as you will shortly realize, is exactly the greatest danger. The police, my dear Dick, are disinclined to waste time on anything they can't prove. Whereas an elderly busybody, poking his nose into my affairs—now that might be tiresome. He can't prove anything either? Possibly, but he can hamper very considerably some of my short-term schemes, a few of which promise to be fruitful— very fruitful, I'm glad to say. And I'm not prepared, I fear, Dick, to allow your imbecilities to destroy much patient work."

"But what could I do? Nothing at all."

"More a question of what you can do. Or, rather, what you are going to do. And I'm very much afraid, Dick, that you haven't any choice. You will do what I tell you to do."

"Well . . . I don't know why you talk like that. You don't boss me around to that extent. I mean hell, at that rate, I'd just tell you up yours and walk out. I mean shit, what do you think—you can't force me into anything."

"No. I can't. I can make you force yourself, though. Shall I tell you?"

"You mean you'd accuse me of pinching that watch? Well, hell, so what? I didn't like it at the time and what's more I told that copper so, and he'd confirm that."

"No, not the watch," gently. "Though of course you are mistaken. I could prove very easily that you stole the watch. And your policeman friend wouldn't stir a finger to help you. You see, whatever you may have told him, you took the watch and kept it. Oh, it wouldn't be worth much. Perhaps six months in jail—a small affair for a boy your age. No, no we'll say nothing about the watch. No threats. But perhaps I might remind you of a detail I once mentioned—that I'd been a medical student. I think I remember telling you that one had to know when to leave alone and when to make an incision. I might find it necessary to incise you just a wee bit." The sound of Saint snapping his lighter reflectively, playing with it, was suddenly very small and very far away.

"Are you telling me you'd kill me or something?" It should have sounded disdainful, even supercilious: Richard was furious at not being able to stop his voice quavering.

"Oh well, one could, you know, without really very much trouble."

The voice was that of somebody complaining that the tea is too weak; and this is a hard thing to understand. Storybook gangsters have made so many melodramatic threats in suave sidling voices that we have every one of us become anesthetized. Suppose we met a real gangster in real life, and he threatened us with a nasty death, and all of a sudden we understood that he meant it. The sensation would be similar to watching an old Harold Lloyd film, in which he clings with fingertips to a flagpole three hundred meters above the street, and being unexpectedly plunged through the looking glass. It is here; it is now; it is happening to me. The relatively trivial acts of violence, which we come across quite frequently, committed by adolescents of retarded mentality have still the power to nauseate and to frighten, so that our whole day is permeated by shock and vertigo. How, then, can we grasp a threat of death which is serious, feasible, immediate? We cannot, and this is why we take refuge in poverty-stricken clichés like "nightmarish."

It is necessary to understand that at the moment he realized Saint was serious Dick disintegrated completely, poor boy.

"But what d'you want me to do?" with hysterical petulance. Anger at his impotence and humiliation before his servility forced his voice up into a shrill wail. "What can I do?"

"Now there you are—look at you," said Saint with chiding gentleness. "You've no control and no courage. The moment a little difficulty presents itself in front of you, what do you do? Collapse and scream about it. Oh, well, that's just inexperience. You're bright enough, and you're able to learn. You ask me what you can do, and you can start by studying how to repair your mistake. You've made a considerable blunder, and you can't mend this fence with just a box of matches. It will need work—in fact, it will need all your free time for a week or more. You'll have to make a project, and then study the means of putting it into practice. Well, well," with condescending amiability, "I'll help you. By the way, Dicky, what is this man's name?"

"Van der Valk."

\* \* \*

Van der Valk was worrying as well about society's anesthesia to violence. Not real, inhuman, extreme, barbaric violence, but the stupid, ignorant, vandalistic greed of a child picking cherries out of a cake, the miserable slaughter of landscape and townscape. What difference is there, he wondered, between a band of suburban youths breaking all the young trees and the speculators who built the suburb in the first place? If you left a child at the controls of a bulldozer, you would be looking out for a smash, no? Similarly, allow people who might have made quite good plumbers' mates the control of vast amounts of money, and the results were identical. He felt disagreeably tired. The way he spent most of his days, shut up inside this odious box, and the problems over which he found himself stooped—all so different from what he had been accustomed to—made up an existence to which he was not yet accustomed, which strained and wearied him very much.

New standards of behavior, for a new kind of society? Reforming the criminal code, he felt inclined to suspect, was a classic example of shutting the stable door after your horse has already knocked down three pedestrians, all of whom have sued you for gigantic damages. And he was sitting there at his desk like King Canute on the beach. Was it Xerxes who ordered the sea to be flogged for disobeying his express orders? Bonne mère, he thought, my mind is wandering.

Xerxes, Canute—several megalomaniac tyrants, and, come to that, vast numbers of bureaucrats, oil executives, municipal engineers concerned about sewage, people interested in building marinas on picturesque coastal sites, all had the same reaction: getting extremely cross with the sea for refusing to obey their convenience and profit.

As a lawmaker, one was exactly like a general who

91

always understood exactly how to fight wars fifteen years after the wars were finished. Propose changing anything at all and you got looked on as the worst kind of woolly permissive liberal. The way to stop the sea— he had been told that morning by a committee member —was, as all good Dutchmen knew, to build a dike to hold it back. He had kept quiet, himself. He knew little enough about law, despite several diplomas; though, he had to admit, he was learning. And what about all those years of experience? He shrugged: as a police- man, he had spent all those years applying regulations; nothing at all to do with law.

He walked home: he had got into the habit in his last job, where his house had only been five minutes from the office. Here it was twenty-five, and through ex- tremely crowded streets, but he had too little exercise. Mm, law. These laws, had remarked another colleague, a progressive one, are about as out of date as the dietary observances of orthodox Jewry. Van der Valk said he agreed, but wasn't sure he had yet been given any really good reasons for changing them, either. What was law, anyway: wasn't it moral law? I suppose, he had been told impatiently, that you're in favor of stoning adulterers. These people were very unreason- able. Now you're stoning me, he complained, only half laughing, or at least riding me on a cart and pelting me with rotten vegetables, as in Staphorst—with a placard round my neck saying, "Regressive Reactionary Fascist."

There, he had crossed a road without looking, thoroughly distrait if not distraught, and if he had been hit he would have taken no further interest in the problem.

He had not really learned yet how to look round problems; he had been too recently released from the little pragmatic details of how things would look to his superiors. This horse was still turning round from force of habit to shut the stable door itself.

"Don't be so preoccupied with detail," his neighbor, Professor de Hartog, had said to him today, quite kindly. They had been talking about punishment, and he had given rather a lamentable demonstration of not seeing the wood for the trees. "You're not in the police now. Never mind who fills the forms in; your job is to draft the texts."

He came to another crossing, waited patiently till the lights gave him permission. Nearly home already. This little stroll was no more than therapeutic, a moment for distancing, for getting the things into perspective that had crept too close during the day, gone blurred and out of focus. Promoters of eyestrain; he pinched the bridge of his nose automatically. This wasn't exercise, anyhow—breathing exhaust gases. Since being here, he had got into the way of taking another stroll at night, through the wooded outskirts of the town where The Hague slithers out to the sea and Scheveningen. At that time there were no hurrying crowds jostling him or treading on his toes: much these typists cared for the important committee member! He liked those solitary strolls: there were long weekends now to spend with Arlette, and she had never been much of a one for walks at night—been on her feet all day. . . .

He wished, though, that a little restaurant existed somewhere, something unpretentious, a place to go when one just didn't feel like cooking supper. A place to sit and eat shellfish with one's fingers, to look out at a darkened harbor and hear the thudding of a belated fish-boat's diesel, and the slap of the tide against the slimy jetty. Had it been a mistake, the Vosges cottage, drowned in woods and silence, a place where deer strolled up to your kitchen window and stared inquisitively in?

Couldn't help that now—it had been all they could afford, and lucky to have that—bought half a dozen years ago, too, when they were still in Amsterdam, with a lump gratuity payment made after his big bullet wound.

It would cost double now.

It had been the summit of his ambition then to grow his own fruit, chop his own wood, strap on skis in winter for when snow smothered the mossy forest paths. Well, perhaps it still was. Three years to go. They had spent their holidays there for five years now, and the little house was nearly ready—and more home than anything here in The Hague. Wine in the cellar, and a marvelous fruitwood bed with pineapples carved on the headposts. He wrinkled his nose at the smell of car exhaust and wished he was there now, crossing the road for the last time, entering the bleak hermetic hallway of his building, unlocking his letter box to see if anything had come, pressing the lift call button with the tip of his stick.

He was disappointed at not finding Arlette home. Still, the stove had switched itself on under the soup. No warmth, no joy, but a smell of supper, and the narrow living room smelt of her, faintly. He wandered about, wanting a drink but deciding to wait with pouring it out till he heard her key in the door. What was biting him? He brought it home suddenly: something he had glimpsed vaguely in the street, absent-mindedly, without interest. Someone, to be exact: it had only been the back of a head. Recalled some person he had had dealings with—remote?—less remote?

Of course—the boy from that jeweler's: his little personal problem, his experiment in private detection.

94

Dear, dear, this last couple of weeks he had had no time. It had gone cold on him now; the private detective needed lots of leisure! There was something there of interest, all right, but hell, he had so little to go on. Two or three times, he had been on the verge of ringing up Amsterdam and asking them to take a closer look, but he had no really convincing premise to offer them. Fidgety little heap of fragments—coincidental, for the most part.

A tedious little affair, anyway. It wasn't even any of his business, strictly speaking; he was no longer an active policeman, with reports coming in upon his desk and subordinates to carry out the chores, and this was a chore. To be sure, that had been the point originally: he had welcomed this little actuality as something that engrossed and puzzled—a box, with a trick opening to fiddle at, and perhaps a few thorns to prick one's fingers. He had needed that at first, a counterpoise to the load of purely theoretical work, stuff with no name on it, with which he had no personal involvement.

But there, he wasn't getting paid to have personal involvements; he had been told that clearly enough, and reminded only today. And to get anywhere with the experiment, he had to go stumping about Amsterdam. For a fortnight he had been there almost daily, in a series of meetings and consultations, as well as that archive stuff he had been working on, but for the last ten days he hadn't been there at all and had been glad of it, having a formidable pile of desk work getting fed him daily by the ineffable Wassermann. He had made notes—scattered, alas, through two or three of his books—half-hearted and incompetent work, which had never been more than a fantasy, really.

There was something there . . . yes. But it was a tiresome little problem. Not a box—more of an egg: all

95

smooth curves. You couldn't get inside without breaking the egg. A smooth, self-satisfied, slippery fellow, that whatshisname, and there would have been a certain enjoyment in giving him a tap with the egg spoon, but really it was all too much trouble.

There was Arlette, slightly late, he thought irritably, smelling the soup suddenly, realizing that he had turned it up too high and that it was now boiling over. She would tell him off! He poured two glasses of port and picked up *Le Monde*.

Larry Saint braked the car gently to a stop and glanced in the rear mirror, suppressing a small smile as the boy caught up, opened the door, and got in.

"A snip," he said quietly, giving a tiny touch to the accelerator to start it rolling again. "A man of habit, bless his heart. I had one moment of disquiet when you let him catch up with you a bit awkwardly, but he stared straight through the back of your neck and hadn't a clue. Seemed almost a bit too easy. You see, a policeman is not exactly altogether a soft touch, because of his training—there's an instinctive layer of observation and inquiry beneath the immediate surface that one does well to be wary of. But in ten days I haven't seen this fellow use his eyes."

"I'd like to be sure of that," muttered Richard.

"I had no intention of letting you make the slightest movement before I was sure of it," retorted Saint tranquilly. "Why d'you think I've been so careful? I've made inquiries. The fellow has been put out to grass. He was in the Criminal Brigade in Amsterdam, and a bit of an original. It wouldn't have been so easy then. He was an unexpected kind of object, who did unexpected things. Then he got shot up—there isn't any secret about it; it's easy to trace back if one takes the trouble. A woman shot him in Spain, good luck to her. They put him out to pasture in the provinces. Now they've moved him again right off the active list onto some committee work for the government—he was past his work, plainly. Now he bums about being the absent-minded professor."

"Then surely he's no risk," argued Dick.

"I would remind you," dryly, "that to succeed in business one takes risks, but not unnecessary ones. This is an unnecessary risk. Why'd he show himself so goddam curious? What's he doing sniffing round Louis? Coming to the shop with a phony tale about a watch? Messing about in the Apples? He wasn't looking for a good girly book, don't imagine it. He's a threat. So are you. I propose to get rid of both. And I wouldn't be at all surprised if tonight wasn't the night. Weather's ideal. We'll just see whether he goes to take his dog for a walk." Saint parked the car, turned out the lights, and looked with approval at the twilight gathering in front of the windscreen, and the fine drizzle, no more than a Scotch mist, blotting out visibility. He reached forward, unlocked the glove compartment, and took out a 9-millimeter pistol. A Luger. It remains one of the simplest, most direct, efficient of weapons. It is only semiautomatic, and hardly ever jams or catches. It balances well, and has a comfortable, secure grip. It has a light pull, takes standard ammunition, and when it hits you you stay hit. It is not the fussy, fashionable little gun—the Walthers and the Sauers—of fictional secret agents and snobbish private eyes. It was one of Mr. Saint's little objects of art—so much better designed than all those other things. . . . "Now don't go blazing away," said Saint. "Three or four at the very most, and sight at the small of the back."

* * *

97

"You don't feel like a stroll?" asked Van der Valk hopefully. He did not know why, but he would enjoy her company this evening. Arlette was stacking things in the dishwasher. They had never before had a dishwasher; never before had she had so easy a flat to keep and to clean. She loathed it as much as he did. There was every comfort and no luxury, every sensible idea and nothing of any interest. No character, charm, breadth, or generosity. No sense of proportion and quite unfurnishable. Everything here was predigested; there was one place you could hang your hat and one position for your bed. No wonder, said Van der Valk, that, once on the street or in a car, people who live in these places become utterly demented.

"Sorry," she said, "but I've ironing to do, and I haven't read the paper yet, and it's raining—I had my hair done yesterday and I'm not in the mood to stagger about under an umbrella. Anyway, I've only one comfortable pair of walking shoes and they need to go to the mender's. I've been looking for others," vaguely, "but they're all so hideous this year." It was all unutterably unanswerable. But when he came back he would find the place livable for once, with a smell of ironing, clothes in piles, and a wife in a housecoat, all nicely stuffy and reactionary: a wife-slave, and happy about it.

Not much fresh air, out here. Real February night. Very low cloud ceiling and rain that is part of it. No sea wind despite a westerly air stream, no smell of sea, no smell of spring either to hope for; not for about another month, at this rate.

It was the evening of March 3rd.

There was a smell of rotted dead leaves from last autumn, of rain-slimed and exhaust-blackened tree trunks, of sodden muddy grass alongside the pavements. The street lamps had a depressed droop like undernourished tulips: the shimmering halo of light, reflected off raindrops, hung around them like bad breath. But this is part of it, thought Van der Valk, not discontented; without this there would be no spring, no hairy pussy willows reminding him of the scent of mimosa far down in the South. He had bought some mimosa that morning for his wife; it had been in cellophane, already desiccated from the long weary voyage that Arlette, too, had made, the wonderful scent long departed. Just as well, she had said, pleased, smiling at him—that way she would feel no homesickness. His wife's smile and the scent of mimosa, vividly pictured and for one instant recaptured, would be almost the last things in his life. That, and the moisture on his loden coat, and the dead leaves, and a wet leather glove: the smells of Holland.

There was nothing in the sound of a car to make him turn: a relaxed sound, of a car idling along under no pressure; a contented sound, of a motor turning easily in the moist air. There was no instinct of danger to make him turn—it was the idlest of curiosity when the car slowed behind him. Probably some out-of-season tourist checking whether the road really did lead to Scheveningen. In a years-old police automatism, he did bring his back foot round to narrow the target and start going down to look for cover. There were four shots, and two missed him altogether, but he had no interest in that. He had no interest even in the face: distorted, rigid with fear, with terror at what it was doing, and the complete inability to stop. The pistol had commanded its owner to shoot and there was nothing else for it. An actor for many years, Van der Valk would have been interested in this piece of theatre, but he had a new part to study, the most important of his parts. In the words of the seventeenth-century actor, he was in the way to study a long silence.

So that he had no interest in the rough clash of the transmission and the squeal of the tires pulling away in haste. He was down on his face in the dead leaves. He knew that he was dying and was pleased that he knew, and could say the words he wished to say—very simple words.

And a few simple thoughts. He had never been afraid of dying, and least of all now. He had had a life, married a wife, raised children, dug ground and planted a tree, sailed a boat and skied down hill, eaten and drunk and made love. He was ready for what came next. He felt his life spilling out on the ground and turned his head a little. Bereitsein ist alles. He thought of Arlette without disappointment and without pain.

It wasn't a bad place at all to die. With a last flick of recognition for this world, he remembered Stendhal saying there was no disgrace in dying in the street, when not done on purpose. And he had . . .

Van der Valk began to study his long silence but was interrupted. He was dead.

"The trouble with public-spirited witnesses is that they're such infernal busybodies." Arlette would remember the phrase. Others, too; light-hearted or disillusioned, even slightly soured. "One definition of aristocracy is a person who does not stop to gawk at a street fight." In one of the villas to the side of the road, beyond the strip of sodden poached dog-infected grass, beyond the cyclepath and the row of leafless trees, lived a public-spirited person. He had been in a first-floor front room, and he hadn't had the television on, being absorbed at the moment in his stamp collection. The coppery bonk of pistol shots at thirty meters, however

100

dulled by the saturated air, had startled him, and he had run to his window and jerked the curtain—but he had not seen much through the wavering fine rain which coarsened the grain of the air, so that what he had seen was a worn old gangster movie of the early thirties, made by Warner Brothers. Van der Valk had enjoyed them greatly. George Raft and James Cagney, Paul Muni and Edward G. Robinson; the young Bogart. A man lying face down in the rain, and the dark-colored car accelerating away. Probably with Peter Lorre and Sydney Greenstreet in the back.

Arlette was not a woman of much imagination. She saw the scene quite differently, because she had lived through it as a girl of fifteen, while stopping to drink a cup of coffee on her way home from school. A street corner in Toulon in blinding dusty sunshine, deserted. The spit and snap of an automatic pistol and the squeal of a car furiously driven. Running police and a white képi fallen off and rolling through the heavy lazy air. Most vivid of all, the café owner with the big belly ducking with such unexpected agility.

"A plat ventre tous—on est en train de se faire flinguer." The young girl, as well as everyone else, à plat ventre in a heap; these episodes sometimes involved unpleasantly indiscriminate machine-gun fire.

Most ironic of all, for twenty-five years she had steeled herself for that telephone call from a potato-filled police mouth embarrassed into lumpish incoherence. Since the beginning of the desk job—in the civil service as it were; in The Hague, of all places (that most civil-service-minded of all prim Dutch towns)—she had told herself that at least there was no longer that to be afraid of. And fatally the call had come, and fatally she had not followed the rules she had long rehearsed that would govern her behavior. The car

101

started as though it had been waiting whetted for this moment, and she had driven ridiculously, convinced of her sedate sober mind, congratulating herself on behaving well. The deux-chevaux braked, skidding, to a stop. So silly to have hurried; of course she was much too late, she knew that perfectly, for a lot of time had passed and there was not just a policeman gesticulating in the rain but a whole knot of cars. And the ambulance. And a group of careful middle-aged gentlemen in raincoats, with their hats on because it was still raining. The body was still in place. She did not worry about that or think anything silly like, He'll get wet! She knew about the measurements and the photographs and the conscientiousness displayed by all, even the press. Everyone made way for her politely, and she did not do anything in the least absurd like going down à plat ventre.

But, being in shock, she did not remember properly anything much of what happened, and her next accurate recollection was of sitting in her flat in daylight, dried, dressed, combed, politely pouring a drink for the district commissaire of police. She could not place the time very well, but thought it must have been about midday. So silly a feeling . . . almost as though she were pouring the usual midday drink for her husband, but in that case why was she being so formal and polite?

"I needn't tell you how I feel," he was saying. "Thanks, Mevrouw, no more for me. And, if I may permit myself the remark, you shouldn't be drinking whisky."

"I know. It has no effect upon me whatever."

"But it might later," worried.

"That's as may be."

"Yes. Er—I need hardly say . . . when we lose a man . . . we don't give up."

102

"No," said Arlette, knowing that this meant they had found nothing.

"We have—er—the skid marks, which will tell us what kind of car it was. And—er—ejected cartridge cases, which will give us the gun. When we recover the bullets . . ." He had better not dwell on that detail, he was thinking plainly.

"Yes," said Arlette, knowing that the car would have been stolen and the gun ditched.

"We are, of course, going to examine everyone with whom he may have had—er, dealings and who might have—er, felt a grievance. It may take a long time. We will neglect nothing."

"Quite," brightly. "When can you let me have my husband back?"

"We were thinking, er, the funeral . . ."

"I don't want to seem rude, Commissaire, or ungrateful. He didn't belong here. He came from Amsterdam, but he has no family left there. I know that you will be extremely kind, and that you will want to come, and send big wreaths and everything—forgive me, please. I'm afraid I don't want that. I'm sorry but I want to leave as soon as I can, which is as soon as you'll let me."

"But where will you go?" asked the commissaire, worried. "If it's the press . . ."

"No. He had, you see, a little house in France—for retiring to, you understand? And that is where I'm going, and that's where he's going, and I want to ask you only one thing, which is that you'll please help me with that and see that I have no trouble, with the customs or whoever is responsible for taking dead people across frontiers. I feel sure that they'll be very worried about whether the proper taxes have been paid."

"Try not to be bitter," gently.

She drank some more whisky and grimaced. "You're

103

quite right. I promise I won't be tiresome or troublesome at all."

He found this humility touching; he also felt uneasy. A frightening woman, in a sense; one didn't know what she mightn't be capable of.

"We won't let you down," he said, and really meant it.

# PART TWO

# Neil's Son of Woeful Assynt

IT WAS AT this point that I found myself involved in this story. I must explain myself: the writer is of course always "involved," but he detaches himself as much as possible. This is partly because gossips, and ignorant people—and sometimes malicious people—will invent anything they think makes a crackly bit, a crunchy read in the salted-peanuts section of the press. Thus I have heard, and read, that Van der Valk was nothing but a vehicle for my own little fads and whims—whereas the truth, if it has to be spelt out, is that of course we were friends, we had quite a lot in common, and we had a good deal not in common. That he was Dutch, whereas I am English ("mais si peu," as the malicious tongues insist), is only the start. He insisted naturally on being disguised a bit; who blames him? I added several fictional details—clumsy, no doubt, and blundering and often unconvincing; I don't claim to be a very practiced magician, Willy Maugham or something. But as I became more experienced at the trade of novel-writing, the border between fact and fiction became more blurred as well as more subtle.

Simon (but everyone called him Piet, a more down-to-earth Dutch name that suited him better) was a friend—or, better said, a "copain"; a grand drinking companion, a lot of fun at all times, sometimes infuriating and often irritating, with whom one could quarrel violently without any bloodshed. I did not agree by any means with all his ideas; I found him sometimes crude, barbarian, and offensively "Dutch." I let myself get teased sometimes into losing my temper, which amused him; this kind of teasing is a Dutch national characteristic.

I have never mentioned how I came to meet him. I am not going into details now—they would be of no interest—but briefly, at a time when I was poor, in fact broke, and working as a cook in a Dutch restaurant, I got pinched for taking home food (a thing, of course, all cooks do, but the manager, who disliked me, chose me as a sacrifice). Van der Valk, amused by the situation—I was less amused; I served three weeks in jail—was the local detective officer in the Amsterdam district in question whose responsibility was to type up the dossier after asking me a great many silly questions. His ill-concealed mirth at my being the fall guy, the pigeon, the patsy, made, as one says, my blood boil.

But later he showed kindness. He took the trouble to call on my wife while I was in jail to reassure her and to show her how she could draw a "social security" benefit. Later, during the three years I lived in Holland, we became friends. We were invited to eat one of Arlette's meals, with a good many bad jokes about my being a cook and a severe critic. He was interested in a cook who wanted to "become a writer" floating about in his district—and as a policeman he was discreetly keeping an eye on me, as I afterward realized. We became friends. When I began to write stories with a slightly fictionalized "Piet" as hero, he got extremely indignant but, with his own brand of detachment, he was also amused and would not have allowed himself to interfere with me. I got my own back for his sniggering by inventing discreditable positions for him to get into. When I came to live in France, I saw less of him, but it happened that he had bought a country cottage not very far from me. It is nearly an hour and a half's drive, around seventy kilometers on some very twisty roads, but I buy wine near there and make the trip quite often. In the holidays, we saw quite a bit of one another, and I generally got a book out of it.

Arlette is a different pair of shoes. I am very fond of France, and get on well with the French—from time to time, like most people. I spent much of my childhood here, I have emotional ties, it is easy for me. But I have never been much attracted by Frenchwomen—their wit, "esprit," their funniness and vitality are fine for a few hours, but to live with . . . mm, I am not so sure. There have been times when I actively disliked her.

My wife, too, was sometimes irritated by her. Too French, too noisy, too opinionated—too much in general, even a lot of good qualities. Perhaps there may have been a streak of jealousy here; not that I have ever seriously been accused of overfamiliarity with Arlette —she herself would have had none of that, quite apart from anything else. Her gaiety and vivacity, her intelligence and wit, her strong character as well as her bold, sharp good looks made her an attractive personality, but one who became occasionally a bit too overwhelming.

Well, of such stuff are friendships made. The two women liked, trusted, and respected each other. So did Piet and I. He got extremely indignant with me now and again, especially after I had "made a fool of him," as he thought it, until his humor got the better of him and he saw the comic side of one of my fictional episodes. At least, he said, nobody in Holland would ever recognize him, so that he could not be compromised.

And I got annoyed with him, too: although always pleased to see him, and enjoying nothing more than a night's boozing together, I quickly had enough of crude Dutch jokes and earthy extrovert backslapping. He enjoyed making me cross, laughed uproariously, and was delighted when I got more vexed than ever with his obstreperous ways. He trod with heavy feet upon little egotisms and preciosities of mine—and I learned to value that. He would blow in, with his heavy feet and wind-reddened face, his awful tweed suits and his crude but sensitive hands (there is a drawing somewhere, by Picasso, of Igor Stravinsky's hands which reminded me of him), and bruise my complacent priggeries with a few kicks. "I can't help being fond of old Piet," I hear myself announcing to my wife in sentimental tones.

I was touched at Arlette's coming to see me. I had read of Piet's death in the Dutch daily paper; I had rung her up and stammered out the usual limping and wooden phrases, but I had thought, with no very good reason, that she would be avoiding me for some, at least, and I was very pleased to see her. I found her changed, less buxom, slower-moving, more thoughtful. But her striking Phoenician looks were the same: the tall proud carriage—they have such a good walk—the chignon of fair hair, the bony high-bridged nose, the splendid large eyes of clear bright brown. All that is a familiar enough sight on Mediterranean coastlines, but had always so disconcerted Holland that in nearly thirty years she never felt at home there. Come to that, Holland disconcerted her; she never really understood the

110

place or the people, and did not always make enough of an effort.

She poured out all her tale to me, and very confused it was. And hereabout I have an apology to make for my own narrative, and an explanation of the technically awkward break in the middle of it. This was her suggestion. When all was finished, it was Arlette herself who wanted me to unroll Kai Lung's mat. She wanted me to make a tale of Piet's last adventure, but "leaving me out of it." This was manifestly impossible. So that I have split the tale in two, and used her as protagonist of the second half. She made a great fuss at first, but shrugged finally and gave in. I have felt myself, in a sense, more involved personally; and this, too, needs pointing out. I "arrived upon the scene" halfway through the tale instead of after it was finished, and it was to me that Arlette came for help in puzzling out the notebooks. As she remarked blandly, with a slightly false naïveté, I was a writer; I kept notebooks myself. I am no detective, but I did, I suppose, contribute something to her detective work.

Arlette had sent telegrams to the boys, but it would take them a day or two to come, and in trouble and solitude it was to Ruth she turned, and Ruth who gave her consolation and support. A good deal to her surprise: like all adopted children—and adopted quite late in childhood—Ruth was not an easy child, full of frightful knots and tensions, and had caused much upheaval and heartbreak in her new home. Still, that was comprehensible enough. She had never known her father, her mother had been something of an oddity, and both of them had died by violence. Coming to Piet and Arlette at around twelve years of age, she had brought a lot of this violence with her. Now in her midteens, she had gone in a great deal lately for subterranean adolescent smolderings, and very tiresome they had found it.

But when Arlette broke the news to her, she changed, as it were, in a breath, and the cliché is almost accurate for once.

"Ruth, darling—forgive my blurting it out. But you of all people will understand." The girl—so hard this last year and so fierce—had been so simple with Arlette and gentle. Of course she understood. Her own mother had died with her stomach shot to pieces.

"Ruth—I've nothing left."

"I know. Then I had you. Now you've me. That's nothing much I know—but I'll do my best." She said no more—she didn't, much—and she did not cry—she never did—but she cuddled Arlette. And it helped: she stopped pulling herself to pieces. Odd, she thought; we've changed places, and now I am the girl of fifteen. The girl helped her find her balance.

"I can't stay in this awful place," she told the boys. They were strangers now, both in their twenties, though both were still in some vague way students. Both had hotfooted it out of Holland. She did not know what they did, any more than what they thought. They were complete strangers, although she knew instinctively that in another few years she would know them better. One was in Bologna, something legal, and the other in Besançon, electrical engineering of a particularly incomprehensible nature. They did not have much time to spare.

"Leave this to us," they said with authority. Limply, she did, and a day or two after found herself translated, transfigured—transmogrified—in the little house which he had chosen and bought, where she was full of him, surrounded by him, with some tea chests full of junk, and a coffin.

112

So there they buried him, in a small awkward little cemetery, squeezed up against a sharp slope of hill and surrounded by rusty railings, smelling of dead leaves. And all the other right things, thought Arlette—metal wreaths and plastic flowers: so economical, so French. A grave lined with spruce branches. Bundles of chrysanthemums, a flower he had always liked the smell and shape of, clumsily and touchingly brought by the boys. A great crown of spring flowers, astonishingly yet characteristically bought, picked, and made by Ruth. An immense wreath of flower-shop flowers with a Dutch tricolor ribbon, brought soberly and so kindly by two local gendarmes in carefully pressed parade uniforms "for a confrère"—hand of the Dutch commissaire of police—but they themselves had taken much trouble, too. And her own small, silly "thing," a handful of little dark-yellow roses in tight bud, the kind that hardly unfurl at all, which she had wanted, and which she now threw into the grave. The curé, with a hand protecting the pages of his missal from the spots of rain that were falling again; the garde champêtre, that French village figure who is also road mender and gravedigger, standing professionally at ease with his shovel; and the gendarmerie, as professionally at attention, and the salute. He would have enjoyed them. He had always liked French military ceremonial, and would greatly have liked a bugler to sound "Aux Morts." . . . For a second, Arlette was standing as she had often stood as a child on Armistice Day, during the awkward silence before the tatty, ragged—but somehow more enobled clash of the "Marseillaise." She had fallen, she realized, into a trance. She glanced at the two boys, standing bowed, with hands clasped, in the attitude of resigned embarrassment with which boys in their early twenties attend a funeral: they themselves are going to live for-

113

ever and it is all rather unreal as well as folklore. Ruth, head well up, eyes shut, and lips moving through the multiplication table, was thinking of her mother, at whose grave she and Van der Valk had stood side by side. A gang of village schoolchildren, on their way home to dinner, were gazing through the railings and whispering. Arlette was holding everybody up.

She threw in the last rose; the curé gave a little cough, the shovel squeaked on pebbles, and the cantonnier, brave homme, grunted at the wet soil.

She shook hands with everyone, gave the right tips, and watched the Law, all three of it, retiring rapidly toward the café; the two schoolchildren who had served the mass rushing to spoil their dinner with a Milky Way. The curé was saying something and she was answering. Ruth had taken a glove off and pushed a warm, damp adolescent hand into her own cold, bare hand. She took off her mantilla, which still smelt slightly of incense. She got into the self-drive car the boys had hired, and was driven back to her new home, where Ruth had a daube of beef, not very nice: she was not a good cook. Arlette ground coffee afterward, and they drank it while the boys talked with exaggerated, emphatic gestures until she asked them what their train times were, whereupon they looked relieved, and only slightly ashamed when they became conscious of relief. There was a distribution of Van der Valk's last bottle of brandy, to which Arlette felt an idiotic sentimental attachment but which the boys polished off ruthlessly. Later that afternoon, the two women were left alone to their new life. For Ruth had asked to stay. There was a school to which she could go, over half an hour away, which would be grim in winter, but if that was what she wanted. . . .

"So please, Mama, if you would buy me a scooter?"

Ruth had never called her anything but her name before.

One of these days, the stonemason came to call, anxious to sell them a nice piece of marble or polished granite, and was vexed at Arlette's wanting nothing but a big lump of rough sandstone.

"A bank where the wild thyme grows." Ruth had been doing Shakespeare.

"Doesn't grow here," said the stonecutter loftily.

"No," said Arlette, a bit tart. "Moss will, though."

"And the inscription, Madame?"

The two girls looked at each other. Arlette had not found anything of sufficient simplicity. The best she knew of was the symbol, in music, for a pause, which is on the tomb of the conductor Erich Kleiber. As for epitaphs . . . the briefest and best is surely the three-word expression of happiness which Stendhal found for himself? "Lived, wrote, loved." Ruth, going through an exceedingly literary phase, nourishing the desire to be an actress that went with her age, had suggested several flaming lines, ranging from "Sous le pont Mirabeau coule la Seine" down as far as "Our revels now are ended." Arlette had put a firm stop to these effusions with a faintly evil-minded remark: "At that rate, one could put 'Vous lui remettrez son uniforme blanc.' "

"Nothing," she said now; "that is to say, the name and the dates. Leave a space below, in case I think of something. And, of course," dryly, "space for me."

"Will we put 'Mort en service commandé'?" asked the stonecutter hopefully.

"No," said Arlette.

Really these women had no sense of what was proper.

It was many months (time indeed of the Toussaint, the first of November, a day in France of remembering

115

and visiting our dead) before the stonemason felt inclined to change his poor opinion.

Arlette had come to see us; it was only then that I heard this story. We said we would come over, to look at the grave and go back with her to her house for dinner.

"The moss is growing," she said contentedly.

The quietness in her voice: was it this which sent me to Horace, searching for the poetry that went with this hard-bought calm? Some almost-effaced memory told me that the old poet, better than any other, had known that justice, which we long for, which Van der Valk had spent a life trying to understand, belongs only to God. But that by surrendering ourselves we can put ourselves in harmony, and at peace.

I stumbled clumsily through these most compressed of all lines, mouthing forgotten Latin, sprawling awkward upon the elegant eighteenth-century French of Monsieur Dacier and le Père Sanadon, last read as a raw little boy, in my own eighteenth century.

When I found what I was searching for—one of the presents poetry makes us—I, too, felt at peace with myself.

> Quam si clientum longa negotia
> Dijudicata lite relinqueret . . .

"I don't in all honesty . . ." began my wife . . .

Regulus, a Roman general, went to his death at the hands of the executioner with the serenity, says Horace, of a lawyer who has wound up a tedious business affair, and leaves for a pleasant weekend in his country house.

At finding an epitaph I was a poor substitute for Stendhal, but Arlette was pleased, I think, most with the classical (in the antique, Mediterranean sense) simplicity of it.

116

"I love it," she said, "and I'll have it done."

When it had sunk into the stonecutter's mind—leisurely, as was proper—he, too, was satisfied.

"That's something more like." The phrase might have given pleasure to Horace.

In her country house, having wound up the tedious affairs of her clients, Arlette also had thought of an epitaph. But hadn't felt able to cut it on a stone. It had run, she said, and rung and sung through her head all through those months.

The marching song which dates back to the campaigns of the Great Louis, in Holland. Yes: "Auprès de ma blonde."

> Qui chante pour les filles
> qui n'ont pas de mari—
> Ne chante pas pour elle:
> elle en a un joli! . . .

I could see, I said.

"He is in Holland," said Arlette, staring at the stone where the moss was beginning.

"But you have him here."

"No. Il est dans la Hollande: les Hollandais l'ont pris. They took him." Well . . . he was Dutch, after all.

Driving home afterward, through rain, the car still full of the scent of chrysanthemums, I thought of the girl's words when she is asked, "What would you give to have him back?" She sings:

> Je donnerai Versailles,
> Paris et Saint-Denis,
> Les tours de Notre-Dame,
> le clocher de mon pays. . . .

We know the lines as a "nursery rhyme" ourselves. They are in *Rondes et Chansons de la France,* on records we bought for our children when they were tiny.

Arlette was right, I suppose, to take the classical line from Horace. But the other, I can't help thinking, would have been as good. Both indeed have the same antique nobility "more durable than bronze."

For about six weeks after the funeral, the snow lay round Arlette, and this, she thought, was as it should be. She shoveled snow from in front of the house, and the shed where the deux-chevaux lived with the sawed logs and Ruth's new scooter. She chopped wood for the kitchen range and the big porcelain stove, cursed about this—it is, after all, a man's work—and determined to have central heating for next year. She wished she lived on a tropical island, the way one always does in March in Central Europe, where winter has the tenacity of a marathon runner. She often went to ski: this had been planned with her husband, to make long raids along the spider's web of woodcutters' paths which enlace every hill in the Vosges. These make good natural pistes for Nordic skis, for the paths were made when the wood was hauled by the timber-tug with powerful slow horses, and the slopes are never too steep. But she found she had not the heart to do it alone, and changed the light narrow skis for Alpine "planks" and drove the deux-chevaux day after day up to the Markstein, to ski there in the sun, on pistes as hard and bare as bleached bones and, when the wind finally went round into the west, sticky like decaying flesh.

Tall blondes in ski clothes, even when they are well over forty, do not find it difficult to attract admirers. Arlette found herself the object of amorous address from a quantity of earnest Germans; even the instructors, notoriously spoilt where women are concerned, notoriously fussy about their women being very youthful and alarmingly nubile, invented pretexts for correct-

118

ing her style. This was very good for her. After peeling off layers of sun cream, she found herself still a good-looking woman despite lines around the eyes.

She had looked forward to the quiet of winter evenings. Ruth muttering over her math and her Montaigne, herself embedded in all the books he had collected "to read when I'm retired." But she found her eyes lifting restlessly to the shelves he had built himself, rather badly but with great glee, boasting about having learned to join two bits of wood in the Depression time, from his father the carpenter, mending broken kitchen chairs for out-of-work Amsterdamers. She found that the quiet of the snow-filled valley irritated her, and when the Paris planes slid over, unseen above the heavy cloud cover, she welcomed the sound.

Admittedly the town was only an hour's drive, and one went there often enough, for fresher vegetables and cheaper fruit, to get one's hair done, to get stockings and a new record, to dress up and go in the evening with Ruth to the theatre, which tended to bore her, or to concerts, which tended to bore Ruth. But she felt distorted, jangled, jarred by voices out of key and a music out of tune; she was upset at even a dearly loved pianist sounding gritty, as though the great black piano appassionato had got left out in a sandstorm.

She missed her hospital work, too: the tottery old men it had been her job to re-educate to walk after an operation, listening to their tedious talk about football and how they were being deliberately and systematically starved by Sister; the women who got so petty, cherishing their varicose veins as though they were jewels; the children with broken limbs, driven into becoming exceedingly tedious by their itchy plasters; the squalors, the stupidities, the incompetencies and vanities of doctors, nurses, patients, and herself: she missed them.

Skiing, chopping, shoveling, a great deal of hard work and fresh air had fined her down so much that she suddenly found herself much too thin, produced some alarming female symptoms, and ran anxiously to a gynecologist with gory fears which she knew to be ridiculous, and laughed at, but she became unaccountably cross when he laughed at them, too.

"The damn thing's not prolapsed or something?"

"Not at all, my dear girl; all your little affairs are offensively healthy and that's just the point: when offensively healthy women of your age suddenly lose their husbands, they get their nice delicate little balance into a horrible great turmoil. My goodness," as she heaved an inelegant nudity off the horrid table, "you're muscled like a tennis player. I'm writing you some nice pills, but I'd love you to have a job, really, and when you're trained as a physiotherapist it seems a pity—but let's get you quietened down first, and then you can think it over."

Arlette went home vexed, as though she had been told to get a man, but it was all perfectly true. What was she doing in the country, anyway? Pure laziness and selfishness. She would get a job, and a little flat, and then Ruth wouldn't have to plow to and fro on that horrible bike. Everybody's too tactful to say so, but the rate she was going on, there was nothing to look forward to but baby-sitting.

Why was it that she clung irritably to living in the little crouched stone house, pottering anxiously around it as though there were still a floor to be polished somewhere but she couldn't remember which?

Spring came with its marvelous suddenness, halfway through April. A flood of hot sun swept the snow away overnight except for the north face of the hillside, in the shadowed rocky hollows where only moss flourished.

120

Dead beech leaves were dry and hard as potato crisps, bleaching to gray, and the new buds were as sexy as anything one could hope for. A big drift of snowdrops Arlette had not known existed appeared behind the woodshed, the field where in summers past they had picked wild strawberries filled with pale wood anemones, and all the garden thrust out clumps of green spears, happily identified as crocus, jonquil, iris, and narcissus.

Arlette had been dreaming of the wild strawberries. She was in the field hunting for them. The plants were there, and it was June, she knew, feeling the hot sun. She was in a cotton frock and a straw hat, bending to search. The leaves of the strawberry plants formed a stiff barrier, prickly and heraldic, hurting her hands when she tried to lift them. There was no fruit at all; she was more angry than disappointed—it was so unfair somehow. And then, with an extraordinary sense of relief, she was lying on bare ground, hard and reddish land she knew lay between La Seyne and Cassis, land from her childhood. She was lying on her back looking up at the plants, large now like vines, the huge leaves throwing dappled shadows—and, yes, there were the strawberries, just above her face, thousands and thousands, and as big as peaches. Arlette woke up. The April sunshine had heaved itself over the shoulder of the hill, and lay hot upon her yellow blanket: she was boiling. She jumped up and opened the window wide to look out: the still cool air blew through her nightdress in slow affectionate breaths, and her bare arms got gooseflesh. She looked with an intensity only a spring morning in Central Europe can bring. In the South the spring is banal. Almond blossom everywhere, and to a child Christmas was only yesterday. In the North the spring comes as acid and shuddering as a bite into a green apple. It seemed to Arlette that she was seeing the spring for the first time, with an eye as fresh as a child's.

Outside her window, the shiny gray grass of the year before (the new green showing through clearly now) was grayer and shinier with dew. Birds were making a monstrous racket. Because her top half was flooded full of sun, the rest of her, from the point where her pelvis pressed against the window sill, felt chilled. It was Thursday: Ruth was free; they could have breakfast out of doors. If he were here, she thought, he would have been up and roaming about; one would smell bacon being fried and hear the clonk of the cork being pulled from a bottle of white wine. The thought did not hurt her, and she was grateful for feeling so generously warmed.

The postman's yellow deux-chevaux, more clattering and unbridled than her prim white one, a vulgar big daffodil to a frail narcissus, arrived while they were sitting lazily having a cigarette, relaxed and heavy.

"Alors, Mesdames," with a jolly leer, "la grasse matinée, ça fait du bien." Yesterday's *Monde* and a postcard from one of the boys in Zagreb, and what on earth could he be doing there? A mail-order catalogue; oh, how dull, a bank statement from the computer in Melun; a large square envelop with a Dutch stamp. She grimaced, snicked it open, and sat staring dully. Ruth got up and began clearing; the clink of teaspoons roused Arlette to begin giving proper attention to the prickly stiffness of written Dutch. The commissaire of police—embarrassed, poor man; it showed in the contents, as stiff and prickly as the style.

He has promised to write, to keep her informed, but he is sorry to say that the inquiry has not so far given the results hoped for. They have used every diligence, but the affair is very puzzling. Since (ha hum) the deceased was not on active duty, the presumption was and remains that of some certainly pathological act of vengeance from the past. This has been most minutely pursued: every file he ever handled has been turned up and the present whereabouts and activities of each and every subject have been verified. Particular attention has been paid to all persons recently released from prison. Everything has been done that could possibly be done using the very considerable resources of filing systems (just ask the computer in Melun), archives, a most comprehensive routine, and large numbers of persons. On the technical side, the forensic science laboratory has done wonders: the gun has been identified but not, alas, discovered; the car could be identified but is unfortunately a commonplace model. Now, as Mevrouw doubtless knows, such cases are never classified, and every hope exists that in the near future further indices will appear leading to identification and apprehension. . . .

Arlette sat with her eyes shut, turning her head from side to side, trying to wipe away these clinging cobwebs. She knew nothing about crime, and very little about detection, for her husband had never believed in involving her with his work or his worries, but she had heard him often enough remarking ironically upon the official passion for files, archives, and routines. They were indispensable but incomplete; they deadened the imagination and paralyzed all unconventional approach. How often had he not remarked that the interesting things about people didn't get into files.

The clatter of the deux-chevaux roused her: the postman had forgotten something—ah, he'd had a parcel in the back and had neglected, sorry, to give it to her. "Bonne journée, Madame."

"Pareillement," said Arlette automatically, reading the last paragraph of her commissaire's letter.

A quantity of personal papers relative to Mr. van der

Valk's work for the Commission had been forwarded to him by the secretary of the same. He had had these examined for anything which could conceivably advance the inquiry with unfortunately no positive result, and since they were personal things he had taken the liberty of sending them on; with his respectful and profound sympathies, he was hers with the utmost reverence.

Arlette opened the parcel, and felt the clutch of a living man who had scribbled in these living notebooks. One of them slipped and fell on the floor; the fall jerked a piece of folded paper loose, and she picked it up and opened it, reading with a smile that grew gradually more sour. It appeared to be the rough draft of a written report made by some desk-bound policeman. A conscientious man, he had typed a fine copy, and had certainly eliminated a few rough edges. But—as does happen sometimes—his polished phrases were wasted, because he had forgotten to destroy his rough.

"I have been over these manuscript notebooks in an effort to discover whether any of the material therein could be in any way conducive toward further light being shed." (He had spelt the word "condusive.") "Some of the official work could be of value, and might be construed with the aid of his secretary, colleagues, etc. I understand, however, that this has been done. The remainder, however, amounts to no more than disjointed scribbles in a kind of personal shorthand, containing what appear to be cross-referenced scraps of personal memo regarding conversations held with colleagues, sketches for a variety of highly metaphysical and personal theories, aide-mémoires concerning library research, and much of an oversubjective and therefore hermetic nature. Most of these notes are further confused and consequently vitiated by being

mingled with what I can only call the raw material of
his private life in its more trivial aspects (jokes about
the Ministry, puns on his secretary's name, and even
shopping lists, to give a few examples) and a great deal
of this is quite incomprehensible, apart from being of
interest to nobody but perhaps a psychiatrist. I knew
Van der Valk quite well at one time, and was familiar
with this habit of making private footnotes to his work.
In justice to him, his written reports were models of
concision (consicion?) and legibility, but these notes
present a state of confusion inextricable, probably, to
anyone but himself. It is therefore concluded that unless we are interested in his having needed a haircut on
January 4th or the fact that his wife has the deplorable
habit of squeezing the toothpaste tube from the top,"
(this whole phrase had been crossed out as an unjustifi-
able piece of sarcasm) "we are unlikely to find anything herein of relevance to the inquiry afoot."

Blood had been steadily mounting in Arlette's head.
She was not really very cross with this little man, despite a smack of complacency and preciseness about
him, and she was not cross at all with the commissaire,
who had done his best with his enormous wooden
machine, was now paralyzed by embarrassment at the
fiasco, and had summoned the honesty and the courage
to tell her a fact painful to both of them and to him
extremely humiliating. But she was furious. Her husband had been so quickly downgraded to a pension, a
posthumous medal, a photograph in a black frame of
officers-fallen-on-the-field-of-honor. A cipher. The
moment he was no longer alive, to these writers of
reports he was no longer human. How often had he not
said that it was the victim who counted—whereas in all
the detective stories, and in all too many murder cases,
the victim is a mere peg on which to hang a plot, a

125

tiresome, uncomfortable, embarrassing preliminary detail, to be hushed up and tidied away as soon as possible?

Arlette opened a notebook.

"Dropping a watch on the tramline—how is it possible just mechanically? I would never have believed it—I could have cried. Odd how even a frightful catastrophe can give one a notion. But I'm not buying one here; too bloody dear. Mem: A. ask boys get a nice classic one in Schweiz Land für mich anniversaire."

She shut the notebook and started to cry.

"All the same," asked Ruth, "where did that other one come from, that pretty one with the enameled numerals? It must have been awfully dear."

"He told me he'd got it remarkably cheap, so I suppose it was secondhand or something, but, now you mention it, he was very mysterious about it, said it had been a lucky break in something he was puzzling out."

"Could that have been, do you think—?"

"I don't know," said Arlette. "But I want to read these notebooks. I'm not inclined to shrug all this off with airy disdain, the way those clowns did, just because they couldn't read them." She said it frivolously enough, but a resolution was beginning to form somewhere down inside her. Not to revenge, avenge, whatever they called it. But to strike a blow, somehow, for the victim, so ignominiously diminished and dismissed. There was an explanation to that assassination, and she intended to find it. And she felt convinced that it must be there in the notebooks. For Van der Valk had written everything down. It was his method and always had been. Whatever it was—trivial, irrelevant, or confused—he wrote it down, and at night he spent hours brooding over that confusion of scribbles, and surprisingly often a pattern would begin to appear in the

126

blurred and blotted lettering, and things he did not understand at all started to fall into place.

"Odd how even a frightful catastrophe can give one a notion."

The most flippant, unconnected, illogical remarks—they had a link which he had known. He probably did not know his assassin . . . but he would have known how to go about finding out.

That evening, Arlette took a clean notebook from a suitcase of junk she had packed without looking at it in the little flat, chose one of his ball-point pens, and began to go over the notebooks, line by line. It would be flattering at this point to say she asked for my advice at once, but it is typical of her that she didn't. She was first going to worry it out, stupidly, individually, honestly, personally. I find this altogether in character. I had never thought about her very much before, I am sorry to say, and this was lazy of me, as well as singularly stupid, because I was interested in Piet, with whom I felt sympathy, but on the whole uninterested in her, with whom I did not; and I never properly understood Piet because I consistently underestimated the influence she had upon him. This led me, certainly, to a deal of bad writing. I have defended this upon occasion (both to myself in private and to others in conversation) by remarks like "Well, in a crime story, you have to keep the action moving and not get too wound up in the interaction of characters." And yet I have sometimes made pretty vain claims that I was practically the inventor of crime stories based on character. (A damn-fool claim as well as vain, because there is never any inventor of anything. "Inventions" are made simultaneously by twenty or more people, simply because the time is ripe. A well-known example in the technical field is the invention of television, claimed by the Russians, the Americans, the English, and the French, all

127

of them with perfect accuracy.) So that throughout a dozen books I left Arlette as a minor character, shoving her in when a bit of color seemed indicated, and in a superficial way: she was a skillful cook and liked music.

I can only excuse myself by saying that this was the way I knew her. We used, when we met, to talk about cooking, a craft I am interested in, and about music, which I love but know nothing about, whereas she knew a lot, and this amused me because it is rare for French "femmes d'intérieur" of humble countrified background and unsophisticated upbringing to have any taste for music at all beyond, perhaps, Gilbert Bécaud, who is talented as well as good-looking.

I never troubled to look more closely at the way in which this ordinary married couple had grown into and developed one another, and yet this is one of the most basic elements in any serious attempt at fiction. We see—to take a well-known and obvious example—that Soames Forsyte is a tragic figure because there is no contact at all between himself and either of his wives (that infinitely tiresome Irene isn't even any good in bed), but we never get further. What did the damn fool marry them for—what did he see in them? Galsworthy funked the issue, from fastidiousness, convention, and—one is bound to say—stupidity or incompetence. The relation between Michael Mont and Fleur is equally superficial, and we cannot help concluding that here is a second-rate novelist.

I do not want to go too deeply into this, because a lot of it is irrelevant to this story: a point weighing much heavier with me is that I do not want to intrude upon Arlette's privacy, or hurt her feelings with some remarks she might find gratuitously personal. But it is perfectly reasonable to notice a few of the ways in which these two complemented each other. I did not know Piet as a young man, but it is obvious enough that he was an uneasy, awkward young man, aggressive about being "working class," ashamed at once of his crude physique and of his intelligence, which he tended to hide, even when I knew him, behind a yobbo act that was nothing more than inverted snobbery. Being a bright boy, he had gone to the Hogere Burger School, a sort of superior Dutch grammar school akin to a lycée, where he had been surrounded by boys of a petit-bourgeois, successful-shopkeeper class, jeered at for his accent and his street manners. He lost his father, an artisan carpenter from the poor and crowded Amsterdam district of the "Pijp," during the war, and his mother soon after, when he was barely out of his teens. He himself ran away around 1943, got to Sweden, and reached England, where for several months he was kept shut up in an internment camp and treated with owlish suspicion—a boy of eighteen. . . . Once back in Amsterdam after the war, his education, his aptitude for foreign languages, his military service record, his quickness at study, and an interest in law—all this led him to be accepted as a trainee officer of police.

Of the Amsterdam police corps at that time, the less said the better. Several notoriously corrupt and incompetent elements were purged, for real or pretended collaboration: a few case-hardened old commissaires were put on the shelf. Other, and often equally undesirable, persons took advantage of the times—a hysterical and most unpleasant atmosphere of vendetta—to ensconce themselves in positions of comfort.

The young Van der Valk early learned a sort of homespun cynicism, and he was delighted when I quoted him the fierce lines from Kipling:

How smoothly and how swiftly they have sidled back
  to power
By the favor and contrivance of their kind.

Arlette came from a family of landowners in a small way, almost a petty aristocracy in the well-brought-up traditional Catholic and conservative French style, and she followed the path of her class: lycée des jeunes filles, Faculty of Letters at Aix, the literary-philo formation then still undecayed. Rebellion seized her, too, and she, too, ran away, but she never liked to talk much about this, and I do not know the exact circumstances of how she came to meet and marry Piet, except that it was in Paris, in the heady atmosphere of 1947, where he was celebrating the passing of some examination with a pathetic three-day moment of freedom. They got married, probably very ill-advisedly, and lived in Amsterdam thenceforward in considerable poverty. They clung to each other fiercely. She civilized him, and he rubbed the corners off her. He learned not to be ashamed of his streak of sensitivity toward "art." She did not like Holland, never really understood it, and probably would have been miserable were it not for her passion for music—and the Concertgebouw Orchestra of Amsterdam, of which she was a faithful follower, was and is one of the most enchanting there is, with a nervous and wonderfully transparent sound, exquisitely sensitive: "Not at all Dutch," she used to say crudely; still, she did learn to like and appreciate Amsterdam.

Poor or not, she was an excellent homemaker, good at cooking and sewing, disciplined by early years at keeping silent and sitting upright, and with a real imaginative talent for bringing warmth, love, and gaiety into her surroundings, which however tatty or penurious had always the glow and patina of a piece of good old furniture. The equilibrium and support Piet got from all this brought him through many hard years: although good at his work, conscientious, and un-

130

deniably clever, he had moments of irresponsibility, a tactless lack of respect for superior mediocrities, and above all a tendency to indiscretion, which did him much harm professionally, made him more than one highly placed enemy, and interfered grievously with his otherwise bright prospects of promotion. A few spectacular and brilliant successes, brought about, he said himself, more by strokes of luck than anything else, saved him from dusty obscurity and an embittering sense of failure which would have destroyed him as a person. She kept him from becoming hardened and coarsened: his own optimism, and a sunny spontaneity, as well as being a generous, kind, and humble person, preserved him from becoming sour and discouraged.

When I was myself poor, miserable, and disappointed, as well as singularly ill-educated and ill-prepared for life, they showed me much kindness—I owe them both a great deal.

Closing this parenthesis, which has been inexcusably impudent, I risk one more personal remark. This is that when I learned about Arlette's behavior it left me open-mouthed. It still astonishes me. I have heard before of instances in which she displayed a reckless personal courage that sometimes—as he himself admitted—frightened Van der Valk.

We were discussing criminals, murders, and suchlike things, riding our favorite hobby-horses and generally enjoying ourselves, when suddenly—"Arlette," he said, "is capable of anything." Respect in his voice, and also a real fear, which took me aback and embarrassed me.

"The female of the species," I said.

"In defense of her home, yes, of course. And the woman criminal who has an implacability, a ferocity, and a cunning superior to anything a man seems capable of—yes, there are well-documented descriptions.

And there are examples of women as guerrilla fighters, or in resistance movements—one is astounded. Why should that be, do you think? Is it biological? I mean the so-called feeble sex, with weaker muscles and all those awkward bumps, tender breasts and a big behind; look how idiotic and repellent the sight of a woman footballer—or wrestlers: unspeakable . . . The female animal—I mean tigresses and wildcats or whatnot —is as active and muscled as the male, maybe slimmer and lighter, but just as active and well-armed. So that the legendary viciousness is not a compensation for being weaker. But in the human species, which is altogether different—I mean so much more vulnerable . . . I've no idea, really. . . . Arlette—a couple of times, I tell you, she's raised the hair on my neck all the way down my spine."

I have since been reminded vividly of this remark.

Arlette walked slowly along the echoing wooden platforms of the Central Station in Amsterdam, carrying her own suitcase, down the tunnel, through the hall, noticing nothing. She felt tired, stale, disillusioned. Why had she come? What good should she possibly be able to do? She did not even have any idea of where to go, how to start, although she had worried about it all the way in the train, turning over and over the few rags and scraps of uncertain fact she possessed—or hoped she did. The journey had been like a sleepless night, waking constantly from an uneasy, unrefreshing doze and finding no advance in thought, which flickered eccentrically without any logical progress whatever, or in the lagging hands of the clock. She had come here, though she did not know what she was going to do.

She had spent hours with the notebooks, not eating, drinking too much, staring about, lighting cigarettes and throwing them away, frightening Ruth. Sometimes it had all seemed clear and reasonable, and half an hour after she would again be plunged into blind ignorance and indecision. After two days she had said to Ruth suddenly, with a snap, throwing herself into a pattern of action abruptly, as though afraid that if she hesitated longer she would never budge at all: "Ruth."

"Yes."

"Darling—I'm going to leave you alone. I don't know for how long. A week, fortnight, I just don't know. I'm going to see this through. I'm going to Amsterdam. I can't give you any address—I've no idea even where I'll be staying or anything. I'm sorry." She did not inquire whether Ruth would be frightened alone in a country cottage at night—a girl of not yet sixteen. It is quite possible that this did not even occur to her.

One must say that Ruth was splendid. She said, "Yes, of course, darling, don't worry, I'll be perfectly all right." As though Arlette, at this moment probably quite mad, even in the clinical sense, had ever thought of that!

Ruth did the sensible thing and rang up my wife. Who told her to come over, of course. "The woman's round the bend," she said to me, much alarmed. "What should we do?"

Ruth rode her scooter all the way over. It was not too terrible for her to stay with us, as her school is not much further away than from her own home. Plenty of other children living in the country have as far to go, and the train service is designed for this. We weren't worried about her.

"Arlette's gone mataglap" was the first thing she said. It is one of the Malay words that have crept into the Dutch vocabulary, like "amok"—it means much the same: a temporary insanity during which the sufferer notices nothing, neither pain, fatigue, nor fear, and is totally unamenable to reason.

"What shall we do?" asked my wife again.

I thought. "Nothing, I think," I said at last. I tried to explain.

Arlette came out into the open air and saw that spring had arrived in Amsterdam. The pale, acid sun of late afternoon lay on the inner harbor beyond the Prins Hendrik Kade; the wind off the water was sharp. It gave her a shock. A succession of quick rhythmic taps, as at the start of the violin concerto of Beethoven. That she noticed this means, I think, that from that moment she was sane again. But it is possible that I am mistaken. Even if insane, one can have, surely, the same perceptions as other people, and this "click" is a familiar thing. Exactly the same happens when one takes the night train down from Paris to the coast, and one wakes somewhere between Saint-Raphaël and Cannes, and looks out, and there is the Mediterranean. Or was.

The pungent salt smell, the northern maritime keynotes of sea gull and herring, the pointed brick buildings, tall and narrow like herons, with their mosaic of particolored shutters, eaves, sills, that give the landscapes their stiff, medieval look. (One is back beyond Breughel, beyond van Eyck, to the primitives whose artists we do not know, so that they have names like the Master of the Saint Ursula Legend.) The lavish use of paint in flat bright primary colors which typifies these Baltic Hanseatic quaysides is startling to the visitor from Central Europe. Even the Dutch flags waving everywhere (there are no more determined flag wavers) upset and worried Arlette; she had not realized how in a short time her eye had accustomed itself to the subtle and faded colorings of France, so that it was as though she had never before left home. The sharp flat brightness of Holland! The painters' light which hurts the unaccustomed eye. . . . Arlette never wore sunglasses in France, except on the sea or on the snow, but here, she remembered suddenly, she had practically gone to bed in them. Yet it was all so familiar. She had lived here, she had to keep reminding herself, for twenty years.

She had no notion of where she wanted to go, but she knew that now she was here, a small pause would bring the spinning, whirling patterns of the kaleidoscope to rest. She crossed the road and went down the steps to the little wooden terrace—a drink, and get her breath back! Everything was new—the pale heavy squatness of a Dutch café's cup and saucer, left on her table by the last occupant; the delightful rhythmic skyline across the harbor of the Saint Nicolas Church and the corner of the Zeedijk! Tourists were flocking into water buses, and now she was a tourist, too. An old waiter was wiping the table while holding a tray full of empty bottles which wavered in front of her eye.

"Mevrouw?"

"Give me a Chocomilk, at least if you've got one that's good and cold." Another click! She was talking Dutch, and as fluently as ever she had!

He was back before she had got over it. "Nou, Mevrouwtje—cold as Finnegan's feet." His voice had the real Amsterdam caw to it. "You aren't Dutch, though, are you now?"

"Only a tourist," smiling.

"Well, now, by your leave: proper-sounding Dutch you talk there," chattily, bumping the glass down and pouring in the clawky Chocomilk.

"Thank you very much."

"Tot Uw dienst. Ja, ja, ja, kom er aan," to a fussy man waving and banging his saucer with a coin.

Neem mij niet kwa-a-lijk; een be-hoor-lijk Nederlands spreekt U daar. Like a flock of rooks. Yah, yah, ya-ah, kom er a-an. And she was blinded by tears again, hearing her husband's exact intonation; when with her, he spoke a Dutch whose accent sometimes unconsciously—ludicrously—copied hers, but when with the real thing, the "rasecht" like himself, his accent would begin to caw, too, as though in self-parody.

Next door to her were sitting two American girls, earnest, quiet, looking quite clean, though their hair was dusty and their jeans were as darkly greasy as the mud the dredger over there was turning up off the harbor bottom. Scraps of conversation floated across.

"She's a lovely person, terribly quiet but really mature, you know what I mean; yes, from Toledo." Arlette knew that Van der Valk would have guffawed and her eyes cleared.

I see her there, at the start of her absurd and terrifying mission. She has the characteristic feminine memory for detail, the naïvely earnest certainty that she has to get everything right. Had I asked her what those two girls were drinking, she would have known for sure, and been delighted at my asking.

I have not seen Amsterdam for four or five years, and it might be as long again before I shall. This is just as well. I do not want my imagination to get in the way of Arlette's senses. Piet, whose imagination worked like mine, saw things in an entirely different way to her.

We were sitting, once, together on that same terrace. "Look at that damn building," pointing at the Central Station, a construction I am fond of, built with loving attention to every useless detail by an architect of the last century whose name I have forgotten (a Dutch

136

equivalent of Sir Giles Gilbert Scott). "Isn't it lovely?" Lovely is not the word I would have chosen, but it is oddly right.

"The Railway Age," he went on. "Make a wonderful museum—old wooden carriages, tuff-tuff locos with long funnels, Madame Tussaud figures of station-masters with beards, policemen wearing helmets, huge great soup-strainer mustaches, women with bustles and reticules . . ." Yes, indeed, and children in sailor suits. Arlette's mind does not behave like this.

I am changed, thought Arlette, and unchanged. I am the same housewife, familiar with these streets, this people. I am not pricked or tickled by anything here, like a tourist. I see all this with the coolness and objec-tivity of experience; I am not going to rush into any-thing stupid or imprudent. This is a town I know, and I am going to find myself perfectly able to cope with the problem. I am not alone or helpless; I have many friends here, and there are many more who were Piet's friends and who will help me for his sake. But I am no longer the thoughtless and innocent little wife of a little man in a little job, standing on the corner with my shopping bag wondering whether to have a cabbage or a cauli. I am a liberated woman, and that is going to make a difference.

A tout was circling around the cluster of tables, sizing up likely suckers. A year or so ago, he would have been handing out cards for a restaurant or a hotel, booking for quickie trips around the sights, with water bus, Anne Frank, and the Rembrandthuis all thrown in for only ten gulden. Now—he had closed in on the two American girls, and she could hear him, in the pidgin German-American patois that is the international language of the European tout, selling live sex shows. The two girls glanced up for a second with polite in-difference, and went back to their earnest, careful, in-

137

tense conversation, paying no further attention to him at all. He broke off the patter, circled backward like a boxer, and gave Arlette a careful glance: French-women, generally fascinated by the immoralities and debaucheries of the English and the Scandinavians—likely buyers, as long as they have first done their duty with a really good orgy at Marks & Spencer's. Arlette met his eye with such a chill and knowing look that he shuffled back into the ropes and made off sideways: the cow has been to the sex show and has no money left. Amsterdam, too, has changed and not changed, she thought. "Raffishness" was always a cliché tourists used; the Amsterdamers were intensely, idiotically proud of their red-light district, and since time im-memorial a stroll to look at "the ladies behind the win-dows" was proposed to every eager tourist the very first night.

Now they have taken with such relish to the new role of exhibitionist shopwindow that it is hard not to laugh—the visitor's first reaction generally is roars of laughter. The Dutch have a belief that sex has made them less provincial, somehow—for few attitudes are more provincial than the anxious striving to be modern-and-progressive. Paris doesn't exist any more and Lon-don is slipping, they will tell one with a boastful pathos, and Holland is where it's at. A bit immature, really, as the two nineteen-year-olds from Dubuque were prob-ably at that moment saying.

Arlette was a humble woman. She saw herself as a snobbish, narrow, rigid French provincial bourgeois. Piet, born and bred in Amsterdam, used to describe himself as a peasant. This humility gave them both an unusual breadth, stability, and balance. I remember his telling me once how, to his mind, his career if not his life had been an abject failure.

138

"But there," drinking brandy reflectively, being indeed a real soak and loving it, "what else could I have done?"

Arlette, walking slowly through the lazy, dirty sunshine of late afternoon in Amsterdam, was thinking, too, What else could I have done?

She had come to lay a ghost. Not that she—hardheaded woman—believed in ghosts, but she had lived long enough to know they were there.

Piet was a believer in ghosts. "I have known malign influences outside the bathroom door," he used to say. He was delighted when I gave him to read the finely made old thriller of Mr. A. E. W. Mason, which is called *The Prisoner in the Opal:* he saw the point at once, and when he brought it back he said that he, too, with the most sordid, materialistic, bourgeois of inquiries, always made the effort "to pierce the opal crust." Poor old Piet.

Once we were having dinner together in a Japanese restaurant. We had had three Pernods, big ones, the ones Piet, with his horrible Dutch ideas of wit that he took for esprit, described as "des grands Pers." We were watching the cook slicing raw fish into fine transparent slices.

"There is poetry," said Piet suddenly, "in those fingers." I turned around suspiciously, because this is a paraphrase from a good writer whom Piet had certainly not read. I used the phrase as an epigraph to a book I once wrote about cooks—which Piet had not read, either. "Poetry in the fat fingers of cooks."

I looked at Piet suspiciously. "So," with tactful calm, "is that a quotation?"

"No," innocent. "Just a phrase. Thought it would please you, haw."

That crude guffaw; completely Piet. The stinker, to

this day I don't know whether he was kidding me. A skillful user of flattery, but damn it, a friend.

The Damrak; the Dam, the Rokin. Squalid remnants of food flung upon the pavements. The young were unable or unwilling to spend much on food, she thought, and what they got for their money probably deserved to be flung; one could not blame them too much, just because one felt revolted.

But one did blame them: beastly children.

The Utrechtsestraat. The Frederiksplein. And, once out of the tourist stamping ground, Arlette knew suddenly where she was going. She was heading, unerringly and as though she had never been away, straight toward the flat where she had lived for twenty years. It was a longish way to walk, all the way from the Central Station and carrying a suitcase, too. Why had she done it? She would have said crossly, "What else could I have done?" For when she got there she was very tired and slightly footsore, disheveled, smelling of sweat, and ready to cry.

"Arlette! My dear girl! What *are* you doing? But come in! I'm so happy to see you—and at the same time, my poor child, I'm so sad! Not that we know *anything*—what one reads in the paper nowadays—*pah!* And again *pah!* Come in, my dear girl, come in—you don't mean to say you walked . . . from the *station?* You *didn't!* You *couldn't!* Sit down, child, do. The lavy? But of course—you know where it is, that's not something you'll have forgotten. I'll make some coffee. My dear girl, *marvelous* to see you, and the dear boys? No, no, I must be patient, go and have a pee, child, and a wash, do you good." The old biddy who had always had the ground-floor flat, and still did . . . She taught the piano. It had been the most familiar background noise to Arlette's life throughout the boys' childhood; her voice carried tremendously.

140

"One, Two, not so hasty. Pedal there, you're not giving those notes their value; that's a sharp, can't you hear it?" And coming back from shopping an hour later, one found another was being put through its hoops.

"Watch your tempo, not so much espressivo, you're sentimentalizing; this is the Ruysdaelkade, not the Wiener Wald or something."

"Lumpenpack," she would mutter, coming out on the landing for a breather and finding Arlette emptying the dustbin.

Old Mother Counterpoint, Piet always called her, and sometimes, in deference to Jane Austen, "Bates." ("Mother hears perfectly well; you only have to shout a little and say it two or at the most three times.")

A wonderful person, really. A mine of information on the quarter, possessor of efficient intelligence networks in every shop, an endless gabble on the telephone, forever fixing things for someone, pulling strings for someone else. She could find anything for you: a furnished room, a secondhand pram scarcely used, a boy's bike, a shop where they were having a sale of wonderful materials ever so cheap; even if she didn't have her finger on it herself, she knew a man who would let you have it wholesale. Warm-hearted old girl. Gushing, but wonderfully kind, and gentle, and sometimes even tactful.

"You take yours black, dear—oh, yes, I hadn't forgotten—you think I'd forget a thing like that? Not gaga yet, thank God. Good heaven, it must be seven years. But you haven't aged, dear—a few lines, yes—badges of honor, my pet, that's what I call them. Tell me—can you bear to talk about it? Where are you staying? By the look of you, you could do with a square meal."

"I don't know, I was wondering . . ."

"But, my poor pet, of course; how can you ask, you

141

know I'd be more than pleased and I've plenty of room; it's just can you bear all the little fussinesses of a frightful old maid—oh nonsense, child, now don't be tiresome. Now I'll tell you what—no, don't interrupt. I'm going to go to the butcher—yes, still the same, awful fellow; all those terrible people, how they'll be thrilled, just wait till he hears; I'll frighten him, the wretch, he gave me an escalope last week and tough; my poor girl, since you left he thinks everything is permitted him. I'll get a couple of nice veal cutlets and we'll have dinner; just you wait and I'll get something to drink, too; oh rubbish, I love the excuse, and what's more I'll make pancakes, I never bother by myself; you take your shoes off and put your feet up and read the paper; nonsense you'll do no such thing, I want to and anyway I'll enjoy it: would you perhaps love a bath, my pet?" The voice floated off into the hallway. "Where's my galoshes, oh dear, oh here they are now how did they get that way; oh wait till I tell the wretch the cutlets are for you, he'll jump out of his skin. . . ." The front door slammed. Arlette was home.

It was a nice evening. Bates brought Beaujolais—Beaujolais! "I remember you used to buy it, child; I hope you still like it."

Cutlets. "He practically went on his knees when he heard; with the tears in his eyes he swore on his mother's grave you'd be able to cut them with a fork, and I just looked and said 'She'd better' that's all."

"Bananas—I've got some rum somewhere, hasn't been touched in five years, I'd say; pah, all dusty, do you think it'll still be all right, dear—not gone poisonous or anything; one never knows now, they put chemicals in to make things smell better; awful man in the supermarket and I swear he squirts the oranges with an aerosol thing to make them smell like oranges, forlorn

142

hope is all I can say." The rum was tasted, and pronounced fit for pancakes.

"And how's Amsterdam?" asked Arlette, laughing.

It isn't what it was; it wasn't what it had been.

Arlette had prepared to be bored with old-maidish gush about how we don't sleep safe in our bed of nights, not like when we had a policeman in the house, which did give one a sense of security somehow. She ought to have known better, really, because Old Mother Counterpoint had the tough dryness, the voluble energy, the inconsequent loquacity she expected—and indeed remembered—but the warm-hearted kindness was illumined by a shrewd observation she had never given the old biddy credit for.

"Well, my dear, it would ill become me to complain. I'll have this flat for as long as I live and they can't put my rent up. I have to spread my butter thinner but I'm getting old and I need less of it. I have the sunshine still and the plants and my birds, and they'll all last my time. I think it comes much harder on a girl your age, who can remember what things used to be, and who still has to move with the changes and accept them, whereas people expect me to be eccentric and silly. And I'm sorrier still for the young ones. They don't have any patterns to move by; it must give a terrible sense of insecurity, and I think that's what makes them so unhappy. Everyone kowtows to them and it must be horrid, really. Look at the word 'young,' I mean it used to mean what it said and no more, young cheese or a young woman and that was that—and now they talk about a young chair or a young frock and it's supposed to mean good, and when you keep ascribing virtue to people, and implying all the time that they should be admired and imitated—well, dear, it makes their life very difficult and wearisome; I used to know a holy

143

nun and she said sometimes that everybody being convinced one was good made a heavy cross to carry. When the young do wicked things, I can't help the feeling that it's because they're dreadfully unhappy. Of course there's progress, lots and lots of progress, and it makes me very happy. I don't have many pupils now, but I'm always struck when they come, so tall and healthy and active, so unlike the pale little tots when I was a young woman, and I remember very hard times, my dear—the men always drunk because their lives were so hard—but they don't seem to me any happier or more contented, and they complain more because they expect much more. I can't really see what they mean talking about progress, because that seems to me to presuppose that people are good and get better, and the fact is, my pet, as you and I know, people are born bad and tend to get worse, and putting good before evil is always a dreadful struggle, dear, whatever they say. One is so vain, and so selfish."

And Arlette, who had had a good rest, a delicious bath, and a good supper, found herself pouring out her whole tale, and most of her heart.

"Well," said Bates at the end, with great common sense, "that has done you a great deal of good, my dear, and that's a fact, just like taking off one's stays; girls don't wear stays any more and don't know what they miss."

Arlette felt inclined to argue that it was a good thing to be no longer obliged to wear stays.

"Of course, dear, don't think I don't agree with you, healthy girls with good stomach muscles playing tennis, and no more of that fainting and vaporing. But I maintain that it was a good thing for a girl to know constraint. Sex education and women's lib, all dreadful cant. Girls who married without knowing the meaning of the word 'sex' were sometimes very happy and sometimes very unhappy, and I don't believe they are any happier now. I married a sailor, dear, and learned how to go without."

"It doesn't make me any happier now," said Arlette dryly.

"No, dear, and that's just what I felt in 1940 when my ship got torpedoed. So now let's be very sensible. You've come here very confused and embittered, and you don't want anything to do with the police, and you're probably quite right, because really, poor dears, they've simply no notion, but at the present you've no notion either. You'd never have thought of asking my advice, because I'm a silly old bag, but I'll give it to you, and it is that you probably can find out who killed your husband, because it's surprising what you can do when you try, but it's as well to have friends one can count on, and you can count on me for a start—and with that, my dear, we'll go to bed, your eyes are dropping out."

"Did you join the Resistance—in 1940, I mean?" asked Arlette.

"Yes, I did, and what's more once I threw a bomb at a bad man in the Euterpestraat, and that was the dreadful place, the Gestapo headquarters here in Amsterdam, and it was very hard because I was horribly frightened of the bomb, and even more frightened of the bad man, who had soldiers with him, and most of all because I knew they would take hostages and execute them, but it had to be done, you see."

"I do see," said Arlette seriously. "It wasn't the moment to take off one's stays and feel comfortable."

"Right, my pet, right," said Old Mother Counterpoint.

Called in the morning with a nice cup of tea, sniffing

145

with pleasure the solid, stuffy smell of an Amsterdam flat whose furniture has not changed its position in forty years, stirring her tea with a silver teaspoon got from saving up the tokens on Douwe Egbert coffee packets, washing in a well-remembered sploshy way because the Dutch are as bad as the English at believing it to be less indecent to scrub standing up than to sit on a bidet, in a house she had lived in, in pain, poverty, and happiness for twenty years, Arlette felt strangely consoled and at peace. Here above her head, on the other side of that dingy stucco ceiling with early-nineteenth-century baroque ornaments, her husband's feet had made the floorboards squeak, and between the two of them they had made the bedsprings squeak, too, and the thought stayed with her through breakfast, so that she asked Bates, "Who has the flat now?"

"Yours? Some artists; she's very sweet, Hilary, though I'm bound to say as an artist I don't think much of her."

"What does she do?"

"She hammers at things," said Bates vaguely. "But he's really very good—such a comic little man, just like Mr. Gandhi, or is it Mr. Kipling?"

"Does one get them confused?" asked Arlette, startled.

"Oh, one does, dear. India, you know. Oh, I know I'm being silly; one is Simla and polo ponies and not a bit sitting on the floor with a tiny fire made of cow dung, but somehow they're just the same. One had a mustache, but I never can remember which." It meant little to Arlette, who was vague about both personages, but when taking the milk in—"I wouldn't do anything this morning if I were you; just potter, and let ideas come to you"—she met Mr. Kipling, or was it Mr. Gandhi, in the hall, and instantly understood: a little bald nut-brown man with steel-rimmed glasses, a shaggy mustache like Monsieur Clemenceau, dirty overalls, and very bright sharp eyes which glanced at her, registered astonishment, and instantly assumed a dramatic expression of delight and enjoyment.

"Good morning," said Arlette feebly.

"Quelle immense surprise, do you play the piano?"

"I used to live in your flat."

"No! Don't tell me—you must be Mrs. van der Valk."

"That's right."

"I know all about you: you are French, you smell delicious, you used to keep the whole neighborhood in gales of laughter, and you had dreadful fights with the butcher, whom you detested because he used to call you 'schat.' "

"How do you know all that?" Fourth feeble remark in a row.

"From Marguérite Long, of course."

"Hush."

"Oh, she knows perfectly well we call her that, and isn't offended a bit; quite the contrary, immensely flattered. Come upstairs and have a drink—oh, don't worry I won't seduce you, although I'd simply love it. My wife's upstairs, she'll be delighted, we've both always longed to meet you."

"I was just going out for a walk."

"You come upstairs."

"Very well," and she did.

"Your husband was assassinated," he said abruptly on the landing. "I am so very sorry. Please go in; I don't need to tell you the way."

And the sight of the hideous Victorian hatstand, which she had been so glad to say goodbye to, made her burst embarrassingly into floods. Mr. Gandhi, whose name he had told her was Dan de Vries, was perfect: he paid no attention at all but said, "Can you drink Pernod at this hour of the day?"

"Of course I can," roared Arlette, adding, "It's nearly lunchtime," in a sort of muffled squawk.

"It's breakfast time," corrected Mr. de Vries severely. "Hilary, this is Arlette van der Valk; she's crying because she used to live here, and her husband as you know got killed; put a stop to it, will you, while I get us a drink?"

"Whatever you want," said Mrs. de Vries. "We've got it or can shoplift it. Cold water, Kleenex, Tampax, several lipsticks, a fried egg . . ."

"A drink," said Arlette, and got a whopper pushed firmly in her hand, took a pull that nearly stood her on her ear, accepted a bent Gauloise, wiped her eyes, and said, "Talk about making a fool of myself."

"Not in the slightest," said Dan, sitting down. "I would be doing the identical things in your place, and probably take a great deal longer recovering."

"Do you like peanuts?" asked Hilary, delighting Arlette by producing instead of a saucerful, or a horrid plastic packet in a vacuum, a large glass jar holding at least five kilos.

"Brings back one's childhood," said Arlette. "Sweet shops. Peppermint bull's-eyes."

"Precisely," said Dan. "Now classed as works of art, and probably auctioned for vast sums. Christie's was flogging sets of cigarette cards just the other day. And twopenny bloods. The Hotspur, the Wizard, and the Champion; Biggles, with his jaw set, behind the twin Vickers. At the time I was the schoolboy genius, four feet high, looking much the way I do now except that my glasses were horn-rimmed, the terrifying trick-spin bowler at cricket. I got Stan McCabe and Don Brad-

148

man with successive balls because my shoulder, my elbow, and my wrist were all double-jointed and still are, thank god; it's my conscience that's so stiff. Shooting policemen in the street—I have upon occasion imagined myself partisan, but faced with it in the flesh, I discovered a kind of moral revulsion; must be the result of reading Biggles as a child."

"Not having been a boy," said Hilary mildly, "it's likely that she doesn't know what you are talking about. He's trying to tell you that he wasn't at all happy about your husband, whose ghost is here present."

"I know," said Arlette. "I've come to lay it but I don't know how; perhaps you can advise me."

"We never advise anybody," said Hilary, "but we'll help you."

"So you've come here to get to the bottom of this," said Dan in a completely different voice.

"Yes," said Arlette.

"Police no good?"

"It's not the word I'd use. Earnest, perhaps, but misguided."

"They never can see the wood for the trees."

"My sentiment."

"Have you anything they haven't? I'm not talking about intelligence, of course. Anything factual."

"I'm not able to say. I think I'd be very glad of your opinion."

"Come to dinner tonight."

"If you like curry, that is," added Hilary.

"Yes," said Arlette. "To both."

That afternoon Arlette went into the butcher's. She was going for a good long walk, anyway, all around her quarter and further, to look at things old and new, things familiar and things startlingly unexpected: it would, she thought, put her in proportion, arrange her ideas, show her what she wanted; she had still no clear notion what this was. To find out who had killed her husband? It sounded easy, until one reflected that the police, however wooden, were not exclusively composed of people who had fallen on the back of their heads in childhood. What could she think of that they had not already thought of? The few uneasy threads of suspicion she had found in her readings of the notebooks, back there in France in solitude and neurosis, here seemed exceedingly feeble, scrappy, and inconsequent. And even if she found out? What did one do? One didn't just lay one's hand solemnly on a shoulder and say, "I arrest you in the name of the law." And suppose there was no proof? Little as she knew of police procedures, she knew from her husband that quite often there isn't any proof. One can know, the police and the judge and the Prime Minister can all know with absolute certainty, and they can't do anything about it at all, and some really nasty people walk about in arrogant ease and careless splendor, vastly rich and respected, laughing their heads off. A depressing prospect.

She went to the butcher to buy something nice for Bates, who had been full of approval at Arlette's eating curry upstairs.

"She's very women's-lib, but I think she must be a nice woman, and Danny is a sweetie—really so polite it's rather touching."

She would go, too, say a polite word. They knew she was around, they had asked kindly after her. She couldn't go dodging about the quarter pretending they didn't exist, avoiding their street like Dick Swiveller. She would walk in, swallow a lot of guff, and walk out again. After all, that butcher had been one of her great enemies for years and years, was a pig-faced swine, a money-grubbing pig, a thoroughly swine-moraled and swine-countenanced swine, expert in every kind of foul fiddle—but still: he had sent "heartiest greetings and profoundest sympathies" through Bates. And the veal cutlets, she was bound to admit, had been perfect. She would do her duty.

She hardly recognized the shop—in fact, she didn't recognize it and, for an idiot moment, thought she had somehow taken the wrong turning and was not in the right street. But there was the dry cleaner's opposite, and the bicycle shop next door, utterly unchanged, not even a coat of new paint in seven years. Her eyes were not deceiving her. The butcher had simply made a lot of money, and that was the explanation of these palatial marble halls. Bates had forgotten to warn her. She walked in bravely, with an air of preparing to give battle, just like in the old days when she used to go behind his counter and right into the villain's coldroom to teach him how to hang steak. There the swine was, holding his great chopper, as swinish and as piggy-eyed as ever. As he saw her, the pig blossomed into a lovely, happy, candid, blue-eyed television ad.

"Mrs. van der Valk!" he shouted, dropping his chopper, pushing a heap of mince out of the way, wiping his hands on his apron, carting out from behind his counter, and shaking hands with vast enthusiasm and a bit too much muscular force, roaring the while, "Schatje, schatje, look who's here." Which, as it always had, made her want to giggle. He had always called her—or, indeed, any other woman customer at all— "schat," which means "treasure." But his wife, who was mountainous, he always called "schatje" which means "tiny treas." Treas was a dreadful great cow who sat enthroned in a glass cage where she could keep both hands firmly on the cash and still have an eye upon any jiggery-pokery on either side of the counter, in the street, along the pavement, and up through the ceiling into her flat, where the hired girl might be stealing bonbons out of the cupboard, but not if she knew what was good for her, because they were counted and so, by god, was everything else. Schatje's real name was Trixie, and the Swine's was Willy, and there stood Arlette, both hands firmly clutched by one while she was slobbered on by the other, astonished to find herself touched, moved, and finally quite swept away. It was all genuine! They were delighted to see her. That hard, tricky, wicked French cow from a stunted, shifty, crooked race which wore berets, smoked opium, and lay about all day in the sunshine in whatever time there was left over from swilling pastis, playing pétanque, and stuffing itself with veal liver—they loved her. . . .

Trixie's eyes were full of tears. "The dreadful thing—I opened the paper—and there's not a day goes by without something horrible—and there it was staring me in the face—but if it's someone you don't know somehow it doesn't hit you, love, does it?—and my heart turned over—and I dropped the paper and I screamed—'Willy,' I shrieked, 'come quick'—my whole day—couldn't eat a thing—I gave a customer change of a hundred instead of fifty, my hands were trembling—and I wished you were here so's I could tell you, love, we've had some fights but suffering wipes out everything, I say."

"I was that angry," Willy had taken it up, "and the whole day I thought if I had who done that filthy cowardly trick, shooting in the back like that, if I had him under my hand—well, schat, I thought, I wished I was in France, that's all, where you still got capital punishment, that's all; there's only one thing for people like that and that's the chop. I told everyone who came in, I said, Piet van der Valk was my neighbor here in this quarter twenty year—no, tell a lie, thirty year; we grew up together and there never was a straighter, no."

What a foul bitch I am, thought Arlette. These people are thinking of absolutely nothing but to show me kindness and love and loyalty. I came in thinking of a polite word and a handshake with two pigs who never thought of anything but money, and I'm so cold and selfish myself that it simply never occurred to me. Look at schatje there, her tears are utterly genuine, coming from spontaneous simplicity, and I couldn't cry at all except maybe from humiliation and shame.

Trix was saying, "You had the funeral private—Willy, there's a customer—and I don't blame you; I wanted to come, I would have come, but I don't blame you, one wants to be alone with one's grief, and the same time, love, when your friends stand by you it's a good thing sometimes, share your burdens and heaven knows they're heavy enough. Now isn't that fine, love, that's grand, you've come back to spend a bit of time in your old quarter, and you'll find we don't forget our neighbors round here, love, say what you like; this is Amsterdam, hippies and the like we may have, dirty long-haired work-shy ruck it is, but we're plain and we speak our mind; are you going to stay a day or so, love—come on up tonight, do, and have a cup of coffee."

"I'm staying with my old neighbor downstairs—yes, I hope I'll be here a few days. That reminds me I came in to get her something. Oh, I'd love to come and have a cup of coffee, but I can't tonight, I'm afraid."

"Then tomorrow" said Trix firmly. "You'll come tomorrow, and I'll show you the flat; it's all new done up, real nice it is, and we'll have a laugh over old times;

153

remember the time, love, you said the steak was horse and poor old Willy got that mad?"

"I'll come tomorrow," promised Arlette.

"You won't forget?" asked Trix humbly, meaning, "You won't be too toffee-nosed?"

"I won't forget," promised Arlette absolutely sincerely, and got a hug. "But I mustn't forget my errand; I want a sweetbread."

"Sweetbread, of course, I'd get it myself but," whispering, "I've got to get back to the desk, love; that old mare there's waiting to tell me off; just ask Willy."

"Sweetbread?" said Willy, as though he had never heard of it, "calves' sweetbread?" in disbelief. "Now you know, dear, they all goes to France."

"Willy!" warningly from the cash desk.

"Willy!" said Arlette, shocked.

"Yes, of course, schat, you know I'm only joking. It just happens I do have one; come on in the coldroom."

"No," said Arlette—now that she was a widow, Trix wouldn't care for that! "Too much draft, and I trust you."

"Well, well," said Willy, delighted at the thought of her suspecting him of wishing to kiss her in the coldroom, "that's a change, ha-ha."

"Oh lovely, dear," said Bates happily. "I do love them, and he always pretends they go to France. You know—he keeps them for black-market customers; it took you to get one. Delicious—I'll enjoy that. You go on upstairs and have a party, my pet. I'm sure you'll enjoy yourself." And so she did.

Arlette had come to Amsterdam without any clear ideas at all. While in the train on the way up, she had thought in a vague and probably dotty way about a number of people she knew in Amsterdam. People

154

who would be pleased to have her to stay, who would give her excellent advice and sympathetic help—who would use their influence . . . that was it, really, that was why she had turned them all down one after another: they were all of them vaguely "important people," with high intelligence, trained minds, and logical reasoning powers, and frequently with various useful official connections—hell, that was just what was wrong with them. She didn't want anything to do with the police, and supposed that was fair enough, but plenty of these people did not have anything to do with the police: what was wrong with *them*, then? She didn't know; just somehow that they would interfere with her muddled mind, make her do things that were probably very sensible but she didn't want to do them. They would see her problem backward—worse still, they would take it away from her and rearrange it till it was tidy: that was no good to her. . . .

So what had she got? Old Mother Counterpoint. Kind, certainly, and in her limited way shrewd enough. But not what you'd call very much of an ally, hmm, for breaking up a logjam that had left the policemen saying, "Well, now, Mevrouw, we don't think there is much more that can usefully be done just at present; we think perhaps time will tell, and patience will be rewarded."

And who else did she know? Sympathetic neighbors in the quarter who had known Piet and liked him—Trix and Willy, for instance. She tried to explain something of this to Dan and Hilary de Vries.

She had taken an instant liking to them, and hoped they liked her. They understood everything, and asked no unnecessary questions. They were perfectly relaxed; they had all the time in the world, did not jump about worrying because the ashtrays weren't emptied. The

155

cooking was all done, except for the rice, which was going to get shoved on when everyone felt hungry and not before. In the meantime, there were drinks, conversation, leisure: what more did anybody want? So they talked about cooking—like all artists, Dan was interested in cooking, and held stern ideas about it. About the smell of sculptors' clay. About the way Arlette had had the flat arranged when it was hers; Hilary had never been able to find a good place to keep the sewing machine, either—one kept tripping over it, tiresome thing. Nobody pushed her; nobody said, "Now you have to get yourself sorted out—you've got to get *organized*." Dan sat and wrinkled his odd brown bald forehead, cocked the head, picked at peanuts, switched the bright small bird's eyes up and down behind the steel rims. Hilary, a quiet-moving rather massive young woman, with a square plain face, an untidy boy's hair, and no dress sense, smoked and said almost nothing. She might have been one of those placid persons whose main purpose seems to be to provide a center to other people who don't have one if it had not been for the evident intelligence which shone out all round, and the careful courtesy with which she would always listen to other people's arguments before opening her own mouth. Arlette found herself slowly loosening and untying, able to say something about the character of her husband, the way he had thought about things, the way he went about a problem.

"He didn't believe in regretting things," she said, "but I wonder whether he felt rather sad. At dying, I mean. He used to say he'd wasted incredible amounts of time and energy on things he'd never properly understood, and toward the end he remarked quite often that he thought he was beginning to understand but didn't feel at all sure of it."

Dan nodded. "All artists are like that if they're any good. Sit there wondering about the form of something and being hopeful that next time they really will get it right at last—ask what and they don't know. Not a thing one *knows*. In the wrong job, your man."

"I wouldn't know that I'd agree," said Hilary. "Why should there be a rule saying the police is a reserved occupation for people who'd never be any use at anything else? Who was it anyway that said the ruler of the ideal state would be an artist?"

"Wouldn't a good artist have too much humility?" said Arlette. "Didn't Renoir die muttering something about he was beginning to get the hang of it?"

"Auto-satisfaction enemy of art," said Dan. "First truism and soonest forgotten. Arlette's quite right: police investigation is a work of art. Attempt to impose form upon immaterial. Chap died in the middle of it, like as not. Why was he shot, after all? Came too close perhaps to understanding something, we might be allowed to guess. Right. Official police mechanisms turning on computers, whirring away there, vastly astonished when no work of art disgorged at the end, only vast quantity of irrelevant rubbish. You want to find out what happened," to Arlette, "but you don't really have any interest in who did it."

"Not really—only like—oh, you know, what's the end of Edwin Drood."

"Exactly. You're not feeling revengeful, are you? Want to see the fellow hanged or something?"

"I don't mind thinking about it—which isn't to say I could do it or allow of its being done."

"Ha," said Hilary.

"I think," said Dan, "you feel you have to make the effort to understand because you think that hell, that's the least you can do."

157

"I can't feel able to go tracking anybody down, being an instrument of punishment or redress or something."

"I think perhaps you damn well should," said Hilary.

"Oh nonsense," said Dan. "What is she, the *Four Just Men?*—easy for you, you're not involved."

"Well," asked Hilary, "why shouldn't I be involved? If Arlette allowed me to or asked me to, I'd try my best to pin the bastard down, not hang about reveling in the tenderness of my conscience."

"Perhaps she will allow you to," crossly, "and then you can put it to the proof."

"I don't know what I want," said Arlette dolorously, "but perhaps I'll know better after I've made a start."

"Very well," almost both together, "then let's make a start."

"I've nothing to go on at all, except some old notebooks."

"Right," firmly, "then go and get them. No, on second thought, let's eat first. I'll go and do the rice."

"The women," said Hilary, "will hang about being decorative while the Deity does the rice and gets beer. Do you want to pee or anything?"

"I'm like the royal family," said Arlette. "I never miss an opportunity."

"Do one for me while you're at it. I'll tidy a bit. Men do the cooking but the sink's left crammed with dirty dishes."

Arlette was not a Janeite, and when describing Old Mother Counterpoint, it was accidentally that she let slip the fact, which I had never known, that Piet used to call her "Bates." Rather typical, though I do not think he can have been a true Janeite, either, but it helped me to get behind Arlette's descriptions. Similarly, it was Bates's phrase about Mr. Gandhi which allowed me to discover something about Danny de Vries. Arlette described him eating curry, lavishly, in corduroy trousers

158

—not in the least like Mr. Gandhi, and not very like
Mr. Kipling either!—and I was puzzled until I learned
that both he and Hilary had lived in England, and that
Hilary was in fact half English, which perhaps explains
her name. It became at once much easier to see them,
as well as to understand what happened. For Arlette,
you must understand, was tiresomely vague about how
things came to happen. Who was it, for instance, that
began making jokes about the *Four Just Men?* I had
thought perhaps it was Piet, presumably an Edgar Wal-
lace fan as well as a Janeite, but, no, it was of course
Danny de Vries, and it was, I am inclined to think,
Hilary who turned it from being a joke into a reality.
The "moral question" was probably introduced by
Arlette herself, who, being French, loves discussions
about ethics, but it was Hilary, with her share of "Brit-
ish bloody-mindedness," who began the weird idea,
amusing me later with its undeniably comic overtones
of "the committee." One recalls the man (he must
surely, too, have had English blood?) who waged, and
won, single-handed warfare against General Motors
and whose "committee" became known as Nader's
Raiders. Very like the *Four Just Men!* Only the English,
one feels certain, have the stubborn awkwardness, and
the courage, as well as the lunatic poetic vision, to do
such things. Though perhaps it took Arlette to include
Bates, as well as Willy the butcher, in her schemes.
Setting out like that to execute private justice—yes, it
must have been Hilary who was at the bottom of that.
Very English with her badly bobbed hair and dressed in
sackcloth, very English in her artistic "hammering at
things"—barbaric kinds of silver and copper jewelry no
doubt—and most English of all in her tenacious pursuit
of the object.

The curry was very good, Arlette told me, but the
coffee bloody awful. Perhaps that is English, too.

"We must find out," said Danny firmly. "You're obviously the only person who can interpret these notebooks, as well as read your husband's writing, and translate this sort of shorthand, but perhaps an objective mind—after all, we never knew him and that's sometimes an advantage—can place a construction on the interpretations that you could not arrive at in solitude. Like a crossword puzzle—you know, you sit gazing at something like 'Warmed-up rum issue in an African kraal' utterly flummoxed, and Hilary, for instance, just glances over your shoulder and says straight out, 'Hottentot.'" Arlette looked blank, as well she might.

"There may be disconnected remarks in these notes," explained Dan patiently, "which, if juxtaposed, make up a clue to something. You said yourself that there were references to the watch which you felt sure meant something."

"Yes," said Arlette. "I'm convinced that's at the bottom of it somehow. He broke his watch and there's a note on it. It was ridiculous, because he said it was an extraordinary accident which could only happen to him. He was winding it or something and dropped it because his fingers were cold. It all hung together somehow, he said; he'd lost his gloves or left them somewhere. . . ."

"Left them *where*? Winding it or *what*? Hung together *how*?" Dan rapped it out in a really impatient, inquisitorial voice, and she realized she was blithering.

"I'm sorry; I'll try and be as precise as I can. Left them on the train. Waiting for a tram, he dropped the watch; it got wedged somehow in the tramline, got run over before he could stop to pick it up, and he wrote in his book, 'Odd how a stupid catastrophe can give one a notion,' and I wondered what notion, because he came home with a new watch and was mysterious about it.

160

Very pretty watch it was, sort of antique. I gave it to Ruth, our daughter, as a souvenir."

"Where did that happen? By the station?"

"Where he bought it? I don't know. He dropped it by the Koningsplein, that's all I know."

"We write it all down," said Dan, fetching a sketching block and a felt pen, "and we look later for things which might fit together."

"I looked for any note to do with a watch. I found an odd thing about some private experiment or theory of his, to do with his criminology work, which said, 'Tale about stolen watch supposed planted. Why come to me?' But I don't know what it means."

"Well, that at least is clear as daylight," said Danny without hesitation. "Somebody came to him—right?—with a tale about a stolen watch, which might not have been stolen—or why would he write supposed?—but might have been planted. He was interested because something was funny and didn't hang together. Else why write, 'Why come to me?' And indeed why write a note at all about something so trivial?"

"Yes, that struck me. It seemed so trivial, and that's why I thought the watch must have some significance. But the two are unconnected. I mean the stolen watch and the broken watch."

"We don't know. Anything else about watches?"

"Yes, but not much help. It is isolated, in another book, and says just 'Richard, A'dam, Lindengracht, watch plant fiddle, what's in it?' "

"Well, that's something, but why another book?"

"Oh, that doesn't mean anything, or not necessarily, because he had several of these notebooks; they're just exercise books, really, and often he had the wrong one or just a different one and wrote things down just the same."

"Mm—nothing else about watches? Well, what

about Richard, since we know there's a Richard linked with the watch. Or about the Lindengracht?"

"No Lindengracht. One Richard, since I followed that up, of course. 'Richard Oddinga, age twenty-two, student,' as though he'd checked an identity card, and after that, 'Pa dead in Friesland; suddenly offered job thought fishy,' which is part of the same note."

"Well, one looks in the Lindengracht and tries to find Richard—easy with a description that detailed. Ask Richard whether he knows anything about it and Bob's your uncle."

"Doesn't it strike you that if it were that easy she'd have done it?" put in Hilary tartly. "Nor does it strike you that somebody shot her husband, and possibly because of something concerning a watch. So you'll go asking, too. Seems to me," sarcastically, "a thought risky."

"There's that," admitted Dan, taken aback at the possibility of Lord Peter Wimsey getting shot at. "Nothing else that could be Richard—I mean students, or Friesland, or aged twenty-two, or—?"

"The only thing I could possibly find is a longish note about pictures, which goes on about a fiddle, and an illegal deal, and somebody called B., and another called Louis, and an addition: 'What can he need the boy for?' But that's awfully tenuous."

"It is," wrinkling and looking more like Grandhi than usual. "Nothing else on pictures or B. or Louis to give a link?"

"No. Or at least—pictures of pictures."

"Huh?"

"Drawings. Doodles. Several pictures all over a page, in baroque frames, just sketched in, but it means nothing to me."

"No," agreed Dan unwillingly, "one might say he'd been looking at pictures, but going on like that we'd

162

end up finding he'd been assassinated by a painter for saying his pictures were no good, and I'd find myself pleading extenuation. No, I do agree, that doesn't get us very far."

"One has to admit, too, that the police have had these notebooks and must as well have checked up anything that would look like a lead or even a link."

"Well, we just have to use more imagination than they did, that's all."

"About the watch," said Hilary suddenly, "you said 'a pretty one, sort of antique,' but was it an antique?"

"No, it was new; that's to say, he said it was second-hand and that it had been a bargain. It was made in imitation of an antique model, more—it must have been expensive. I mean originally."

"It wasn't bought in an antique shop? I was thinking about pictures."

"I think he'd have said. He told me he'd picked it up by accident—by coincidence, I mean—from a man whom he'd been talking to."

"Anyway, it wasn't antique," said Dan with an air of logic, "so if he didn't get it," sarcastically, "from an antique shop, it'd be slightly more likely he got it from a jeweler."

"Or, if it was secondhand, from a watch repairer, if we're going to be so devastatingly logical," said Hilary, refusing to be snubbed.

"That's a thing, though—any note about either of those, or a watchmaker or anything?"

"No, I looked."

"So all we've got is that Richard was involved in a supposed watch fiddle, age twenty-two, student, Pa dead, suddenly offered job—"

"A job," rapped out Hilary suddenly, "in a jeweler's."

"She's right, you know," said Dan in the pause that

followed this. "I mean where else, a stolen watch or possibly planted—it would be a jeweler's."

"So we look for a jeweler's in the Lindengracht. And if there isn't any we're back to square one."

"I'll go over the notebooks again. But I don't think there can be anything else. I've marked all the bits with pieces of paper."

"Have a look," said Dan, reading the scribble laboriously. "It goes, 'This boy Odd, odd-ball odd boy'; yes, a play on words just, but he does say 'this boy,' so the other boy could be the same boy."

"There isn't any jeweler's in the Lindengracht," Trixie was saying in a conclusive tone of voice, which might not have meant much by itself, because people very often do speak conclusively, the most so when they have no earthly idea what they are talking about. But as she was explaining—at a good deal of length—she had been brought up "around the corner" and still had a married sister in the quarter whom she visited once a week.

Arlette had come for the promised coffee-drinking, a Dutch rite which takes place at any hour of the day guests happen to drop in and is "de rigueur." Arlette might not much enjoy sweet, pale, milky coffee at half past seven in the evening, but she knew what was expected of her, and was lavish in admiration of all the domestic arrangements. In fact, she was not at all ill at ease or unhappy. Once away from the cash desk and the abattoir, they became simple, truthful, thoughtful, and affectionate. When younger, Arlette would have thought that their taste in interior decoration, which was atrocious, made such folk permanently uneatable and unspeakable, but with experience she had learned better manners. Simply bursting with innocent vanity,

164

Trix had started with the "salon," dwelt none too briefly on objects of art brought back from holidays in Majorca, Bavaria, and an area apparently bounded by St. Ives, Stratford-on-Avon, and Buckingham Palace, and gone on to an exhaustive coverage of every room in the house, with special emphasis on every detail of the ruby-tiled bathroom and the turquoise-tiled kitchen. During this tour, which ended with the fur coat in the bedroom cupboard, Willy sat upon cushions in the living room with a tolerantly uxorious expression and a bottle of beer. I suppose nothing could be more vulgar, ostentatious, and ridiculous, thought Arlette; I wonder why I'm not nauseated. She had refused the offer of more coffee, and was being given a choice between crème de cacao, crème de banane, and a mauve concoction known to Holland as Parfait Amour.

"You're trying to work it all out, aren't you?" asked Willy with a shrewd directness which would have upset her ordinarily; she detested nothing more than the Dutch taste for personal questions.

"If I can."

"Track it down, like. Not wanting anything more to do with the police neither, are you?"

"How do you know?"

"I'd be the same. I reckon it could be done, too." He stopped talking abruptly, as though afraid he'd said too much, and opened another beer.

"We were talking about it," admitted Trix. "Working it out, like. There must be something to find out. People don't just come up and shoot you with no explanation. Not like that. If they were chased, or sort of pushed into a corner, then maybe. But not like that. Oh, I know the paper said it could happen."

"Paper'll say anything," muttered Willy. "Sneaking up in a car like that? Never on your nelly. Somebody

165

who knew him and had a grievance—and that means he's there somewhere and could be found."

"But the police have tried everything."

"Hmm," said Willy darkly, withholding the average Amsterdamer's opinion of the police, the built-in readiness to accept all sorts of nonsense which Van der Valk had never found a really good answer for.

"Remember that book there was after the war? *The Commissaire Tells*—fella's life story?" Arlette did; also Van der Valk's opinion of it. "Know what we said? We said, 'Yeh, and the Commissaire could tell a lot more, too.'" An explosive grunt, partly beer and partly indignation. "What I was thinking was . . ." He trailed away into silence.

"Well, stop turning around the pot, then," said Trixie coarsely. "Y'made up y'mind t'say it, say it."

"We'd like to help you," said Willy, covering his confusion in beer.

Arlette was surprised and touched, but nowhere near as much as before she had gone to eat curry with Dan and Hilary. People did want to help, and they weren't bad at it, either. And plenty of people were less shrewd and less sensible than these, as well as less simple.

"So you can," she said.

"You bet," said Trixie with emphasis, "but you know, duck, we didn't want you to think we were sticking our nose in."

"Anything we can do, you just say. I mean, I'm just a butcher, but there's not many knows the quarter better than Treas and me."

"Who says it was anything to do with this quarter?" asked Trix.

"Nobody knows," said Arlette, "but the funny thing is, some other friends said the same. We're trying to work it out."

"We ought to put our heads together," said Willy. "Many hands make the work light."

"One can't have too many friends," said Trix sententiously, "but hereabout is where you'll find 'em. Not in The Hague," with deep distrust.

"You don't really think it was anything in The Hague, do you?" asked Willy. "Here was where we've always thought it must belong." An Amsterdamer's chauvinism, thought Arlette, tickled. In those other, provincial towns, they're even too stupid to commit crimes.

"I must say I think myself it was something here. But it's terribly vague, and we've got nothing to go on, really, just a few vague shadows. Like an idea that it's something to do with a jeweler's, which we think must be in the Lindengracht."

"Isn't any jeweler's in the Lindengracht," said Trix.

"Well," said Bates, "I call that very sensible as well as very decent of them, and I'm very pleased myself to be given a better opinion of these people; one just can't tell, dear, the piggishness just goes with the meat."

"But isn't it awfully silly and childish?" said Arlette uncertainly. "I mean just like children. *Emil and the Detectives?*" And at the same second she could hear her husband's voice.

"Emil was probably the best detective ever," Van der valk had said more than once. "Children are, you know. They're marvelously observant, and nobody notices them. They're rapid, flexible, and marvelously inventive. They'd make perfect criminals if it wasn't for the chatter."

Well, here we are, Arlette told herself, but where's Emil?

"That's great rubbish, dear, if you won't mind my

167

saying so. It's a pity to have a lot of people trying to do something, because they do talk so, but what strikes me, dear, is that it could be very handy. People will talk to me, for instance, quite without suspicion where they'd never utter a word to you—no fault of yours, just that they'd be wondering what you were getting at."

"You mean you want to help, too?" asked Arlette stupidly.

"I'm going to be Emily," said Bates, giggling. "But to be serious, my pet, just ask these people in for a drink, and then we'll see what forming a gang can do to help."

"Not the *Four Just Men*," remarked Danny de Vries, "but *Swallows and Amazons*."

"Please shut up," said his wife crushingly. "I don't think we ought to chat or make jokes. This is a very serious thing, and we shouldn't talk without something essential to say."

"Sorry," said Danny humbly. "I was only being frivolous from a sense of embarrassment."

"No use being embarrassed," said Bates briskly. She had "taken the chair" because they were in her work-room. It was the revolving stool, really, on which she sat next to débutant piano players. Everybody was looking sheepish, feeling like a child that has neglected its practicing this week. Sensing this, Arlette had produced whisky. "There's nothing even to be formal about," Bates went on. "We were all the Commissaire's friends and we're all Arlette's friends, and that goes for you two"—looking at Danny and Hilary—"even if you never knew him, and we are simply resolved to find out who killed him and why." She said it in a firm matter-of-fact tone, brooking no contradiction and admitting no

168

drama. She might have been saying, "Now, then, key of
E flat, keep a nice steady tempo, and don't emotion-
alize."

"It's a committee," said Willy, who sat on several,
looking round severely, but there was no sniggering.
And Willy it was who produced the first constructive
idea. "This watch, now, Mrs.—er, Arlette, that he
brought back and that was secondhand; I mean we
don't know if he bought it in a jeweler's or what, but I
mean, we can find out surely if he gave a check.
Course, if it was cash . . ."

"No, he paid a check. I've seen the duplicate, but it
just said 'watch.' "

"Not the payee?"

"I know the police looked at all his checks to find if
there was anything unusual—but of course this wasn't.
I mean a payment for a watch, and so what? I never
thought of it before."

"If it was crossed, we could trace it back." It had
been so obvious, thought Arlette, no wonder we never
thought of it. At the same time . . .

"When it's that easy," said Dan soberly, "it might
give us the famous Richard, but it's not likely to give us
a murderer."

"Doesn't matter," said Bates, brisk. "We've got to go
by elimination, anyway, and that's the only way to narrow it down. And I may as well say, too, that we'll have
to face some discouragements and mistakes; that's
inevitable surely. I've made a note. Arlette, my pet, if
you ring up the bank manager he'll tell you if you
haven't already had a statement."

"Of course I had one, but didn't look at it." Trixie
looked a bit shocked at that but kept quiet.

"Well, a phone call will fix that. Now what else is
there?"

169

"The thing about the pictures, and the name Louis, and B. and 'the boy,' who might be Richard and might not." Dan, who had been studying the notebooks all day, had all this at his finger ends.

"Now that really is vague."

"Doesn't matter. We've agreed that anything at all might give an opening. It might be nothing, but it must have been something on his mind, because there are drawings of pictures, like one does of a subject that is occupying one's thoughts."

"When it's something to do with pictures," said Arlette, "I could always try a man we used to know, a picture dealer, who gave him advice sometimes about a question of faking, but that's quite forlorn of course. No earthly reason to believe . . ."

"Nothing's a forlorn hope," said Hilary sternly.

"And there's always an earthly reason to believe," said Bates, who was a firm churchgoer despite schisms, heresies, errors, delusions, and much of which one disapproved most emphatically.

"What else?"

"Well, there's the poetry one. It's a bit offbeat—the thing about the stripped tree and the false apples."

"No use," said Arlette. "I know what it's about, or vaguely—something about politics in Scotland a couple of centuries ago." This cast a chill.

"No matter," said Dan, recovering. "It must have another reference, to something or someone else. Or why would he have written it down in a working notebook? All these things mean something," stubbornly. There was a silence. Everybody was feeling that the remark had been made already, and hadn't been especially helpful then.

"We're agreed to disregard just names and telephone numbers. We'd never get far with them."

170

"The police will have checked them, anyway. That's the kind of thing they do well—much better than we could."

"Sorry, but just in the notebooks, there's not very much else." Light was shed by Trix. She had kept quiet, feeling perhaps a scrap out of her depth. But the word "books" stirred something. She fidgeted, looked around, and spoke suddenly.

"Er—I know it must sound silly—but are we sure we do have all the notebooks?" Everyone looked at her.

"I only meant, sometimes like, one keeps other ones, private like."

Nobody laughed, though a slow grin went across Dan de Vries's face as he thought that this would be the nearest that Trixie, a most able bookkeeper, would ever get to admitting that tax evasion existed.

"Well, upon my word. Are we sure, Arlette?"

"I don't know at all," said Arlette slowly. "I'd never thought about it. I've no real means of knowing. Nobody ever counted them. It wouldn't have occurred to me that they might not all be there—the police sent me back a packet, with a note about this was personal stuff they were returning to me. I can hardly believe they'd keep anything back—I mean they'd have sent all or nothing."

Deep bass grunt from Willy, indicating skepticism.

"No, honestly I can't believe that," said Arlette seriously. "There was a service memo inside, which they'd overlooked, saying they'd been through all this and nothing in it was of any help."

"A remark which we, by definition, do not accept." Dan, tartly.

"They did, though, say that anything relevant to the work he was doing had been passed on to some col-

171

league. That might mean there were more books. I could find out from his secretary, I suppose. I'll go to The Hague. And I'll talk to the bank. And, just on the off chance, I'll try the picture man."

"Meeting adjourned for twenty-four hours," said Dan, businesslike.

"Come to my place," said Trix. Nobody queried this—that it was "her turn to make the coffee." Not even Arlette noticed. A single-minded person, the only thing that mattered to her was that she was no longer alone. She had found solidarity, friends, people both competent and intelligent, who out of the sheer kindness of their hearts were sorting out her confusions and setting forth to right an injustice. Not even Dan and Hilary de Vries thought anything in the situation at all unusual, and would have been taken aback, even vastly indignant, at anyone finding it funny.

Van der Valk would have found it funny, though. And "very Dutch"; even when being very Dutch himself, he never lost a sense of detachment, and a highly developed sense of the ridiculous. "It takes the Dutch to do a thing like that," he would have said. "There's nothing they like better than forming committees, preferably of protest. A wonder that while they were at it they didn't elect a secretary to keep minutes."

Arlette's flying in the face of her prejudices—bitterly maintained and dearly cherished for twenty years—Van der Valk would have found uproarious. Just as well, really, that he wasn't there! He would have made coarse jokes about this new passion for togetherness, and the utterly astounding consent of people like the butcher to take a hand in her personal life, and then she would have flown into a tremendous fury. . . . Had it been nothing more than the pilgrimage made to The

172

Hague next day, he would have been shaking his head with a skeptical grin.

"I hope I'm not disturbing you—may I come in?"

"Oh!" Miss Wattermann leapt to her feet in an agony of nervous embarrassment. "Mrs. van der Valk!" A folder of papers by her typewriter fell to the floor. "I am so . . . I don't know what . . . I mean I never did get an opportunity to tell you how very . . ." The telephone rang, flustering her further. "Oh dear, please excuse me . . . just a sec . . . Who is that? Ring me back, I'm extremely busy," in a steely rap. Well, maybe I do intimidate her, at that, thought Arlette cheerfully, and a good job, too. She was aware of looking good— well, handsome—or, uh, distinguished: she had taken pains with her appearance, and knew the black suit showed her to advantage.

"How nice of you to come and see us," said Watter-mann shyly.

"Not very disinterested, I'm afraid."

"Oh, if there's anything at all I can possibly do . . ."

"It's that I'm told there were some papers my hus-band had been working on which got passed on to some colleague."

"You mean in one of my files? I typed everything of his, so we'd find it here."

"More in the nature of just rough notes was what I was thinking of."

"You mean the manuscript notes—the famous school exercise books? But the police took them all— they thought, I mean they were hoping—" She had got embarrassed again.

"I know; they sent them on to me. But they did say there was some stuff with work materials which . . ."

"Oh, I know—it's perfectly true—oh, what a fortu-nate coincidence . . ." The door had opened with a

173

breeze and a man come in with it, hands full of papers, pipe, and a handkerchief, on which he was blowing his nose. He stopped dead when he caught sight of Arlette, and said, "I beg your pardon," politely, bright eyes behind the hanky approving of her figure. "This is the man you want," said Wattermann and, aware of a certain coyness in her voice, added hurriedly, "Oh, Professor de Hartog, this is Mrs. van der Valk."

The man got rid of everything neatly: the hanky flashed into one pocket, the pipe still smoking into another, the papers changed hands and were thrust abruptly at the secretary.

He bowed formally. "Extremely happy to meet you and only saddened by the circumstances."

"You are very kind," said Arlette, pulling her glove off and giving her hand.

"But what's the fortunate coincidence, Miss Wattermann—is it that I can be of some service?"

"If you can find ten minutes?" Arlette asked.

"Ten minutes, stuff—as long as you please. Forgive me one second. Nell, I've had this memo for some jack-in-office hiding behind a reference number—will you kindly draft one in return saying that if they have matters for my attention that's one thing, but if they embody suggestions in these impertinent terms I refuse to discuss or even to read their remarks. A bit sharpish, backhand cross-court. Always make a return of service a passing shot. Sorry, Mevrouw, civil servants; we mustn't let them trample on us—such insolence. Do please come into my office—I won't take any calls, Nell. . . . Do please sit down, Mevrouw," with a look of gallantry, "and tell me how I may serve you."

Arlette was immensely encouraged. Everybody—everybody—is so nice! And how especially nice to be looked at with wicked sexy eyes by a Herr Professor

174

Doktor. How nice to be enjoyed; it is dreadfully good for the morale. She crossed her knees, which the man studied with pleasurable attention.

He was large but not fat, a high forehead without being bald, tanned without being brown. The studious look of the horn-rimmed glasses and the pipe was not pedantic, but sat agreeably with an unlined and youthful look. He was her own age, a plainly mature and responsible person of intellectual distinction and academic eminence, but had kept a trace of undergraduate jauntiness and enthusiasm which was appealing.

"Oh, I forgot," picking up his house telephone. "Nell, cups of coffee, please." He started hunting in a drawer for cigarettes.

She began, "There were some notebooks—no, thanks, I've my own; do smoke your pipe—which had business stuff, and that's no concern of mine, but I wanted to ask one thing, and that's if there were any irrelevant notes or scribbles in any of them."

"Yes, there were," said de Hartog with a crisp rapidity and precision that filled her with hope. "In all of them."

"Would it be unreasonable of me to ask to have them back when you're finished with them?"

"You shall have them now," getting up and striding to a file cabinet. "I am finished, and I have prepared a précis of some basic work that will be very valuable to me—to us. I'd like to say this, Mevrouw—you'll virtually never get a scientist to admit that another scientist could conceivably be both brilliant and sound. While he was alive, my colleagues would have qualified both. They would have said he was occasionally brilliant and in general unsound. I'm modifying that, and saying he was frequently brilliant and might well be sounder than most, only for the fact that nobody knows either way. I liked your husband greatly and miss him profoundly. Please don't cry. It is a compliment to me to come near making you cry with a sincerely meant remark, but it causes me much pain."

"I'm not going to cry."

"The notebooks are tangled but to anyone of imagination perfectly lucid—and quite consequential. He followed no special code—I mean that there are heaps of interpolations and irrelevancies in different-colored inks, or upside down or whatnot, but he did not lose his thread, and when I compared the finished work he left me with these roughs, I was struck— Hell's bells, I am making you cry. Will you have dinner with me tonight?"

Arlette stopped crying at once and took a cigarette out of her bag. De Hartog leapt up, struck a match dramatically, and held it.

"I refuse to cry. No, I've got to go to Amsterdam. But when this is finished—then, yes, with pleasure."

He sat down, struck another match, and relit his pipe with nervous, excited gestures.

"You're detecting," he said suddenly.

"Yes. With what success I cannot tell."

"The police investigation fell flat. Yes, of course. Well, I'm not going to inquire. If I can at any time be of assistance to you—will you call me? I'm not becoming the protective male; it strikes me you don't need one. But if you want a legal opinion—or, ach, I hesitate to say advice—or a push in let's call it the burden of establishing proof—or just a hand or a leg—will you say so, and I will be happy? . . . Ah, that makes me proud. Here are the books, with my faith, hope, and, may I say, affectionate confidence."

"I receive and feel all three," said Arlette, and meant it.

* * *

176

The bank manager listened with the stony immobility which is neither polite nor impolite, took off his glasses, lifted his telephone, mumbled something that was to her unintelligible, said "That presents no particular problem," asked politely whether the arrangements for transferring funds to France gave her any cause for concern, said "Come in" to a knock, received a dossier from a pale and effaced young man who looked at her with curiosity, put his glasses back on again, said "Ah" twice, took out a silver pencil to help him, cleared his throat, and said "A certain Mr. Bosboom. Cleared through the Plantage Middenlaan branch of the Netherlands Credit Bank to the credit of a Mr. Bosboom. No trouble at all, Mevrouw, only too pleased to be of service."

"Mr. van Deijssel? Charles? Arlette van der Valk. Yes, I'm in Amsterdam. No, I'm at the station; I've just got in from The Hague. No, it's kind, but I can get a taxi. No, I'd rather speak to you at home if that's the same to you. May I come over? Yes, of course I would."

Charles van Deijssel had neither gallery nor shop but, like most art middlemen, managed very well in his own flat. When Arlette arrived, he was standing on a chair, getting a good light on a picture he was photographing.

"I think I'll have to look at that with a bit of infrared. There is a most suspicious quantity of overpainting. My dear Arlette, just looking at you gives me an appetite for dinner, which will, alas, be a disappointment. My dear girl—a real Chanel. Don't talk nonsense, I can tell by the cutting. I hope and trust that your knickers are black crêpe de Chine."

"White cotton with Swiss embroidery."

"Detestable. Anisette with lots of ice cubes?"

"Oh, yes. Lovely, Charles, delicious. Tell me, did you see Piet in the six weeks or so before?"

"I wasn't able to say anything or do anything. Yes, I know I'm a selfish, superficial, egotistical little nasty, but I was utterly paralyzed. I think though, you won't hold it agin me. You should have been cross, you know, if I had appeared with a long face and a bunch of gladioli—oh, how I hate them, so fleshy. So smelling of anesthetics and starched white coats and clinics in Neuilly. Bitte-bitte, darling, you're not cross."

"No, but I asked you a question."

"Why, I did. Yes, so I did. He asked me out for a drink. Brain-picking, as usual, the old bastard—sorry, darling, but to me, honest, he's not dead at all. I keep thinking he'll roll in any moment with one of those Picassos they paint down there in Ibiza and try and flog it me. Oh well, now you mention it, I'd quite forgotten but he had something to ask me."

"Can you remember what it was about?"

"Of course. Ordinarily not in all likelihood, but murders do fix things in one's mind—hmm, Dr. Johnson, wasn't it? However, it wasn't anything at all thrilling; he only wanted to know whether I knew Louis Prinz."

"Name means something, but I don't know what."

"Ach, it's that jewelry shop on the Spui. Lot of antique bric-à-brac which looks good but isn't, if you take me—you'd never bother looking at it seriously." The name, the address—Arlette scarcely noticed. The word "jeweler" was ringing loud bells, though she hardly knew why. Some theory of Danny de Vries, but what . . . Her mind was in too much confusion to recall.

"But what was it about?" Arlette asked.

"I shouldn't be saying it ordinarily, but you I can

178

trust. Libelous, you see. He was asking me whether old Louis was fiddling on pictures, and I said, oh, yes, be sure of that, but no proof, of course, so I better warn you: don't repeat that and if you did I'd have to repudiate, swear I'd never said anything of the sort; no such thing, melord; the police is putting the words what I never said in me mouth."

"Pictures—phony pictures?"

"Not at all, ducks. Louis is high class, he wouldn't touch a phony—no, just mucking about with invoices to avoid income tax and not get fucked about either by earnest people who think the national patrimony of art's getting dilapidated; and that's what I told Piet and he just grunted that way of his, so I couldn't for the life of me say was he excited or was he bored stiff. I remember thinking it offbeat, because he was one of these rarefied-atmosphere types, and what the hell interest could he possibly have had in somebody's piddling income tax; good grief, he'd have been taking an interest in mine at that rate. I'm glad I saw you, my love; I can tell you without blushing that I was most overthrown and hamstrung by that beastly happening—poor old Piet, always did have a taste for low life and people who shoot at one. You've gone back to France, of course: what are you doing here? Sentimental pilgrimage, or are you applying a little ginger to the leisurely bureaucracies?"

"That's about it," said Arlette vaguely. She wasn't going to tell him—not that he would have been interested, anyhow. Dear Charles, standing on his chair in his cocoa-colored linen trousers and an oatmeal cardigan, and a raspberry shirt—pretty, but not serious.

Danny de Vries she found plunged in contemplation in front of a picture, but looking too cross to be

179

Gandhi, and slumped anyway on his shoulders in a broken cane chair. He cheered up when she came in and stood gawking at the picture.

"It's just about good enough to throw darts at," he said. "Hilary's out shopping. Like some brandy?—you rescue me from deep despair. Don't stand about there looking irresolute; it's what I've been doing for an hour or more. Bring home any bacon?"

"I've been too flustered to sort anything out, but I do believe so." Arlette had felt ashamed at not thinking of anything during the "meeting," and had passed the day with the embarrassed sensation of being the captain of the team but playing badly, and getting on this account into a tangle of impotence. She launched upon a confused and boring tale, in the middle of which Hilary came back and made tea. "I don't know if it really is of any use," she finished lamely.

Hilary was looking at her with an affectionate but much-tried patience, like an elementary-school teacher with a charming, slightly retarded small child.

"But, darling—don't you see that it hangs together?"

"What?" glumly and obstinately incapable.

"Oh, sweetie!—the pictures, Louis, the boy, B. It's that antique shop on the Spui—Louis Prinz. This Mr. Bosboom must be B."

"Do you really think so?"

"Oh, lovey," exasperated, "don't be so *thick*."

Dan, who had been listening with half an ear while scrabbling in the notebooks Arlette had brought, gave a great bellow.

"Take away that filthy tea—I said I wanted brandy, didn't I? Here it is—it's all here—by god, that great cow Treas was quite right." He was brandishing "English Criminal Precedents" and had turned back into Mr. Kipling, all fierce eyes and mustache.

"Don't sputter," said Hilary, chill. "You're spitting all over us."

"Down here, black on white: 'Sole fact—the boy came to see me.' All there: the jeweler, the Spui, the old man—can that be Bosboom, or perhaps Louis?—reference to a retired manager. Pictures—they sell pictures there, and furniture, as well as jewelry and all that junk—you know, antique paperweights and silver sugar sprinklers. Listen—he says 'Observation Spui unlikely to tell anyone much'—that's as may be—and then, 'Larry Saint, some personal observation.' Now who is Larry Saint? Does that mean anything to you, Arlette?"

"Nothing whatever, I'm afraid."

"It does to me, though," said Danny.

"Oh crap," said Hilary. "Stop drinking that brandy, you're getting overexcited. You've never been near the place—I see you there, with half a crown in your pocket, whipping in because you saw a Japanese sword that pleased you."

"Woman," said Dan with horrid quiet, "I wish I had one; I'd disembowel you on the spot. I'm perhaps a bloody lousy artist, and I've spent all day painting that thing which if a dog saw it he'd piss up against it first moment. But I'm a painter and that means I see things."

"Seeing things, is it now?—oh, all right, tell us. What is it that it sees?" still with the retarded children, this time one having a temper tantrum.

"Neil's son of woeful Assynt." It was launched with a voice of Churchillian resonance, pregnant with doom, but it fell flat. The women looked at each other.

"Huh?"

"The stupidity of you females, good for nothing but making this unspeakable tea and showing a bit of bum from time to time—aren't I telling you I'm a painter?

181

This boy Piet van der Valk was in the wrong job, I've said it. It's like a crossword—if you understand his mentality, you can read the clues. Assynt—assonance —Saint."

"Oh my gawd," said Hilary rudely.

"Surely the boy . . ." began Arlette.

Dan got into a rage, looked about for something to break, found nothing, saw the cup of cold tea, and threw it violently at the bad picture.

"Ah," he said, in a voice of great auto-satisfaction, "that's what I needed."

The bright, sunny, warm afternoon in late April had been slowly turning black without any of them noticing. In the silence that had fallen came a huge slow rumble of thunder, and the same moment, like a good actor, a drenching downpour of rain came slap against the window. They looked at each other.

"There," said Dan magnificently, "is God telling me I'm right."


Trixie's coffee was absolutely horrible—she had the bad Dutch habit of making a piddle extremely strong and then filling up the cup with clawky hot milk. They were all drinking it politely.

"Something factual."

"Something to go on at last."

"But we don't know yet. No certainty."

"We don't *know*, but there's a strong probability."

"How so? I mean, why more probable than something else?"

"Because all the other probabilities have been exhausted."

"By the police, he means: they've been over everything."

"But they'd missed this. It's the only thing left,

really, I mean there's nothing else even terribly remote."

"Even hinted at."

"Anyway, there's all sorts of other indirect pointers. He was conducting a private experiment. He didn't make any solid notes, and he didn't ask the police for anything. It was something quite small and unimportant. He never took it very seriously."

"But I don't understand—in that case, how did he get killed?"

"Well, that's what we'd like to know, isn't it?"

"That's what we're intending to find out."

"But we can't be *sure,* can we? I mean, if only we could be *sure* . . ."

"If we were sure, we'd only have to go to the police. Wouldn't be anything for us to do at all."

"But if he got killed for something so small . . ."

"Must be a loony. There doesn't have to be any motive at all."

"Surely that's where the police went wrong—looking for a motive."

"One looks for *cui bono*—whom could it possibly have advantaged? Who could possibly have gained by such an act?"

"Whereas if it were a loony . . ."

"Don't you see—just because in some obscure loony way he felt menaced, or interfered with or something."

"But in that case he might feel threatened by us, too, no? We might get murdered, too."

"That's ridiculous—we can't sit here getting frightened about what might happen if something else utterly hypothetical were conceivably to happen."

"There's always an element of risk. Why else have police?"

"Yes, they're paid to stick their neck out."

"Not paid much, poor dears."

"So they stick their neck out half-heartedly and who can blame them? They don't have our motives."

"We mustn't have any motives. Or even any fixed ideas at all."

"Except not getting shot at."

"Oh well, if you're just going to be frivolous . . ."

They weren't getting anywhere, and were becoming cross with each other. It was Bates who put an end to this, in a tone so downright that the nonsense stopped abruptly.

"We feel sure that we're on the right track, so we have to pursue that. And even if there were some risk, what would that amount to? Whoever or whatever it is can't shoot all of us, even if it is a bad person, or somebody insane, or even both together. If we all have a go at him, he's bound to get rattled and that would make him give himself away sooner or later."

"That sounds reasonable enough, but how is one, as you describe it, to have a go at anyone, and why should he get rattled?"

"Suppose we were wrong?" said Bates soberly. "We can't exclude that, can we? Suppose a lot of people, all apparently unconnected, came to you and showed suspicion of your having committed a crime—I don't know what, being a burglar or something—why, if you were innocent you wouldn't take any notice, except that you'd get cross at being persecuted, but I mean, they're not *accusing* you, they're just showing suspicion. Whereas if you were guilty you'd be very frightened."

"I'd start feeling guilty even if I were innocent," said Dan.

"Now, Danny, stop being tiresome. The point is that if several people seemed to have knowledge of your having done something disreputable, you couldn't at-tack them or anything. You wouldn't dare, because you

184

couldn't be sure how many people were involved or had knowledge of your guilt. You would break down."

"A loony doesn't necessarily work like that. They react quite unpredictably."

"It's much too easy to call all criminals loony," said Bates firmly. "All criminals pretend they're loony once they're caught. It's the easiest way of evading responsibility. They say they can't remember or they must have had a blackout."

"But that's often true."

"It's true because they want it to be true. They don't remember because they don't want to remember. It's easy to obliterate something disgraceful or unpleasant from one's memory; otherwise we would all be tormented by remorse. They first blunt and then destroy their own moral sense."

"So what do we do?"

"We all go to this man on some pretext, which we will invent. We're inventive enough, I should think."

"Danny is."

"Is he, now?"

"Too much so sometimes."

"Now, now. Don't you see, on rather ridiculous pretexts. Ridiculous enough that the man would understand—if he's guilty, that is."

"We all go."

"Except Arlette."

"That's true. She might be recognized."

"Isn't that the idea?"

"No, no. That might be putting too much pressure on. If the horrible man saw her coming . . ."

"That's true. We can't risk her life."

"Why not?" said Arlette in a sharp, grating voice. "My husband risked his." There was a silence, as though she had said something shocking.

"She's right, you know," said Dan. "He may have

185

done just that—coming with a silly story to show suspicion because he had no proof. And provoked whoever into an act of violence."

"An act of fear," corrected Bates. "But it won't happen to us—safety in numbers."

"But we won't let Arlette run that risk."

"It seems to me," said Willy, "that we need some extra proof first, and what about this Bosboom? Since anyway it was he who sold the watch. He might well be the murderer."

"Having endorsed and cashed a check—don't be so damned ridiculous," said his wife. "It would lead straight to him. It led us straight to him."

"Not yet, it hasn't. It's a common name."

"The woods are full of them," said Danny. Arlette got a nervous giggle which she was unable to stop. "Bosboom" in Dutch means "forest tree."

"Arlette could check that."

"There's a risk."

"Stop telling me there's a risk," yapped Arlette furiously. "What about the risk for you?"

"There isn't any risk," said Dan. "It's true; if we go with silly stories—'I got recommended to you by my friend the Commissaire'—he'd not be able to sit thinking up ways of assassinating people; he'd quite literally be far too scared."

"Scared—quite literally—out of his wits," remarked Hilary.

"That's settled, then—we'll all go for him," said Willy in a vengeful voice. "I want to see the bastard sweat. Nonsense, Treas, there's no risk."

"Except perhaps for the last one who goes," said Trix unhappily. "Because by that time he'll be a very badly frightened man."

"The last to go will be me," said Bates.

186

All of them looked at the others. There was some embarrassed coughing, but nobody contested this honorable position. It was just as though she had said, "I will be the last to leave the sunken submarine." Who would have thought it, wondered Arlette, of Old Mother Counterpoint? The fact is that she has more character than the other four put together.

It was true that the Amsterdam wood was full of trees. The phone book was full of Bosbooms. Arlette went to the branch of the Nederlands Credit Bank in the Plantage Middenlaan and was received with chill formality.

"We regard the addresses of our customers as confidential information." Tell that to the marines, Van der Valk would have said coarsely. Arlette adopted a feminine, emotional approach.

"May I have a word with you in private?"

"I see little use in that, Mevrouw." He was the stiffest, most wooden, most proper kind of Dutchman.

"It costs you nothing to listen." I see her, her big Phoenician nose sticking out arrogantly, her splendidly straight body tense with the reined-in desire to slap this proper little man spinning and throw his polite little plaque saying "Chief Cashier" at a nearby clerk eying her with a nasty mixture of lechery and disapproval.

"If you insist, though I'm bound to say . . ."

"Just hear me out. I am the widow of Commissaire van der Valk, a policeman who was assassinated in the streets of The Hague while going for an evening stroll."

"Er—my respectful sympathies, Mevrouw."

"Your respectful sympathies are, I'm afraid, no good to me. I am asking you for nothing but the address of a man to whom my husband paid some money." It might have been the key word "money."

187

"Naturally, Mevrouw, you have our sympathetic consideration."

"I'm asking you nothing but an address."

"Our rules of confidentiality, Mevrouw . . ."

"I'm asking you, will you or won't you give me this piece of simple harmless information?"

Awful woman was showing signs of screaming. "Mevrouw, I beg you, there is no need of—"

"There is great need. If your wife had been killed by an armed robber, would *you* be satisfied with people's rules and regulations?"

"Mevrouw, really . . ."

"I'm not asking you for the front-door key."

"Hush, Mevrouw, please. In the circumstances, I will make an exception. But you do understand—"

"Man," wearily, "don't torment me further."

The roses were shooting with a force undaunted by any rules. A cramped situation, a polluted atmosphere, a heavy layer of dark gray cloud, a cold northwesterly wind coming down from Scapa Flow, where it was still winter at the very end of April—some of the roses were already showing buds. Mr. Bosboom had met her with an aggressive roughness that startled her. Why should he be hostile? He was just a man who had sold her husband a watch.

"I can see no way in which I can be of service to you."

"Will you at least listen? Politely or anyway patiently."

"I should hope so at least. I wouldn't wish you to think me lacking in common courtesy. But as regards your husband's most untimely and unhappy death—it is as though you appear to believe, if you will pardon me, that I had withheld information from the police."

"I have nothing whatever to do with the police. They

188

know nothing about this. I have nothing to say to them. This is purely personal. I have no reproach or even remark to make to you which you could possibly find offensive."

"I am bound to believe you, Mevrouw, and to listen, naturally, with proper courtesy, to anything you may wish to say. I cannot believe that I can help you."

"Will you at least ask me in off the doorstep?"

"I beg your pardon. . . . Won't you please sit down?"

"I am not trying to enlist your sympathy," she said slowly. "Nor seeking to commit you in anything. I've no reason whatever to believe there's anything you can tell me that you wouldn't have told the police—that is, assuming you had anything to tell them."

"Which I did not."

"Just so."

"So if I may ask what your purpose is in doing me the honor of a visit?"

"Don't be too formal," said Arlette sadly. "Try to believe me—I've no ax to grind." He bowed his head, and said nothing.

"You sold my husband a watch."

"I do not contest it. An innocent transaction, I should imagine."

"I've no reason to believe anything else."

His bow was sardonic.

"You see, he wrote something down in a notebook. Something about a boy who worked in a jeweler's, who was suspected or thought himself suspected of stealing. Very vague, and one would say quite unimportant."

"I have no doubt of that."

"But he thought it important enough—I don't know, it seemed worth asking, that's all—to come and see you."

"He asked me," said Bosboom carefully, "and my

189

memory serves me well upon the subject, whether there was any likelihood in a tale told him of a watch unaccounted for in a jeweler's inventory—a jeweler's where, as he had learned, I had worked for numerous years. I gave him my opinion, which was that I thought the story exceedingly unlikely, and that the young man in question, who remained unnamed, and whom I may say I do not know, was fabulating. That is all. I still see no relevance to any subsequent happening. I have no means of saying, of course, whether he gave my simple opinion on a matter of conjecture any credence."

"Mr. Bosboom—please, I'm not trying to make any more of this than you tell me there was."

"I am grateful to you."

"Do you know a man called Saint?"

Bosboom's large gardener's hand, which was rubbing his jaw, gave a nervous jerk. "Now why do you ask me that?"

"Just because in the note my husband wrote, which was in a pile of notes he wrote concerning his work, your name and this one are mentioned in the same context. These notes were part of a pile of manuscript—they just got stuck in a file. Nobody read them, you see, till after. The police thought them of no importance."

"In what context?" asked Bosboom slowly.

She wasn't being very good at this, she thought, and stopped to think. The long pause, and her concentration, seemed to have a reassuring effect upon Bosboom, who became less still and stony, and arranged his features into a less forbidding pattern.

"In the context of a rhetorical question," she said at last, "asking himself what conclusions to draw from a situation which wasn't clear to him, and which is that much more obscure to anyone trying to piece things together."

"As you are—that is the obvious inference."

"Yes."

"Because—this is your inference—this diary or memorandum, or whatever it is, contains the germ of explanations—why he was killed, to put it bluntly. And you are trying to make this outline, call it, of an idea into something evidential. Now be quite honest with yourself. You are most anxious, and I can understand that and sympathize, to find something with which to go to the police and say to them, 'Here is matter for inquiry, which you have hitherto neglected.' Now isn't that an accurate summing-up of your thoughts?"

"Except that I have no intention whatever of going to the police with any suggestion or complaint or argument at all, it is accurate as far as it goes."

He knitted his big bristly eyebrows together. "If you are not trying to stir up the police—I would understand it if you were—I don't grasp your purpose."

"I wish to find out. I feel strongly that there are things to find out, that it can be done, and that I have the right to do it. It is personal to me. Police and courts and judges don't enter into it at all."

He looked at her, studying her, taking his time about answering. "Forgive me, but have you really thought this out? I don't wish to appear insulting. You certainly aren't behaving—shall I say overexcitably. May I, in a friendly way, because I wish you nothing but good, beg you to ask youself what it is you hope to gain?"

"You believe that I have a suppressed hysteria, don't you?"

He puffed a bit, taken aback and unwilling to say either yes or no.

"I couldn't have answered you a day or so ago. All I could see then was that my husband had been assassinated. I was determined to use any means to identify the assassin. I've learned a good deal since. This for a

191

start, that my husband was a policeman, but he wasn't working on an investigation, so it can't have been anything criminal. He kept it quite private; that seems clear. He did not apply to any official instrument for help or cooperation; he did not use any official machinery. The notes we've found are fragmentary and confusing, but go to show that whatever this was he had made some kind of bargain with himself, that he hadn't grounds for an official inquiry. He was working something out—we don't know what—in his spare time. I intend to find out what and why. If it led to his death, then that might be a matter for legal justice, I don't know, but it isn't my affair. I don't believe in private police forces. Bringing people to judgment isn't my job—or my intention."

"Then what is your intention? I may ask that, mayn't I? Since, after all, you have come to me for information."

"Just as my husband came to you—unless I am very much mistaken—for private information. It was a private affair between him and some person, or maybe some people. Now he is dead. So that now it is between me and this person. Whoever," she finished tranquilly, "killed him." The level tone she was able to speak in had surprised herself as much as it had Bosboom.

"Hmm," he went slowly, and again, "Hmm. You see, I've been a businessman all my life, and as far as I know an honest one. You won't take it amiss that I should be hesitant in beginning anything, or contributing toward anything that I can't see the end of, and whose consequences I can't judge. You understand that I—like your husband, if you wish—or like you, if you prefer—have as well ethical hesitations. Your husband came to see me. That is true. But he certainly gave me no reason to suppose that he was pursuing anything in

192

the nature of a criminal inquiry. Nor did I have the slightest base for a supposition that there could be any connection at all with his subsequent death. After thought, I felt satisfied that this must be coincidence. I did ask myself whether I should go to the police. But what had I to tell them? I didn't feel it to be anything but confusion and irrelevance. All it boiled down to was a question about jewelers' stocktaking, a thing inside my experience, and that was why he came to me. As a sidelight—he happened to have broken his watch. I happened to have one I had no real use for. I sold it him in a casual neighborhood transaction. There was no matter in this for police inquiries."

"I think I understand," said Arlette. "I'm not trying to put any pressure on you. Perhaps you feel that if you now told me anything, and I were to use that to create some sort of scandal or uproar, you might be put in an uncomfortable situation. As though you had had some knowledge and suppressed it, which might come to appear discreditable—is that it, perhaps, a bit?"

"Possibly . . . partially . . ."

"Or that you have no definite knowledge, and that something you could perhaps tell me could come to appear mischievous, or even libelous because of what I might repeat or insinuate?"

"There might be something in that, too."

"Would it help you if I gave you my word that I will not make anything you tell me public?"

"It would help . . . yes."

"Then I've only one thing left—a remark, not an argument. My husband was killed. Will you not do what you can to help me? For nothing, for no motive, but only as an act of generosity or, if you prefer, pity toward a woman who has lost her husband."

Bosboom was silent while the antique pendulum

clock in the comfortable, chintzy little living room ticked quietly and the traffic outside boomed suddenly loud at the corner and decrescendo as it passed by. A far-off airliner circling above Schiphol added its distant screech. Then he said abruptly, "My wife is out. May I offer you something? She will be back very soon. I should like to put this to her, and hear what she has to say. Would you agree to my doing that?"

"Yes," said Arlette.

That evening around rush hour, she was standing in the Spui, while the pedestrian traffic, swelled by the mounting tide of tourists, eddied past her. She gazed at the windows and the door for a long time, but did not go into the shop.

A little while later, after the shops had closed, she was in the Leliegracht. She had followed a young man. Was that Saint? It seemed too young. Was it perhaps Richard, "the boy"? It seemed too old, or perhaps too sophisticated, a poised languid figure which had strolled negligently through the ten minutes of bridge and waterside between the two points, sniffing pleasurably at the freshness of a spring evening which had turned out nice after the rain.

Arlette found herself outside a sex shop. She glanced with a scrap of distaste, for she had really no desire to catch herself loitering outside a sex shop, and crossed the road. From there she glanced up at the windows above, and suddenly down at the shop again, for something had caught her eye. These places—in her limited experience—were generally given a name combining prudery and prurience; "Eros" or suchlike, culled from the superficial popularizations of Freud and Frazer with which they gave themselves an air of respectability. She grinned a little—these people and their classical myths!

194

Really—The Golden Apples of the Hesperides: now that was affectation.

Suddenly the grin froze around her mouth; she turned abruptly and walked with a quick, stiff action out of the street.

She had just discovered the stripped tree of the false apples.

She knew.

I know, she told herself, over and over, as she walked back toward the Ruysdaelkade. I know. What am I going to do?

She did not wish to tell her confederates at all. They had helped her, undoubtedly, immensely. They had comforted and quieted her, found out the material points and pointers without which she would not have known what to look for, crystallized her shapeless thoughts and canalized her turmoil of unbalanced emotion and uncontrolled wishes. They had surrounded her with an affectionate understanding and solidarity in a way that Ruth, for instance, who was too close to her, could not do. They had shown her that the police work, however concentrated and carefully directed, could strike nothing but empty air, and that this was nobody's fault. Least of all that of the police. Why else had Van der Valk been so careful not to involve any police mechanisms in his "private experiment"?

She had, too, promised Bosboom to respect his confidence. Nobody should find out from her the things he had told her. She could use the things she had learned, but she must respect their source.

Still, she could not let her confederates down. They had promised her true alliance, and given it. Dear old Bates, who had made her understand herself. Dan, who had understood and linked up all the scraps of writing

195

and got it all right before she had been given the thread, by Bosboom, that pulled everything together. And the extraordinary force of Willy and Trix, with their blind loyalty to "one of themselves"—it was that which had given the whole thing, a pretty tangled metaphysical argument in the mind of, say, Hilary, a direction and a dynamic.

"Y'can't just let a thing like that go." Willy had said, trying to understand his own instincts. " 'S like the time of the occupation. Mean t'say, no names, no pack drill now, but I knew plenty who made their pile then and never looked back since. Played their cards clever, y'know? I was only a lad but, I can say, I could have had my own business, had all I got now, near enough fifteen years ago. Or Jews—I mean, we didn't like Jews all that well. Used to make jokes, harmless like, but meaning it a bit, too, about moneylenders an' pawn-brokers an' stuff—you know . . . And, well, I mean, I was a butcher and Jews don't eat our stuff, pork and all, and they got their own slaughterhouse; I mean, what was it to me? The moffen started rounding up all the Jews, and there's nothing but grief for the likes of us to think about it, let alone interfere. Why, we didn't even have hardly any here in the quarter, those days. But it stuck in my gullet somehow. I dunno, in the occupiers' time, I can't say I thought much about patriotism or the Queen or the government. Queen never did anything for me, y'know what I mean, and bloody government, bloodsuckers—anyway, they all run away to England; it was us that had to live with the occupation. So why not go with it, not necessary collaborating, get me—but just ride it out, close your eyes, look after number one? I never did get to work out why I done some things —Willy—Charlie, that's what I should've been called, because that's what I was. But I got noth-

196

ing to regret, never had. Sod it, I just feel that way. If I can do something now about Piet, that's what I'm going to do, and hell with the consequences—don't care if they put me in jail f'r it." Exhausted, he reached for his beer, drank the whole bottle, breathed out heavily, and suddenly said, "I felt like a Jew myself, sometimes. Times I was a Jew, come to that."

No, Arlette had responsibilities both ways. Not just to Bosboom. He had had a wrestle with his conscience, no doubt, but so had Trix, who was accustomed to adding up her comforts and her cash desk, and arriving at a perfectly satisfactory existence. And she had made up her mind a good deal quicker!

"D'ja find this Bosboom?" asked the committee.

"Yes—wasn't much use. Just a confirmation that there was something about the jeweler's—he used to be the manager there. The watch just came up by the way—he happened to have one. He knows nothing about the boy."

"Or Saint?"

"Just knows he exists—he's a nephew of sorts, of old Prinz. But I've got better. I went there myself. I found out what the poem means—the thing about the false apples that puzzled us."

"No!" said Dan, vastly excited.

The house of Louis Prinz was lucky in its cleaning women. There were three of them, noisy and muscular Amsterdam housewives, with tongues that went as fast as their hands: indefatigable climbers upon ladders, whackers of carpets, clatterers of buckets. Louis had had them for many years, and was as proud of them as of anything in the shop. He was fond of telling long comic stories about their terrifying energy, their ap-

197

palling zeal, their shattering tactlessness, the years it had taken him to prevent them taking the cat-o'-nine-tails to his carpets, scrubbing all the patina off faïence, or slapping great wads of polish onto eighteenth-century marquetry. The day Jopie tripped over an easel and spilt a bucket of hot soapy water over a Saenredam canvas, one of his church interiors—"She thought she was scrubbing the pavement; I think she was deceived by the perspective." The day Rinie fell off the ladder clutching an Empire chandelier to her amazing pneumatic bosom. The black Monday when Willie found a piece of Boulle and decided to polish the brass inlays.

Dick stood in the center of his kingdom, his fingers relishing the surface of a fifteenth-century piece of oak found by Louis in a country presbytery in Belgian Limbourg—a bit wormy, but very nice. A grin crept out on his face; he had done the same thing, his first month, with another piece, covered his fingers in dust, and bawled out Jopie—youngest, noisiest, and quickest-tempered of the three. She had piled roaring in upon Louis, along the lines of "If that snot-nose is going to start teaching me my job . . ." The old man had been upset.

"You're a good boy, Dicky, a very good boy, but if I had to choose between losing you and losing my Jopie . . ." But Dick had learned quickly—he had learned everything quickly. Intelligent and sensitive, naturally attracted to objects of worth and beauty, he had attacked his own ignorance and inexperience with a heat of enthusiasm which had made him—well, he thought, grinning, pretty near as indispensable as Jopie, anyhow. He could handle more now than just tourists. True, the older customers insisted on seeing Louis, just like the businessmen who insisted on seeing Larry. And while he had picked up a great deal, he still knew nothing when it came to the buying—linchpin, as he had understood, of an antique business—and that was one thing which couldn't be learned in a hurry.

"Takes years, years; there's no short cut," as Louis said with his heavy, chesty sigh, "and who's to do that after I'm done with, I can't tell. Larry's no good—he's not even interested."

One saw little of Larry nowadays. He had taken a very small margin of time before handing over all the day-to-day routine. It was Dick now who performed the ritual of the keys and the cash float, checked the alarms, did the paperwork of stocktaking and invoicing, and handled all the modern stuff, the watches and knickknacks, reproduction jewelry and silversmithery, and "managed" in rather more than name. He had used charm on the three "girls," made jokes with them, had them eating out of his hand. . . . He had a proper salary now, and a percentage. He had acquired a pair of Cartier links for "an apple and an egg"; he had at last got some decent clothes. The Lindengracht had been left far behind. No more student lodgings! He had, indeed, moved into Larry's flat.

For Larry had been away for lengthening periods, culminating in an absence of three weeks "in the Caribbean," he had said vaguely: certainly he had come back with a beautiful tan, light and unobtrusive, like everything of Larry's.

"I'd really like you to keep the flat warmed and aired. I might even end by handing it over to you altogether, but that's all still in the womb of time, mm?" with a chuckle at "his phrase." "You're doing very well, Dicky, very well. No, you needn't pay me rent. Just keep an eye on the little shop—yes, the apples. I'll show you how; it's quite easy. It's nothing very spectacular, but it earns me a very pretty little dividend: more

199

silly young girls in the world than there are dirty old men, but both have their uses as you'll discover. In the good old phrase, crumpet sells when cotton and corn are a drag on the market. That girl I have running it is ideal—a real fanatic—women's lib," with his easy light laugh. "A treasure. Go easy with her, Dicky-boy; she has a fire in her belly, has our little sister Eileen."

Times, thought Dick, standing dreamily feeling the primitively smoothed surface with its amazing patina, I feel as though I were running a temperature. Almost like someone with TB or something. Bouts of feverish excitement. Learning to keep that easy cool evenness Larry has is the hardest of all when one is a success, has one's foot on the ladder. I contrast myself now with what I was only a few months ago! Knowing nothing, able for nothing, totally empty-headed. Incredible! No wonder I feel the blood going to my head now and again. . . .

It hadn't always been easy! In fact, it had been very hard bought, some of the winnings, taking fearful tolls of nerve, straining every atom of him. There had been Daisy. Lordy, what a fool she had made of him! The reminiscence was just one hot agonized blush. Worse than a tool—a toy he had been in her hard, cunning, oh so skillful fingers. Or the incident, as Larry had called it the only time he had ever referred to it, at the time the heat had really been on, with plainclothes policemen in pairs running around Holland checking everything they could think of and the papers full of mysterious hints about their being hot on the trail of heaven only knew what. It had all blown over, exactly as Larry had prophesied. He had thought of everything! The incident had taken every scrap of nerve he had, as well as all the training Larry had been able to inject into him, but he had managed.

It wasn't a thing he liked to think about, even now. It was a damned unpleasant sore spot, only half cicatrized despite everything. Still, he had to face it now and again, to show he was on top and wasn't letting it get him down. It had been Larry, after all—his idea, his responsibility. His plan and his action in all save "the surgical detail." "I can't hold the scalpel for you, Dicky-boy; that's the one thing one has to learn to do on one's own or the whole exercise is pointless—that's what separates the men from the boys." Well, yes, of course, he'd understood that and accepted it. It was over. That ghost wouldn't come back.

"Mightn't it be a trick?" he asked Larry tensely after it had all disappeared from the press reports, when all the police activity both advertised and unadvertised had died away. Larry knew all about that; he had sources of information everywhere. "I mean, they always say they never close the file, never loosen the teeth."

A shrug. "Teeth have to have a grip, if we're insisting on these emotional metaphors. They've no hold anywhere; nothing at all."

And so it had proved. One couldn't ever relax vigilance, but that was just what Larry called "keeping in training." "Never let yourself get out of training. Especially when—like me, my dear boy—you begin to approach middle age. A real professional can't afford that mistake—gravest one of all, the temptation to get softened by comfort."

And yet with it all Dick had what he could only describe to himself as a sort of uneasy nervous hunger. Very like that first day, which he often thought of, when he had been going to that absurd piddling job and stopped in the Spui to eat a sandwich from the snack bar at the corner! He hadn't needed that sandwich, yet he'd had to have it. The incident was a bit like that. To this day, he was anguished by the thought of not knowing—had nobody, the police or anyone else, really ever had even the wildest or most unconfirmable of "notions"? Larry said of course that they hadn't. Couldn't. Quite out of the question.

"There is of course always one tiny risk," he had said. Before, of course, not after. He had never spoken about it afterward. "As in all surgery, even the most minor—always that one tiny risk. Naturally, one would never accept odds against—that in no circumstances. It's from the departure point of even money that an intelligent man will consent just to look at an operation—any operation. He then works to narrow those odds further in his favor. He gets, let's say, to nine-to-four on. At that point he might accept a bet. But he hedges it, Dick. He lays off—by betting on every other possibility as well. Always back both sides, my boy, and that at a moment when the odds are right for you. Now here, owing to this lamentable blabbermouth of yours, you've stacked cards against you. You went to this man and you told him some silly things. Now the odds are still very considerably in your favor. Point one, the man is not on any active duty. Two, the things you told him are fundamentally so trivial, as well as so silly, that the probability of his disregarding or forgetting the whole thing is overwhelming. He wrote nothing down—you're certain of that. He began to, but stopped. There is no official move afoot, or we'd have learned of it long ago. No button has been pressed, no machinery set in movement. There's nothing except a curiosity aroused by a half-recalled piece of gossip. Those odds are still slightly too large for my liking. We narrow them by removing this awkward grain of sand. That the grain of sand may be followed by others through the same hole—we close the hole. That another grain, too microscopically small to be seen, has already got through—those are the odds now facing you. They are so small as to be negligible. If a surgeon did not neglect the odds on his patient being a dangerous active hemophiliac, there would be no surgery—nobody would dare incise as much as a finger."

"I see all that," muttered Dick. "The only thing that worries me is that he should have spoken to some friend, or acquaintance—or something. I don't know what . . ."

"Hedge your bet," said Larry with his soft gleam of amusement. "Hedge your bet, my boy—as I do. Arm yourself against any other loose-mouthed gossiping fool like yourself—sorry, but face it honestly—who might come floating idly in your direction, carried by some eddy of fantasy or supposition or conjecture—it can never be more than that."

And now weeks had passed. Nothing had happened. Nobody had appeared. Why had he still this persistent temperature, this chronic low fever? As though he had really caught some infectious disease?

It was enough to make one go and have a chest X-ray, to be quite sure. People simply didn't get TB nowadays.

His reverie was interrupted—and he was grateful, because it had become unpleasant—by the prolonged silvery tinkle of the door chimes. A customer . . .

No, not a customer, Dick's by now trained and sharpened eye told him immediately. Nothing but an artist! He had learned not to despise them, because Louis insisted on keeping a friendly relationship with all artists, however trivial or foolish. . . .

"First, you never know when you'll need a craftsman; do them a favor and they'll do the same for you. Second, whatever you think, it's good publicity—you'd be surprised how often an artist, who has a trained eye, has put me in the way of something good. And commercial artists, who are the most tiresome because they want to borrow things free, can give one in return a commercial puff. I furnished a whole play once for the Stadschouwburg—did me a lot of good, and I recouped the trouble and the damage with no bother at all."

This was one of them, obviously. They came all shapes and sizes, wheedling for a Chinese silk screen "to photograph the model against," putting an antique porcelain pipe with a Delft jar and a seventeenth-century astrolabe for a whisky advertisement, asking to borrow an Empire day bed to help sell innerspring mattresses! This object was typical enough. Small, broad-shouldered, and bowlegged like a Belgian sprint cyclist, a thatch of untidy hair, a bald forehead, those idiot steel-rimmed glasses, a huge walrus mustache. Still, as Larry said—rule number one—"Be courteous, no matter who."

"Good morning; how can I help you?"

"Prinz in?" asked Danny de Vries.

"I'm afraid he's away in the Ardennes all week. Plundering the presbyteries, he calls it."

"How about Saint?"

"Ah, sorry."

"Not in Amsterdam either?"

"Yes, he's back, but we don't see him here much now. Friend of his?" casually. Couldn't be much of an acquaintance of Larry's, or he'd know more of his movements.

"Not really. Recommendation from a friend. Was looking for an Italian Madonna; any at all, provided it's early—quattrocento or thereabouts, something with a gold background; you know, genre Simone Martini, but Cinzano would do, too, n'est-ce-pas? A motif I'm working on."

204

"Sorry, we've nothing like that in. We've an icon, but I don't think I could let that go—the insurance . . . It belongs really to Marianne Colin in Paris. You might try Papenheim in the Leidsestraat."

"He sent me to you. You Richard, by the way?"

"Oddinga—at your service, but I don't know you, do I?"

"Do now," with a rather impudent grin that brushed Dick the wrong way a bit, he didn't know why.

"How so?—that you come to know my name?"

"Oh, a friend—same fellow gave me Larry Saint's name. Suggested you might help me."

"Who's that, then?"

"Bit of an oddball," said Danny, laughing. "Police-man—not a type you'd think knew anything about art." Dick had stiffened up like a fresh-caught mackerel.

"Er—what's his name, then?"

"Rather a tragedy—daresay you read about it in the paper. Got shot over in The Hague by some psychopath —bit of a professional risk, I suppose. Used to be a commissaire in the Criminal Brigade—but you knew him, surely? Piet van der Valk."

"Knew him?" with stiff lips. "No, can't say I did. How come?"

"Oh, well," said Dan, laughing heartily, "he seems to have known you, anyhow. Suggested I look you up, when I was talking one day about antiques—funny, only just before his death. Well, actually it was Saint he mentioned—interesting man, he said, and good at his job. But since he mentioned you in the same context . . ."

"Really? What context was that? I don't know why I'm curious—seems funny, that's all."

"Oh, I forget. Something about a watch, I think, but I can't really recall. Just about antiques. I was inter-

205

ested because old Piet was an absolute mine of information about all sorts of queer things—specially here in Amsterdam. Well, I'll blow; pity about the Madonna, better go and ask Peter Wilson, ha-ha-ha. By the way, tell Larry when you see him Piet was saying give his regards—bit out of date, that; sorry about the joke, it's in bad taste, huh? Still, regards are regards; pass on the message just the same. Bye-bye, hope to have the pleasure of meeting you again sometime." And banged out happily, leaving Dick paralyzed.

He must mention this to Larry. But where was Larry? He didn't know exactly. He was using the flat, but irregularly. He wasn't back every night. But he must know about this, for certain. Who was that chap? Damn it, he hadn't given a name. Said he'd been to Papenheim—try ringing.

"Hallo? Oh, Mr. Papenheim—Oddinga here at Prinz's—you haven't by any chance had an inquiry about a quattrocento Madonna?" Dick had been too disturbed to notice how odd this would sound.

"What?" said the voice at the other end, not believing its ears.

"Well, I had a rather peculiar fellow asking whether we had a . . ."

"Just like that, eh? What did you do—tell him to try Marks & Spencer?"

"No, not an oleo—artist of some kind, by the look; wanted maybe to copy it or something."

"Why'n't he go to the Rijksmuseum?"

"Yes, I thought it odd, too, but maybe—"

"What is all this?" suspiciously—was this a roundabout approach from Louis letting it be known he'd got one, or had a client who wanted one, or—"Why d'you ask me such a thing?"

"Oh, only—er, that of course I said we hadn't and I

206

suggested he ask you, and he said he had." Dick was floundering now.

"Had what? You think I've got one—why'n't Louis ask me himself?"

"No, no—oh hell—look, it was just the fellow seems not all there, and I was a bit puzzled, and since he said he'd asked you, I thought I'd check with you what the fellow could be after, really, since this might be just a pretext for something else."

"I've seen nobody, know nothing of this. Sounds cockeyed to me. You get any loonies, don't send them to me as a way of getting rid of them, my boy, I beg you."

"Yes, of course; sorry I troubled you." There was a grunt and the phone clanked. Dick wiped his forehead, felt for a cigarette he needed, regretting the foolish impulse that had made him ring up without thinking. Papenheim was such a suspicious bastard. He would go on thinking for weeks that there was a real fourteenth-century picture somewhere, perhaps offered for sale, and Louis was trying to find out whether it had been offered to him! People said one thing and meant another, and in this slippery world Richard was not yet altogether always at his ease. He blew out smoke in a noisy puff, rubbed his head, and wondered what it all meant.

Dan, gleefully, was reporting that Saint was not at home, but the young man had nearly had kittens: they were on a hot trail. Trix, it was decided, would be the next attacker. She giggled self-consciously, but said she wouldn't lose her nerve, whoever else might.

Dick had not seen Larry at lunchtime, nor apparently had he been to the flat. Dick thought of leaving a message on the phone pad, but decided not to. He had had time to cool down. Don't get flustered, he told himself. He could imagine Larry's sarcastic eyes being expressive—what, another panic? He decided to do nothing. Just a coincidence which would blow over. Recall—if anything were known, he'd have heard about it long before this.

He was amused at this fine example of slightly over-blown Amsterdam bourgeoisie. Successful shopkeeper a mile off! Trix, much dressed up and heavily perfumed, had difficulty starting, which didn't bother Dick at all. This type of customer, with money to spend and a conviction that antiques would increase her standing as well as prove a good investment, was familiar. Dick was young enough for them to patronize, which gave them confidence: he had made some good sales this way, a thing which had much amused Larry.

"Of course, Mevrouw. A piece of furniture, perhaps? Now this is a striking little piece, and extremely elegant—it opens out to form a writing table, you see. A bonheur-du-jour—genuine Louis Quinze lacquer. It's not signed, but we'll give you our written guarantee. That might look very well in your salon." Like fun it bloody would, Trix was thinking, but what she said was "You see a lot of them faked."

"Not in this house, Mevrouw."

"Yes, but how would you know the difference, huh?"

"An expert can tell, Mevrouw, and Mr. Prinz is recognized as a great authority."

"That's all very well, but—why, I remember as a child there was a cabinetmaker's shop in the quarter, and he used to make these things."

"Naturally. There are numerous reproductions. But both the wood and the methods used are modern."

"That so? Well, let me tell you something, young man—this old chap, old Piet van der Valk, he used to

208

mend chairs and such, but his shop was full of old bits of furniture, and he used to say if you took a piece of old wood and used the traditional methods and such you could make something even an expert couldn't tell the difference." Trix came out with it bravely. The information came from Arlette, who had been told by her husband. These reminiscences had been confirmed by Willy. "I remember the old boy when I was a kid in the street; 's true enough, he had an attic full of old wardrobes and such, used to take them to pieces." But it was not this remark that petrified Dick.

"Really?" he was saying in a light voice with no timbre. "How interesting. One would not think he had sufficient skill. What was the name again?"

"Old Piet van der Valk. Of course, you weren't born then; that was in the old days—I can only just remember them," added Trix in haste. "But his son was well known, too—real Amsterdamer, nice chap; my husband went to school with him," with perfect truth. "You'll know about him—he was that Commissaire of Police got assassinated in the street just the other day, a right filthy trick that was. If my husband got his hands on the one that did that, he said to me at the time . . . Well, young man, how about it?"

"Mr. Prinz will guarantee the authenticity," Dick managed to get out from between his anesthetized jaws.

"He will, will he—well, perhaps I'll talk to him. I'll think it over—thank you, young man." And out Trix flounced. She hadn't done it very well, she thought, but well enough. She'd seen that young cockerel's jaw drop!

"Worked," she announced triumphantly to the committee, "like a bloody great dose of castor oil." Trix felt sufficiently confident in the company to have no scruples at all about lavatory humor. What was more, she was quite right.

Dick had wanted to close the shop, but was frightened of Larry coming past—even dropping in! Or even Louis—who might come back. It was true he was in Belgium, but one never knew how long he would stay away. He felt unable to give explanations. He could say he was sick—it was perfectly true. If there was one thing he wanted, it was to be in bed, in peace, with nobody able to come in and worry him. Time to sleep and relax and knit himself together. Silence. Peace.

The shimmer of light on the black and scarlet lacquer of the bonheur-du-jour—the happiness of the day!—which had pleased him now had a hard and hostile look. A piece of old wood creaked suddenly, the way they sometimes did when the atmosphere was insufficiently humid. He ran to fill the containers on the radiators, and was frightened and alarmed at spilling water on the carpet.

"Now if Hilary goes. Strike while the iron's hot," said Dan, rubbing his hands together.

"That might be extremely dangerous," answered Bates bluntly. "If a young man like that is frightened, who knows what he might do? It was agreed that I should go—I run much less risk."

"He was shook, all right," said Trix with satisfaction. "I think Willy ought to go. He's a man, and strong, and he could handle the situation. I could nip back to the shop, and he could be changed in a few minutes."

"I don't think it's necessary," said Arlette. Everybody looked at her.

"What's the matter, Let?" demanded Dan, who had the Dutch habit of abbreviating proper names. A thing which would ordinarily have infuriated her as much as being called "love" by Willy the butcher.

"I don't know. It seems like hounding people, that's all."

"But there's no doubt at all—this boy must have some guilty knowledge. Just look how he reacts—twice, with separate people—to perfectly harmless remarks."

Bates: Arlette turned to look at her. Strange woman. So gentle, and so kind. So completely the harmless, loquacious, clacking old biddy. And yet, when it was a question of anything she felt strongly about, so very implacable. I understand that, thought Arlette. I would have said I was the same. A principle is a principle, and one cannot yield on that. But when a principle has a personal relevance—no, one can't yield. But surely one has to modify.

"Yes," said Arlette unwillingly.

"Come, my pet, I know what's going on in your head. But think—it might not be only guilty knowledge, you know. Has it struck you that—?"

"Yes. It has."

"Well, then . . . I mean, one hasn't the right to shuffle it off."

"I know."

"Oh, come." It was Hilary, all bracing common sense, as usual. "We can't talk like this. This isn't only theorizing ahead of the data, but really it's outrageous. We can't make suppositions of that kind. This boy, it seems pretty well established, is *the* boy—I mean 'the boy' mentioned in the notes: I'm not denying that, I can't. But, hell, where is the motive? He came to Piet, asking for we don't know quite what. Advice, maybe, or help even. He wasn't an informer about anything criminal—or Piet would certainly have taken steps. And, as we now know, he didn't. So the boy was in some kind of trouble. He'd maybe not pinched this famous watch at all, but just been accused of it. He's just afraid that now we mention the name there's some little thing we know of, some little secret, probably utterly trivial, we know something about—and he feels

211

that as something disgraceful. You know how boys are; they exaggerate out of all proportion. It's probably—much more probably—something absurdly petty."

"I don't agree," said Dan bluntly. "And, remember, I saw him—you didn't."

"Well, where's the motive?" said Hilary.

"If there'd ever been any motive, don't you think the police would have found it? They're not fools, after all. You can bet your behind that if there was one they'd have solved all this and we wouldn't be here now. They'll have gone through everybody's advantage or impulse or motivation like—like that dose of castor oil Trixie was talking about."

"There isn't any motive," said Bates bluntly. "If you'd seen as many pathological people as I've had the misfortune to come across—people do things without any motive. Or that is to say, of course there is one, but the casual observer can't see it. They don't even know it themselves."

"I'm going to go and see this boy," said Arlette, who had not been listening, or had given no sign of doing so.

"Oh, Let, you can't," Danny said.

"I can and I will. You talk as though you were able to stop me or something—now shut up, Danny, my mind's made up. I'm going to find out what it was my husband was interested in."

"This mysterious Saint, no doubt, whom nobody seems able to lay eyes upon."

"She's right," said Hilary with finality. "If it were anybody else, then I'd agree we can't go bullying this wretched boy over something he may not even know the slightest thing about. But *she* has a right to go if she wants."

"In all honesty," said Dan, "the boy may feel worried because Piet got killed, and be wondering quite without rhyme or reason whether it might not have been in some way his fault, because somehow he was at the start of all this."

"That's just what I meant!" shouted Hilary triumphantly. "Quite illogical."

"It doesn't matter," said Arlette quietly. "I'm going to find out. All this speculation gets nobody anywhere. I'll ask. And if necessary I'll find this Saint. And ask him, too. I want to get to the bottom of this. What's the use of talking?"

"But, ducky—the shops will be shutting in a few minutes."

"I know where the boy lives," she said unanswerably.

"Well, I'm going to come with you—or anyway after you," said Dan.

"What for?"

"Just as a witness. I won't interfere. I won't even be there. But just to say afterward, if need be, that you were at such a place at such a time."

"I wish you wouldn't. It makes me feel most uncomfortable."

"That may be so. But all the same I've made up my mind."

"That's reasonable," said Hilary, "just as long as you don't indulge in any heroics."

"If anybody accosts me," said Danny happily, "I'll scream, that's what I'll do."

"And I'll come and rescue you," said Arlette, grinning. "One has to deflate the drama, my husband used to say."

"Are you going at once?"

"I'm going to change. A white blouse will show the blood better."

213

"Don't make jokes like that, pet," said Bates seriously. "I just hope you know what you're doing." She did not say, "I'm the only person here able to realize how serious this is," but her attitude did. To the others it's just a drama, she thought. Almost a game. Arlette guessed this, watching her disapproving eyes on Dan, but said nothing. She could not tell, anyway, what might be at the back of an elderly woman's mind.

"May I come in?" asked Arlette abruptly when the door opened.

"Well—er—were you looking for Mr. Saint? I'm afraid he's not here and I don't quite know when to expect him."

"I don't know yet whether I'm looking for Mr. Saint; I'd like to speak to you first. And since I'm not selling anything, and my business is personal, I'd be grateful if I could come in."

"Sorry—er, of course. Please sit down. A cigarette?"

"Thank you. Why did you ask whether I was looking for Mr. Saint?"

"Well—he lives here—when he's around, that is. Er—I'm just keeping things warm for him."

"I see. You take his place, in a way?"

"I don't see quite what you're getting at."

"You live in his flat. You work in his shop. Isn't that so?"

"Oh, that—yes, yes."

"Sounds as though you're quite a handyman," said Arlette, taking one of her own cigarettes.

"Well—we're friendly. You haven't told me what this is all about?"

"I didn't think I would need to." The boy might have been confused, by her manner, her accent, her appearance. She did not look like a policeman's widow; nor was she playing the part in a conventional manner. She

214

was not, of course, accustomed to playing parts, and too forthright a person to be good at dissimulation. Faced with this boy, in this flat where lived another man connected, she felt certain, with the assassination of her husband, she felt oddly free of emotional pressure. She felt no rancor, no cruel desire for vengeance, no anger, and no fear. It might have been her detached and chilly manner as much as her clothes that confused the boy: they were a little too smart. She had dressed for her own execution rather than for a simple interrogation. Is it possible, too, that her voice, dropping monosyllables with a flat delivery and a metallic timbre, had a resemblance to Saint's?

"You must be a friend of Larry's," said the boy. "I should be offering you a drink. Would you like a glass of champagne?" She heard this with a surprise which brought her sense of detachment—as though she were standing at a distance—a step further toward unreality.

"I think that unlikely." He was already twisting the wire off a half bottle.

"If it's business," with an air of cunning, going back for two glasses, "I daresay you could tell me, you know, and I'll see it's passed on."

"So that you're in his confidence, you'd say."

"Oh, yes," with a self-satisfied chuckle, twisting the cork out carefully and holding it back to make the inrush of air less abrupt.

"Then perhaps," said Arlette, sitting very straight, "you can tell me what happened to my husband, Commissaire van der Valk."

The cork jumped, and champagne dribbled all over his hand and up his sleeve. He stood, and stared. With a housewifely instinct of dislike at the waste of good champagne, Arlette got up, took the bottle, and put it down on the table.

"I see," with her face close to his, "that you know."

215

He looked at her, face like an idiot's. "You see, also, that I know."

He could find nothing better to say than "How?"

Arlette did not become angry, but she lost her detachment. How! As though that mattered. "What are you, then—his handyman, his fancy boy? You were in it together; I can see that."

"That's not true," yelped the boy, who had heard the word "fancy" and missed the rest altogether.

"What's not true?" furious at the stupidity of the denial, catching hold of his tie and wrenching him so that he staggered. "What's not true, little ordure that you are?" speaking French without realizing.

"Larry . . ." he sputtered out. "Stop—you're choking me," like a child when a game has become too violent. It had all been a game—and now the game had suddenly stopped and, like an overexcited child, he began to cry.

"The police . . ." stupidly, as though wondering why they weren't there to help him.

The police . . . what had they to do with it? She lifted her hand to hit him, the disintegrated face of a great blubbering boy, but stopped herself.

"Which of you was it? Or both?"

"Larry . . . I . . . Larry drove the car. . . ."

"And you? What was it you did?"

"I . . ."

"You shot."

The boy fell on the floor, hid his face in his hands, and sobbed.

Arlette wanted to be sick. She turned her back abruptly. Her gloves and bag stood on the table. The bottle stood alongside, in a little pool of champagne; she snatched her gloves up before they got stained. One could do nothing with that invertebrate there. Where was Saint? She looked around the room, dizzy with nausea. This was his flat. Here he would come, sooner or later. She set her teeth hard; she had to get out of here before she became sick. She got control of herself with an effort, took her bag, put her gloves on slowly, the familiar painstaking movement calming her, and forced herself to open the door quietly, and close it quietly after her.

Saint, by one of those coincidences dear to fiction writers, was at the bottom of the stairs but—as should not happen in well-organized fiction—too late to be cued into the scene. He looked at her with interest, wondering what had made her so explosive; with amusement, thinking, Dicky-boy, you've been clumsy; with some enjoyment, thinking, Good-looking woman; with curiosity, wondering, Where did he find that? He did not know who Arlette was. Her picture had not appeared in the paper, thanks to the commissaire of police who had been friendly enough to protect her from the press. And a day later she had been in France. It had deflated somewhat the human-interest side of things.

Arlette, coming down the steep narrow stairway while he flattened himself courteously to allow her to pass, knew at once that this was Saint. Into her mind instantly came "the arsenal." It had been Van der Valk's joking name for the bottom drawer of a big countrified Louis XIV commode. Here he kept his hunting rifle, a Mauser 7.64 with a telescopic sight, with which he had sometimes gone after wild boar; a .22 for sniping at rats, pigeons, and hooded crows; and a variety of "police souvenirs." He had never been one for guns himself, and very rarely carried one, but there were two pistols and the Israeli submachine gun which had killed Esther Marx, Ruth's mother.

217

Arlette, bred in the French countryside where everybody carries a gun, even though the consequences of this are that there is nothing left to shoot at, was not afraid of guns. Once, in the summer, passing by a French garrison barracks on "open-doors day," she had been tempted by him into trying her luck, and had scored forty-six out of fifty with an army rifle on the barracks range. It had been third best, and next day an amused officer had come to call, bringing her her prize of a pocket alarm clock and a pair of sandals. They'd fitted her, too.

"You had a good look at my feet, anyhow," she'd said, entertained. And once, on New Year's Eve, rather drunk, she had complained of having no fireworks. She had fired a magazine-full from the little machine gun at an uncomplaining pine tree; being tracer, the result had been deeply satisfying.

It was not, though, this pleasant memory that was uppermost in her mind right now. It was sheer animal desire for blood.

If she had had a gun, she would have shot Saint there on the stairway. The odd thing was that she could pass him, almost touching him, aware of his appreciative sketch of a half smile, in perfect command of herself.

Danny de Vries was on the pavement opposite, rivers of sweat running down his ribs. He had seen Saint go in, had felt sure he knew who it was, had been very frightened indeed. Arlette was very white but not in the least shaky: his breath came out between his teeth when he saw her, and he rubbed his elbows along his sides to try and stop the secretion of fear. She was self-possessed, too; instead of walking toward him, she crossed the road in a diagonal and walked away toward the corner. He had a moment of alarm before realizing that she did not wish to compromise him, just in case

218

anyone was looking out the window. He breathed deeply and forced himself to stroll along casually.

She was waiting round the corner, leaning against a baker's window, eyes tight shut. He gripped her arm and was relieved when she opened her eyes and smiled at him.

"That was Saint. I'm sure of it."

"I know. Take me to a café, Danny. I've got to have a brandy or something, and I think I've got to be sick."

"You shouldn't drink; you're in shock. Some hot tea . . ."

"Do as I say."

She drank the coarse pub cognac, shook her head, clenched her teeth on the glass—thick enough, luckily, not to break—bolted for the lavatory, and was away so long that Dan began to have lurid visions of having to break the door down. He was just wondering how one should go about this—did one call the fire brigade?— when Arlette came back with her face drawn, certainly, but natural-looking, and said "Sorry."

"If you had a black coffee, or something?"


Saint, with less gentleness, had heaved the still sobbing, shapeless boy to his feet, thrown him roughly into the bathroom, looked with distaste at the puddles of spilt champagne, and gone to his room to change. When he came out again, everything was as he had left it. He made a face, went into the kitchen, got materials to mop up, made a meticulous job of doing so, threw out the dregs of stale champagne, looked around carefully, went and looked in Dick's bedroom, poked over a few papers lying about, frowned, and went into the bathroom. The boy was sitting on the lavatory seat, looking dilapidated past belief.

"You'd better have a shower, tidy yourself, acquire a

proper control, and then come back and give some account of yourself. When I allowed you to use this flat, it wasn't to turn it into a brothel. That pigsty out there—I'm in two minds whether to throw you out of here right now."

The boy looked up, puffy and swollen, as though he had been punched. "Too late," he said. "Too late."

"Comedy!" said Saint with contempt. "Take a shower," he commanded curtly. "You're not even coherent. I'll give you exactly fifteen minutes to make yourself fit for consumption." He turned around and walked out. The boy shambled drearily to his feet and called out "Too late" again after him, but Saint was not bothering to listen.

"I'm perfectly all right now," said Arlette with a slight impatience.

"I don't care," said Danny, "I'm calling a cab." What a fuss. Still, he had been immensely gentle with her. He had asked no questions, made no effort to hurry her. He had suggested again the strong black coffee, and been cheered by her saying, "Yes, but at home. Not that swill here." Her voice strengthened then, and she grinned suddenly. "Not that awful slop Hilary makes, either."

"It's true," said Danny, laughing, relieved at the color coming back in her face and her normal-sounding voice. "Hilary makes ghastly coffee. I'm so accustomed to it I no longer protest. Feminists always make bad coffee, have you noticed?"

"Who ordered a taxi?" bellowed the driver, banging in at the door. "Hurry up, then; going off duty in ten minutes 'n' I ain't going to the airport 'r anything," catching sight of Arlette. Five minutes later, Bates was making coffee with twice as much as she would put in

220

ordinarily, Hilary was saying "You'd better have something to eat," and Willy and Trix appeared bringing a present—two veal kidneys! Dan had rushed to tell them that Arlette had done something but he didn't know what and they'd do well to find out quick, because what she mightn't have provoked lord only knew.

Arlette sipped her coffee and said, "Thank you, it's lovely," although it was much too strong. "I was sick as hell," she said reflectively.

"But, darling—what happened? Get her a glass of water, Hilary, and an aspirin—no, that might upset her stomach."

"I'm perfectly all right," drinking water, "but give me a moment." Bates was producing eau de Cologne, a sinister bottle of marvelous-stuff-for-one's nerves, and threatening a whole pharmacopeia. . . . "I've some terrific pills," yelled Trix. "I can pop round and get them in less than a sec. . . ."

"Do shut up," said Arlette. "All I want is water."

"Sorry, pet, we're making much too much fuss."

"They did it," she said, looking from one anxious face to the other, "the pair of them. One drove the car. The other held the gun. I was going to hit him but I didn't. He fell on the floor and threw a fit. So I walked out. Then I met the other . . . on the stairs. If I'd had a gun . . . luckily I didn't. I was quite out of my mind. I wanted to see him fall into some horrible machine—a harvester or something—that just tears everything up. I wanted blood. I'm all right now. I was mortally sick, and got diarrhea—I didn't know—what it would be like to kill a person. A horrible sort of greedy excitement. Like being raped. Or being possessed by a demon. It's revolting . . . because so degrading."

"Yes," said Hilary, "mankind is a beastly object."

"But you're all wrought up," said Willy kindly.

"It was natural," said Trix, "feeling like that—look what that man did to you."

"You were being subjective," said Bates. Oh my, Van der Valk would have thought; there's that word again.

Arlette fell silent. They didn't understand and she didn't blame them. She had never understood either. If one could, then there would be no crime in the world. Being possessed by a demon . . . I don't know whether there's any demon, she thought: perhaps there isn't any needed. People by themselves are quite enough. . . .

"I haven't got it quite straight," said Dan, who had been quiet in a corner, putting brandy in the strong coffee. "The boy broke down—when he knew who you were, is that it? That's that—we know, then, we were right and there wasn't anything wrong with our idea there. Tapping at him a bit broke his nerve. And the other was in it, too—that's not just aiding and abetting; that's equal guilt, I think, under law. When there's a conspiracy, all are guilty together and who held the gun is irrelevant. What do we do now? I suppose we go to the police. We have what we need."

"That's claptrap," said Hilary. "It wouldn't help us at all. The police wouldn't move: they'd say there was no case. For all they know, it's we who have made the conspiracy. Can't you see—there's no proof."

"Oh, don't be wet—when you've a confession, you need no proof. This boy is broken all to bits. He'd spit it all out to the police in no time."

"Not a legal proof," Hilary objected. "A confession isn't accepted, because it can come out under psychological pressure. People will confess to anything, because they feel obscure guilts and needs to be punished. When a murder is reported in the papers, you get all kinds of cranks turning up to confess to it. Ask Arlette what her husband would say."

"It's true, I think. I've heard him say the same."

"But if the boy really is guilty, and we know he is, there must be some evidence available, now that the police know where to look. They'd turn it up. There must be a motive somewhere, good grief," complained Dan.

"What makes you so sure?" Hilary asked.

"But surely . . ."

"Look, we've been over and over this. A motive—like they'd committed something criminal and he'd find out, so they silenced him. Then why didn't he do something official? He was a policeman, he knew all the ways of pinning a crime on people. Yet he did nothing. Look at the facts. He was killed, and there's still absolutely nothing to show why. You're like these detective stories going on with *cui bono*—I'm absolutely convinced the killing was meaningless."

"Then what's your explanation? Drugs or something?"

"Something pathological. People just do kill for no motive. Just for fun. Or just for the thrill—didn't you hear what Arlette said? Out of perversion—just like concentration camp guards. And when they were tried, half of them got off."

"That's true, I'm afraid," said Bates. "People are just wicked sometimes. I've seen it. It happened here in Amsterdam in the war. Nowadays we say, oh well, poor things, they were exposed to great temptation or they were perverted by their rulers. But we didn't say so then. We just saw wicked people who killed us. So we killed them—when we could. And we don't have it on our conscience."

"We're going all metaphysical," said Dan. "That

223

won't solve anything—we can go on talking here, and get nothing done."

"That's right," said Willy unexpectedly. "Why did we begin this? Because the police got nowhere with it. And what guarantee have we now they'll do anything? Nix. Like you said, there'll be all the legal talky psycho stuff for weeks on end, and the fellow gets off. That's no good."

"Right up," said Trix. "Anybody now who commits a crime says they're mad and gets away with it."

"But hell's delight, they are mad." Hilary could be obstinate, too. "You can't punish people for being mad; that's medieval."

"I don't believe that boy's mad. I saw him," objected Dan, "and you didn't. He didn't act mad. He just acted guilty, frightened of being found out. If you're mad, you're not scared."

"Well, the other one might be mad. He doesn't seem to be scared."

"All right, admit he's dotty, then. But not a legal, certifiable dottiness. Nobody could prove he goes around killing people. You'd never pin it on him. He doesn't even need an alibi—why should he be asked to prove one? He's under no obligation to prove himself innocent."

"We're getting nowhere," said Willy angrily. "Too much talk. You can go on arguing, but where does that get us?"

"I think Arlette should decide," said Trix. "She's the one concerned; she's seen them and talked to them."

They all stopped arguing to look at her. Yes, she thought, you all want me to decide. As though I could. As though I can take such a responsibility. Yet I must, I suppose, I started this.

"I don't know anything," she said. "Since I have to say something—then I think the boy's harmless. I be-

224

lieve he's just a poor silly boy who got tangled up in this somehow and can't get out. The man—no, I've got no proof and I can't be sure. Not reasonably. All I can say is that when I met him—and I nearly touched him—I knew it was him. The moment I saw him. I don't know how or why, but I knew. I'd have killed him then, like a pheasant. Mad? Yes, I suppose he is. Anybody who kills anyone is mad, I suppose."

"No," said Bates, with such decision they all jumped. "Not always. Some men kill from sheer wickedness, and sometimes those men must be removed, and there's no madness in that."

Arlette recollected that she was the only one to know that Bates had killed a Gestapo man. She had better keep her mouth shut. "I've no right to say anything," she said. "I would have killed him."

It was astonishing how Bates took possession of them all. A scraggy old woman . . . She leaned forward in her dowdy sage-green tweed skirt and a shapeless brown pullover: thin, active, decided.

"We've talked and we've talked," she said. "I think we're agreed that the police are no good—not that I haven't great respect for them, but sometimes their hands are tied by all these legal-psychological quibbles or administrative rules, and that's, I'm sure, why my poor old friend, Arlette's dear husband, felt unable to do anything. Mad! I daresay this man is mad; I'm certain too, it's him and not this poor wretched boy—everything points that way. And I say it's up to us to do something. It's not fair to ask Arlette to decide: she can't. We have to. That's our duty, our moral obligation. When anyone is in danger, it is the individual's duty as much as the state's to take action. I'm sure we have to do something and if we can't do it legally we just have to do it illegally. Justice is made by God and imperfectly administered by men. Why? Because men are very weak and generally bad, and have no sense. We have a clear duty to act, and all there is to decide is how."

Not a soul budged.

"Now," said Bates decisively, "as Willy said one day, we're a sort of committee. Or, if you prefer, a jury. What do we do? We vote on it. Not Arlette. Us. There's no way we can hand this man over to justice in the ordinary sense. So what do we do? Punish him ourselves. And how? Kill him? I suppose you'll all be shocked at that coming from me. But it can be done, you know. I've known it done. I've seen it. Now—are we going to do something? Or are we just going to drink tea and shuffle off our responsibilities, and run to the police and tell them, oh well, we're convinced it's so-and-so, but we've absolutely nothing to back that up except one hysterical boy. Now. Danny?"

"We've got to do something—yes. I don't think we can kill him. I think that's judicial murder, as much as if a court did it. I don't believe in capital punishment."

"Willy."

"I say you're dead right. I say whether the man's mad or not, I don't care: he's killed and got away with it. Whether he had the gun, I don't care either. He's the older man and one can't pin it all on this boy. Trix saw him; he's just a boy, scared stiff. And I know nothing about capital punishment—I couldn't argue against all what you say. But I do say you never get to know if a fella's mad or not, because you'll get the shrinks to argue both sides, armies of'm 's likely 's not. And what d'you know at the end of it: damn all. I don't say prison, neither—they serve maybe seven, eight years and they're out again with one idea, that they won't get caught no more. I say chop. But there—I'm no good at arguing that either. Because I couldn't do it m'self,

226

that's why. Might sound silly, because I've killed ani-
mals. But I don't know, might be that—killed too many
calves t'be able t'kill a yuman. I could beat'm up, of
course," reflected Willy, looking at his forearm resting
on the table. "But I don't think putting'm in hospital's
any good, unless you really break him up, and that's
dirty. Kill'm and finish, like you would a tiger that's
broke loose. You don't maybe want to, but you got to.
Only—I don't know how."

"Couldn't we," said Trix diffidently, "get him any
other way? Burn his shop or something. Take away all
his money—that would punish 'm, I'd think."

"Not possible," said Dan, grinning slightly, "without
involving other people who haven't committed any
crime, and who might even have more to lose than he
has. Anyway, you can't take away a tiger's money, can
you?"

"No, I suppose not. Well, I, too, say kill him and I
know what Willy means, but I think I'd be just the
opposite. I mean I've nothing against killing calves—
my living, after all, and not one I'm ashamed of,
neither; but I mean I don't think I'd be able to kill one
myself. But if I had to I suppose I would, that's all. If I
really had to. I'd feel perhaps worse than with a man.
I'm sorry, Hil, I know you'd come down on me for
saying that, but what harm's a calf ever done? I'd tell
myself this was a man what had shot a defenseless
friend of mine in the back, I don't care, he did it or he
got it done, or he was there and didn't stop it; he liked
it. And I'd say just shoot him down the same way. I
agree with Arlette, pity she didn't have a gun; then it
would be done and we wouldn't be tormenting ourselves, right?"

"Hilary?"

"I've said it all already, haven't I? I'm sorry, I can't

227

go along with you. I think it's pathological, and I'd maintain that even if there were fifty shrinks shouting the opposite. I just don't see how it could be anything else."

"So what d'you think we should do, then?"

"I don't know," she admitted. "What about you, then?" she said to Bates.

"It seems to me," answered Bates, "I've even more reason than you for saying no. After all, I believe in God and you don't think He exists. I could think of all sorts of arguments about the value of human life, and it being God's justice and mercy that counts, and our having no right to decide because we can't judge, we don't know. It's wrong to kill people, and just because this man killed one of us—well, two wrongs don't make a right. And you'd tell me that what was done in wartime has nothing to do with it, because we are permitted to kill in wartime. But, against all that, I'd still maintain we have a duty to fight for what is right. What had this bad man done to that poor boy to make him take part in such a dreadful act? Evil is all around us. When we don't do something, we share in the guilt. We can *always* find good reasons for saying no. This or that doesn't concern us, or it's the state's duty to act, or whatnot. Well, I believe in a doctrine of personal responsibility, and that's the responsibility I'm willing to take. I say kill him because we've no other means of action; and because I wouldn't think it fair to expect any of you to go against your rightful scruples, I'll come right out and say I'll do it. The man who's dead took risks all his life to protect us, and finally he took a risk too many, and are we going to stand by and say, oh well, that's what he got paid for? No, and no, and no."

They all sat flabbergasted.

"I haven't any gun or anything," the old woman said,

almost comically, "and truly I wouldn't have much confidence in myself if I had. They're not much good anyhow. You need to get very close, and even then there's the risk of hitting somebody innocent, if it isn't just a tree or a house. One would probably get caught too. Not that I'd complain about that. It's another argument—you've all got responsibilities. But I'm no use to anybody."

"So what do you suggest?" said Dan with an oddly humble simplicity. The old woman had not finished astonishing them.

"I'd say," perfectly clear and decided, "a bomb. I don't mean a grenade; they are very dangerous and indiscriminate. But as I've gathered, this—I won't call him man—lives in a flat alone. One could fix a bomb. I would do it. I don't know how to make it, of course, but I believe it's quite easy. These nasty schoolboys are always making bombs—and blowing themselves up, too, poor lambs."

"I know how to make bombs," said Hilary, and even Dan looked at her in astonishment.

"You do?"

"It isn't difficult. I am quite adept at contrivances— as you're fond of saying, 'I'm always hammering at things.' And I've quite a knowledge of the chemicals—I use several of them."

"And you'd make a bomb?" Dan said. "But I thought you said—"

"When I meet someone with the courage to take up a viewpoint with that much honesty," warmly, "and act with the courage of their conviction, and accept all the responsibility of doing so, am I then to have the moral cowardice to say, well, I won't lift a finger except to hinder you? Little you know me, my lad."

"That's settled, then," said Bates with the greatest coolness. "Who'd like some tea?"

Everyone in the heat of discussion had forgotten Arlette. She got up quietly and said, "Not for me. We can't do anything more now, anyway. Do you mind awfully if I go and take a little walk? I feel dreadful. I want to quieten down and come to my senses, and I don't want any supper."

"Of course, pet. We'll keep those lovely kidneys Willy so kindly brought until tomorrow."

She's even planning the cooking, Arlette said to herself. I must get out of here.

She felt almost paralyzed by terror.

Larry Saint was subject to a certain irritability. He had rationalized it well enough; he had it under good control; still, he could not prevent himself getting irked at the insufficiency and incompetence of the tools with which he worked. People were so incredibly stupid! And so slack! The moment his back was turned, they were taking advantage. This flat, now—he paid that woman a very good wage and asked little enough for it. That the place should be kept scrupulously clean, that his clothes and linen be impeccable, that certain indispensable things like flowers or drinks should be kept freshly renewed. And, look at it—dust there, and he could not abide dust.

And this tiresome boy! A good useful lad—one could not really say more, but there, one could not really ask more. The word "excellence" was one of his favorites; he demanded excellence from himself and from his dealings, but was too aware of the frailties and feeblenesses of the people he dealt with to expect more than a result that was passable.

He couldn't really complain—that very mediocrity made his own excellence so manifest. Now that he was beginning to get a bit of capital behind him and learning how to direct the wind into his sails, his excellence was attracting the attention of some really worthwhile people, men of weight, of substance. They had learned that when Larry offered a package for sale the goods were first-class, the delivery punctual to the second, even the packing razor-sharp and surgically neat. Never a careless knot or a loose thread where Larry was concerned. That was the way; they appreciated that; they were like that themselves, and recognized excellence when they saw it. But one had oneself to have a few reliable servants.

He was being too impatient, no doubt. The boy had only had a few months' training, and even though he had been given a few flicks with the whip his dressage was not complete.

Larry sighed. He was fed up with this piddling town, populated by self-satisfied imbeciles. Alas, it was still the source of virtually all his regular income. Nothing wrong with the picture business; Louis was nicely tamed and the boy admirably plastic. Nothing wrong with the little Apples shop—small fry, but a good sturdy little cow. The young had such very simple needs—and paid well for them. But it was petty, and above all time-wasting. His mind was full of projects, some of them beginning to ripen fruitfully—but one must have leisure, a free hand, relief from that petty paperwork. He sighed again; it would take a few more months.

A good little lad. Bright, quick, nicely willing, and even fervent. And charmingly greedy! How he had snapped at a few elementary creature comforts . . . But alarmingly unstable.

Not for the first time. Mr. Saint reflected, going over the chain he had forged to anchor the boy. It had been bold and well executed, but he had never liked the rather excitable and melodramatic course it had taken: inevitable, he supposed. Had it been a bit too radical,

231

the original conception? Yes, but it had formed a pattern, and one had to accommodate oneself to existing patterns. He had taken out plenty of insurance. The important thing had been to make sure that the leak created by the boy should not only be sealed, but sealed in such a way as to cut off all conceivable hesitations, feebleness, or failures the boy might ever be guilty of.

Like this, for instance. Irritating! That the boy should play with women, no objection. A nicely ripened married woman, so much more satisfying than foolish little girls; fine, the boy needed that. She hadn't looked bad, either, from the glimpse he had caught of her. Still, what were these tantrums? He had thought to have the boy well vaccinated against these emotional upheavals; Daisy had seen to that!

Fact is, concluded Mr. Saint, the boy is sloppy. Spilling champagne on the carpet like that. He detested sloppiness; it was like dust, abhorrent to his wish for excellence, to his insistence on really neat packaging. He would crack the whip!

And satisfied, he found a fresh lemon—the cleaning woman hadn't neglected everything, then!—took the bottle of Cuban rum, made himself a daiquiri, sat down comfortably, and picked up the *New York Times:* it was important to perfect his English.

Richard, with clean clothes, damp hair combed back, a chastened expression, and quiet movements, came in, hesitated, moved over to the cupboard, went digging there at the whisky. A waste, that; it was Chivas Regal.

"I don't want you to drink," said Saint mildly from behind his paper.

"It's already poured out." As though he didn't know!

"Very well, then, drink it. But that will be all. I want you clearheaded, for once. Now come and sit down." He folded the paper carefully, laid it aside, gave the boy the glassy eye.

232

"I think you owe me some explanation, don't you? Quite apart from your own behavior, which was lamentable, when I lent you the use of this flat, it wasn't to destroy the furniture by pouring champagne over it. I don't know who that woman was and don't wish to but—"

"Don't you?" shouted the boy. "Don't you?" with violence.

"Quietly, Richard. I gave you time. Not enough, apparently. You're overexcited. Perhaps you're ill. A few days, perhaps, in a clinic. A little narcotic therapy."

"I'll tell you," more quietly. "You need to know. You'll want to know. So I'll tell you who she is."

"Piano, Richard, piano. Still too frenzied. If you have some interesting experiences, tell me by all means, and if they excuse your barbarian behavior, so much the better; you will find me sympathetic."

Dick took a big drink of the mixture of whisky and ice cubes. False maturity gave him an elaborately studied air of sophistication and poise, a ludicrous copy of Saint's way of holding a glass and drinking from it.

"She's the wife of Commissaire van der Valk. Or, to be more accurate, the widow."

The movement, for Saint, was violent. He got out of his chair, walked over to the window, looked out, fiddled with a curtain that was not hanging quite straight, came back, picked up his drink, sipped it, sat on the arm of the chair, and said, "Really. Did you invite her here?"

"She rang at the door. And guess what—she asked for you."

"Really. Well, well, well, well. And further? What then? She made an appeal to your better nature?"

"Look, stop being sarcastic, it doesn't help. I'm telling you, she knows."

"So you poured her out a glass of champagne?"

"That's idiotic. I took her for a friend of yours. Any-one would—can't you see? She asked where you were."

"I see." Saint was regaining control of himself. "Go on."

"So to be polite I asked her in, of course, and offered her a drink, and said I didn't know when you'd be back. And then she said. 'Which of you killed him?'—just like that. And if you can't understand why I spilt the drink . . ."

"So you told her. With, I hope, some degree of accuracy."

The boy's face broke up suddenly, like splintered glass. "I don't know what I said. I mean, I said it was nonsense; I can't recall the exact words I used."

Saint put his glass down slowly, gently, meticulously. "I'm afraid, Richard, that you're going to have reason to regret this."

The boy took another violent swallow of his whisky and slapped the glass down with an air of making his mind up. "Sounds as though you are, too."

"That's a matter of opinion, isn't it now?"

Dick shook his head. "No go, Larry. I've had time to think this out. Whatever I said, and I don't pretend I can have sounded awfully convincing, it was known before."

"What was known before, and just what basis of fact is there in these conclusions of yours?"

"There were two people in the shop today—sepa-rate, I mean, a couple of hours apart. Ordinary man and woman. Both of them, on some pretext or other, mentioned the fellow . . . you know . . . all just casual and by the way. Man was one of these artists, wanting to borrow a picture; he said he'd been by Papenheim. Well, I thought he seemed phony and I rang up Papenheim, who'd never seen him. This fellow

234

asked after you, said to give regards. And then a woman, one of these shopkeeping women, a lot of money and a vulgar accent—she was looking at furniture, had a long tale about—you know—his father was a carpenter or something. I was here thinking it out, going to tell you when I saw you—and she appeared. That's no coincidence."

Saint, a rare thing for him, was mixing a second drink. He turned round and said slowly, "And you, I suppose, were unable to see that this was pure blatant bluff, and began to blush and stammer and fall upon your knees, the way I found you. Unable to see that this was the oldest, stalest, most threadbare police trick in the world."

"They weren't police."

"Really never heard of that one? The trick of picking you up and announcing solemnly that all is known because so-and-so has confessed all?"

"She didn't say anything of the sort—I tell you she just knew."

"She knew nothing, you little cretin. If anybody knew anything, do you suppose for one moment that all this comedy would be played? But you . . . naturally, typical of the little weakling you are, you burst into tears and wring your hands and say, yes, mum, I did it, with my bow and arrow. Or did you endeavor to take cover behind me? Because if you nourish hopes in that direction, Dicky, I may as well say that deep disillusions await you."

The boy took refuge in anger. "No, I bloody well didn't, but suppose I had; what would that be but the simple truth? Who thought it all up in the first place and why? D'you think I don't understand that? To impress me with how smart you are, and how all-powerful, and what a terrific big shot. It was all unnecessary,

235

the fellow was just curious; but, no, you had to be like a Roman emperor or something and say, oh, that fellow irritates me, throw him to the lions; you're just an egomaniac, that's all. Well, I tell you you needn't think I'm going to be any Christian martyr. I tell you they know something; I don't pretend to know how, nor why it all only comes out now, but for all I know—or you either—the police will be knocking on the door any minute, and what will you do then?"

"Ah. You've got it all worked out, have you?"

"I've had time to think, if that's what you mean. If I'm caught, I'm caught."

"And what will you do then?" mildly.

"I don't rat on my pals, if that's what you're suggesting," reddened and trembling. "I'd clam up, and get a lawyer, and just see what they could prove. You always claimed they couldn't prove anything," sullenly, "but how have they come to know, tell me that. They must have got hold of something, some piece of evidence, or they wouldn't be so certain. If there's something points to me, then it points to you, too. If the police pick me up, then they'll pick you up, too, and I'd like to think then that you wouldn't be trying to shuffle it off on me, that's all. You always expect me to trust you, but the way you're acting makes me wonder, that's all, just how far I can trust you."

"Very neat," said Saint, sitting down again calmly, "but since I do not hear the police hammering at the door, although they've had plenty of time to do so, you will forgive me if I suggest your imagination is, as usual, overheated. But just to get it all settled and cut and dried, so that we can both be easy in our minds, let's assume your hypothesis. Very well, the police arrive, and they utter the usual bullshit about there being a supposition that we are both concerned in some ab-

236

surd conspiracy. And, being their ignorant selves, assume further that they can think of nothing but the usual stale trick that's already been played on you—with, as far as I can see, results exceeding all expectation. So that I'm invited to sit down opposite the desk of some pompous little fuzz-head and told portentously that you have admitted everything. What do I do then?"

"If you're even a tenth of what you claim to be," said Richard quietly, "you'd just shrug it off."

"Very good; I'm glad you give me credit for a few brains. So then they go to you, and say—it's the obvious move—that I've named you. And then?"

"I'd treat it as a lie, naturally."

"Ah. But give them credit for a few brains, too. They can be quite cunning. Suppose they fabricate some piece of evidence—that they claim, for instance, that they'd identified some object—the gun, say. As I told you at the time, it's safely out of harm's way. But if they gave you some piece of information that you thought could only have come from me, being only known to me—and, of course, yourself. You see, Dicky, I think ahead. I take my precautions. What then?"

"I'd say, prove it."

"And suppose," maliciously, "that they did."

"You're getting ready to sell me out, aren't you?"

"That, Dicky, is exactly what I suspected you would think. As you see, your nerves are not strong enough for this exercise in the imagination. I quite see that this must be painful to your new-bought self-esteem. You had quite a rapid little climb, didn't you? You were on the street without a penny, and I found you, and gave you a nice cushy job, and you went to parties, and played about with Daisy, and thought yourself quite a boy, and then—when it comes to a pinch—you show

237

yourself a weak sister. Twice now—twice you've compromised me. Third time, as they say, pays for all. And
I—still following our little hypothesis—find myself, for
the third time, in a position which could compromise
me. You don't seriously suppose that I can allow that."

"You are a proper bastard, aren't you? I never asked
for that job—you forced it on me. I thought that trick
with the watch dodgy, and you've never given me a real
reason to suppose it was anything else. You wanted to
show—it's your own words—that killing someone was
just another business deal. You had all those statistics
about road deaths, and earthquakes, and Vietnam, and
that corny old gag about pressing the button and killing
the Chinaman. And *I* was the sucker. All right, if you
push your famous hypothesis that far, and if everything
you say came about—then, no, I wouldn't just take ten
years in prison or whatever, like something out of the
Mafia or—no, I wouldn't lie down for you. You put me
on the hook, I'd fucking well see *you* were on it, too."

Saint, beaming as though given a birthday present,
leaned a little forward, sipped at his drink, looked with
pleasure at his fingernails, and took his time, sadisti-
cally, about answering.

"And there, Dicky, is the point of our little intellectual exercise. There is where I wished to bring you.
Surgery—I once told you that it was important, and I
gave you a proof. That was a physiological example.
There exists also—and now is the time for lesson
number two—a psychic surgery. The patient, in this
instance, is you. Let us hope that you suffer no excessive shock, and that we effect a quick cure."

Richard looked at the smiling face with glazed eyes.
This fellow's bonkers, he thought. He's out of his goddam mind. There are we don't know how many people
who know he killed a man, whatever I did. But he sits
there gassing about shock.

238

"You see, Richard, the police would have much difficulty in accepting that I should have had any hand in such a thing. I am a respected, well-regarded, highly scrupulous businessman. Part owner of an antique business which, you should know by now, is spotlessly virtuous. Owner of a bit of house property, including this building. And there's a sex shop on the ground floor—dear, dear, the old ladies would tut, but there's nothing—nothing—reprehensible about that: on the contrary, we're in the forefront of liberal beliefs. I have, let me put it, an initial right to the incredulity of a court. Now let's descend from the general to the particular—I employ you. Nice, well-spoken, respectable young man, of good antecedents. I employ you—justifiably—in a position of some confidence. One day you have a moment's slip from grace, and you pick up an expensive watch which is—due entirely to my innocent carelessness—hanging about. Now I can't blame you for that: we agree to say no more about it. But it is a tiny slip from grace, let's say, and goes perhaps to show that you aren't entirely reliable. In fact, as I now learn, you go in an oddly roundabout way to a virtually retired police officer, and you spin him a tale. To cover youself, no doubt, and to satisfy your conscience. But it so happens that he begins to take an undue interest in your activities, and since some of these activities—playing about with dancing girls, and the like—might be thought by the more strait-minded a little out of line, you are a little embarrassed. You have access to my flat—dear, dear, that was perhaps unwise of me. I have—with the benefit of hindsight—noticed some unbalanced behavior. What you have subsequently done is, I fear, unknown to me."

"Is it?" jeeringly. "Including, I suppose, driving a car in the streets of The Hague."

Saint was now powered as though by an electric

239

charge. The voltage, an observer might have thought, was now at its height.

"Ah, yes. Now that you remind me. It had never occurred to me to make such a link. Or else, to be sure, I would have been scrupulous in communicating a certain sense of unease to the authorities. Now that I think of it, you did borrow my car around that time."

Dick looked at him quite calmly. "You really think you'll get away with that?"

"My dear boy. Commissaire van der Valk did not even know I existed. I did not even know he existed. But if we need an item of evidence, I might be able to produce one. What, for example, about the gun?"

"There's no print on it," said Dicky tensely. "I saw you myself. You cleaned it and oiled it and wiped it off. I saw you with my own eyes."

Saint sniggered. "Rather a suspicious circumstance, I feel inclined to believe, myself. The police, you see, have a rigid way of thinking. Everybody has read the little detective stories. Even a kitchenmaid knows now that one must wipe off the prints. I fear, Dicky, that a gun with no prints is a rather more suspicious circumstance than one with any amount. You see, since the gun is mine, and I would not deny the fact, one would ordinarily expect to find prints of my hands upon it. Since, of course, the gun lies about in this flat, where you have been making yourself so conspicuously at home in my absence, the absence of your busy little fingers might appear dubious. They are, after all, on everything else."

"And why am I supposed to have killed this man?"

"Well, now," smilingly, "how can I tell that? It's a question for the shrink, conceivably. It might be thought that, having wormed yourself into a very pleasant situation, you were prepared to go to somewhat paranoid lengths to protect it. And over and above all, my boy, there's one overriding factor. Nobody would care very much why you did such a particularly unbalanced thing. The fact is that you did it. Eh?"

Dick stared at him. Jumped up on his feet. Tried to say something, but the words strangled in his throat. "You . . . you . . ."

"Precisely. Now you're going to go running out in a great rage. Very good for you to go and have a quiet stroll. Think it over. Ask yourself whether it really would be so good an idea as you think to try and involve me in your fantasies. One tiny point before you go . . . Since you go storming out of here in a great state, I will naturally have the locks changed—a simple affair of self-preservation. Since you feel a magnified sense of grievance, do recall, won't you, that this provides an added incentive for you to be thinking up malicious tales and rumors. Even to go accusing me of things. Even to start imagining they were true. The disgruntled-employee syndrome, with the paranoid features already noticed." Saint's warm, happy chuckle of enjoyment. "My poor lad, it would be like jumping head first down the well—an approved form of suicide in medieval times.

"No, Dicky," in his friendliest tone, "be advised by someone of more experience than yourself. Take a nice, long, quiet walk—it's a fine evening. Don't dramatize the situation. If this woman, or any of these other absurd comedians, makes a further appearance, you may be well advised to let me handle them. And, Richard . . . avoid the adolescent temptation to melodrama. You might be attracted by some emotionally satisfying scheme like jumping down the well and leaving a cunning little note behind—just recall that

241

cutting off your nose in order to spite your face is not going to improve your features. Put your jacket on. Have a pleasant stroll. Remind yourself that you are a young man of promise. That you have your foot upon a ladder leading to fortune. That you only have to keep your nerve. Oh, and by the way, Dick—should you find any of these zealous seekers after retribution hanging about, since they seem to be dogging your path—you'll remember what I told you, won't you? No more little fits of hysterics—the one is reparable, and you can safely leave me to deal with it. But a few more unguarded outpourings of your sensitive nature, and one might not be able to guarantee quite so optimistic a prognosis. Bear it in mind."

Dick was sitting with quiet docility, the strained wild look gone from his face. He looked soothed and reassured. "Well, you've got me in a basket, haven't you?"

"True, but that's not the way to look at it. A basket can be a very comfortable conveyance. You've done well, Dick; you've got promise. Accept the idea of a setback here and there; accept that there is a price to pay for all success. Instead of getting tangled in these childish guilt feelings, turn your energies toward advancement. And learn patience, Dick. Take a leaf out of old Louis's book."

"Huh?" The boy was surprised.

"Yes, yes," nodding gently. "I'm not going to give away any little family secrets, and you needn't waste time in speculation. He's an old man now. Looked up to. Admired. Respected. Has a very pleasant existence. Could have had a great deal more, but had no ambition. Patience. Objectivity. The ability to accept small constraints. And you're a very young man. You can go a great deal further. There, I've given you a few themes for meditation. Buzz off now, Dick, like a good boy; I want to be left in peace."

The boy got up and walked to the door, turned with his hand on the knob, and said, "But if these people come hanging round the shop——?"

Saint was giving an example now of patience. He looked up from the *New York Times,* which seemed again to be getting his full attention, and said calmly, "I'll be spending a few days in the shop, Dicky. Don't worry about anything at all. You know that you can rely upon me. You understand that it won't be in my interest to get myself lumbered with these well-meaning persons who have imaginary grievances. I'll get that tidied up. You can relax completely. And in a little while—you've been working very hard, and it is natural that you should be feeling the results of overstrain a little—you can start making plans for a really delightful holiday. There—I've given you a few serious subjects for thought. There's a more pleasant one for your mind to occupy itself. Off you go now." And with perfect docility, the boy opened the door and closed it softly behind him. Saint listened till he heard the thump of the street door below, smiled, put down the paper, and began carefully to mix himself another drink.

There is something comic, almost preposterous, about the idea of those two human beings walking on a fine spring evening around the pavements of Amsterdam, working on the same problem, unaware of each other. They both tacked to and fro undecidedly, something like two chess players on a problem. Now and then, one would pick up a queen, or a knight, and move it thoughtfully to a new square, ponder for a moment, shake his head, and put it back. If so, then so, and if not so, then also so. Difficult. But they were not playing against each other, and there was plenty of time. It was only eight-thirty. All night ahead of them. And though both had had a long day, and had suffered a

243

nervous crisis, both had reserves of nervous energy, and were not yet wearied out. They came, several times, quite close to each other at street crossings without ever actually meeting. Even if they had met, they might not have noticed; both saw very little of what was going on around them. As for Mr. Saint, uppermost in both minds, he was working in very much the same way. He had been going to go out, and phoned to cancel the appointment. He made himself comfortable, instead, with a tin of jellied duck, for, like a prudent man, he always had something in the refrigerator. Afterward he made himself a cup of coffee with his little Vesuvius machine, and glanced over the street from the darkened window of his bedroom before drawing the curtains and going back to the brightly shimmering comfortable living room, gay with sprays of flowers and reflections from the many mirrors, where he stirred his coffee thoughtfully and began to walk softly up and down, preoccupied with the pattern of his carpet and moving chess pieces here and there across it, his hands in his pockets, according to his habit, fingering and turning pieces of small change between his supple fingers.

Louis Prinz was not a very old man; he was only just past sixty and in good sound health. But he had had a long day, driving back all the way from Belgium: four weary hours in the seat of a car had given him a nagging fatigue, and a certain amount of dull pain which, he suspected uncomfortably, could be due to his prostate. He had been to look at a picture that might—just might—have been by Roger van der Weyden and be worth trouble with the prostate. He had been pretty sure in advance that it wasn't and, after looking at it, felt quite satisfied that it was a good seventy years later, just for a start, but he had bought it. One bought anything from that period, and only too pleased to have it. The price was high, and might have been a great deal higher but that it was, as he pointed out, quite unattributed. A simple matter: he kept such pictures for several years, so that he could never be accused of speculation. Meanwhile, he would gather a body of responsible opinion, which would quite certainly not be wasted. The panel was warped, and much of the paint terribly shaky and fragile, and in a couple of places exceedingly badly restored with crude overpainting, but he knew a very good man to see to such things.

On the way back, he had called at three houses from which people had written to him, saying they possessed seventeenth-century candlesticks, a ruby necklace (the collar of Prester John, to hear them talk!), and a Rubens. The one was nineteenth-century plate, but early, pretty, and not worn at all, so that no copper showed—but of course the marks told one at once. The second was heavy but finely set Victorian garnets, lovely craftsmanship—modish stuff, too, now. The third was small and woolly but of the period—their guess hadn't been so bad after all; came from the studio, he thought. He had bought the lot—not at all a bad day.

He had even picked up some china. When in a house, it was always a good rule to be extremely thorough and rummage through the attic since one was there anyhow. They had thought nothing of it at all, but it was famille verte, and a piece or two not even chipped.

In the rush hour on the road outside Amsterdam, he had pulled off to let the flood go by, and had had something to eat. Imitation Indonesian—oh well, it was healthier to eat rice than those detestable fried potatoes. No lover of golf, he found it difficult to get enough exercise, but inside the city of Amsterdam he walked everywhere, and that kept his stomach within bounds. He wasn't old! Still had that powerful appetite for little girls . . . Had had to keep the taste for very little girls within careful bounds since the extremely unpleasant epsiode from which he had only got extracted by the help of that— No, he had learned that it was no use calling the fellow names. A dreadful fellow, and indeed, Louis had decided more recently, a damned unpleasant piece of work. But at least he respected the agreement, and left one in peace. He showed signs nowadays of losing all interest in the business—except, of course, for his cut in the dividend; he didn't neglect that! My god, his own sister's son . . . No real family blood; knew nothing whatever about art. Monetary values—oh, yes, hot on that; could always tell you what a similar piece had fetched at Christie's six months ago. Was showing signs now of wiping the Amsterdam dust off his elegant shoes—good thing, too. By all means, go to wherever it was—Louis didn't know. Saint-Tropez or somewhere, he wouldn't be a bit surprised. And welcome . . . He'd got that boy installed. Seemed to think the lad trustworthy . . . Well, he was, on the whole. Bright and smart and energetic. Knew absolutely nothing, but that, by and large, might be an advantage. A well set-up young fellow, presentable, and—what was a rarity nowadays— nice manners. Called him by his first name—"Louis," as bold as brass, instead of sir—but they all did nowadays. What he liked about the boy was a certain sensitivity. Not really a feeling for art, but at least a notion of what was beautiful, what was honorable. He himself was dishonorable, but not about art. . . . Bosboom had understood that. He regretted Bosboom very much indeed; they had respected each other. This boy was a whippersnapper, but he did seem prepared to learn, to

246

wish to understand. He didn't think he knew it all already, like Larry. Larry! Wasn't Leopold an honest enough name for him, then? It had been good enough for the old King of the Belgians, a much-abused man. It hadn't been his fault that Astrid had died! And when invaded by those Germans, just look at the way the French had behaved! Gave one a respect for a monarchy. But they'd no one like old Wilhelmina now. "The man of the family," Churchill had called her. Still, Juliana was a good woman, a fine woman. He didn't regret coming back. He hadn't liked Washington. Fine pictures there, though . . . Oh, he was tired. He put the car away. The big Citroën Safari station wagon was an impossible thing in towns, and most of all in this once—this town had been progressively ruined, from the moment that ghastly burgomaster had taken the decision to fill in the Rozengracht—but it was a damn fine car on the road. And you could get anything into it—right up to one of those great massive rustic armoires. The cabinetmakers gave good money for those nowadays—cannibalized the wood. That was an old tradition. As far back as before the war, he recalled, there was a cabinetmaker in one of those little streets in the Pijp who used to copy Empire and even eighteenth-century pieces in old wood. What was his name? Nice old man, wonderful craftsman. Van der Velde, Van der Vliet—he couldn't recall. It was so very long ago. Amsterdam had changed so utterly, and was it the loss of the Jews? That extraordinary ant heap around the Waterlooplein, or the Jonas Daniel Meijerplein—there's a good honest name for you. Those Amsterdam Jewish names . . . Komkommer, Augurkiesman! Why, when he was a boy, one of his first girls had been called Bloometje Visschoonmaker! Little Flower Fish-Cleaner!

247

Louis went up his stairs, puffing now and heavy, fumbled with the landing light, the flat-door key, took off his coat, washed his hands, and went to the lavatory—reminded again, unpleasantly, of his prostate gland. One would have to go to Sussman for that—oh well, there were still good doctors in the world. It wasn't a difficult or dangerous operation nowadays. He set down the Flemish painting with great care. That panel is ready to split, and the paint is loose as hell. And it's a very well-made piece, with a lovely feeling. Just look at that little Rubenesque canvas. Not bad—the draperies are quite well painted. But trash, by comparison with the other.

The flat was very still. His old housekeeper was long since gone. In the kitchen, he found an apple tart—dear old girl, she wanted to give him pleasure, and knew how he loved apple tart. He would have a piece of that.

And suddenly the street-door bell went. What was that? He never had visitors. Except for girls, and they came by appointment! A mistake, no doubt. He moved over to the speak box set by the kitchen door, pressed the switch, and said heavily, still a scrap out of breath from the steep stairs, "Who is that?"

"Richard." Distorted by the microphone, the boy's voice sounded breathy and squeaky; for a moment, indeed, Louis found himself wondering who Richard was. Devil take it, he was in no mood to be bothered with nonsense.

"Mm," grudgingly. "Come on up, then." He pushed the release button for the street door in no very sweet frame of mind. Tiresome boy! He went to open the flat door and was shocked at the strained, haggard face.

"Hallo, Richard—what's up? Something gone wrong with the shop?"

"No—no—but can I see you, Mr. Prinz? It's more

'. . . it's more—" The voice shot up and down alarmingly.

Louis scratched the back of his neck. "All right, Richard, all right, go on in. You just caught me—I'm hardly back ten minutes."

"I know—I tried earlier."

"Sit down, boy, then—cool off." The boy did cool off, heaven be thanked. The luxurious shabbiness of the room, the rather stuffy atmosphere, Louis's solid, bulky presence, his trick of brushing along his mustache with a big square forefinger seemed to have a sedative effect that took hold at once. What began as a jerky uncoordinated gabble, with sudden shifts in time, resolved itself all at once into a coherent narrative which kept Louis still and silent until the flow exhausted itself. By then he had not only grasped the situation but knew—it was inevitable—what he had to do. The tale was lunatic—but the boy wasn't. Saint, on the other hand, probably was. With this conclusion, he got up and padded over to the decanter; it was nearly empty and he had to go to the corner cupboard for a full bottle. His conclusion was unexpectedly verified.

"I think he's off his head," Dick offered suddenly, to his back.

Louis turned round slowly. He knew the story was all true. He uncapped the bottle, poured himself a half glass of whisky. "I see. And you come to me. Well, that was quite right."

"You're being very patient," said the boy with a half smile. "He said you were, too. He said I should copy you and be patient."

"Do you know what he meant?"

"No."

"Hmm." He drank some whisky slowly. "I do, though."

"What?" with a touching naïveté.

249

"You'll probably learn, before very long," said the man grimly. "Very well, Richard, you've told me. Put your mind at rest. There's nothing more you can do. I'll handle this." He sat down again heavily, finished the whisky, staring over the rim of the glass at nothing; fell silent.

"You don't think I ought to go—to the police, I mean?" timidly.

Louis came back with a start. "The police—no. Or at least—not yet. You've shown me confidence, Richard, and I'm very grateful. This is your business, too. But will you now trust me further—will you allow me to handle this my own way?"

"Yes—yes, of course. But what am I to do? I mean now." Louis had lit a cigar; it was not drawing very well. He puffed at it, took it out and looked at it with mild annoyance. Wrapper cracked—he threw it away.

"Got any money?"

"Some."

"Go to a hotel. Stay the night. Do nothing. Just go to the shop as usual, in the morning. Open it up as usual. You'll see me very shortly afterward. I'll tell you then what I think best."

"Very well," much relieved. "Er—could I have a drink?"

"I'm sorry. Yes, of course. Help yourself. By the way—you still got the keys?"

"Of the flat? Yes. But he said he'd change the locks, though he probably didn't mean that. I think he feels sure of my coming back."

"He does, yes. But give them to me, would you?" Boy looked as though he were only too glad to get rid of them.

"Suppose he's put the bolt on?"

"Why, then," said Louis reasonably, "I'll ring the bell."

250

"Mr. Prinz . . . what about that woman?"

"Never mind about the woman," testily. "I've no doubt I'll know how to find her. Go on now, Richard," impatiently, "I've a lot to do. Go to the movies." He managed to give the boy a smile, tapped him on the shoulder, assumed a hearty tone. "No further worries for now. Don't bother. I'm an old man—I've seen more queer things in the course of my life. Just leave it to me." The boy got up uncertainly. "Everything will be all right," said Louis with a confidence that surprised him.

Left alone, Louis drank another glass of whisky. It was all quite clear now. He no longer felt tired. He thought for a while, looking around the room and scratching the back of his neck, before padding over to a big régence commode. He opened the bottom drawer and scrabbled about. Awful lot of junk in here. Smoke was getting in his eye; he took the cigar out of his mouth and laid it carefully in an ashtray. There ought to be an oilcan somewhere; now where had he seen that last?

When the doorbell rang, Larry Saint was not surprised; he had been half-expecting something of the sort.

"Yes?" into the speak box.

"Is that Mr. Saint?" Not the boy—the woman! His smile got broader.

"In person."

"This is Mrs. van der Valk. Do I need to introduce myself?"

"One moment, please—I'll be right down." He had blocked the street-door lock, because the little Dicky-boy still had keys, and there were plans made for the little Dicky-boy. But he was glad to see the woman—he'd been wondering where she'd got to! "So sorry,

251

Mevrouw. I was expecting no further visitors. But you don't disturb me at all. Would you like to come upstairs? You know the way, I believe, but permit me to go first. There we are. Do please sit down. And to answer your question—no, you don't need to introduce yourself. It is, I'm afraid, rather belated of me, but I have found out who you are and why you are here. And you must permit me—again, I fear, very late in the day—to offer you my most sincere sorrows and sympathies."

Arlette sat down, where she had been sitting that evening—only three hours before: what a lot had happened since. Or perhaps not that much. Theology! It had taken her far too long to understand that she was responsible for her own sins—not those of other people. And now that she had reached the final step, she wasn't frightened, or confused, or even nervous.

"May I offer you something to drink?"

"Thank you."

"Then a cigarette?"

"If I may, yes." He lit it for her, eyes all shiny and delighted. I wouldn't put anything past him, she thought. Not even his trying to seduce me. She looked at him, remotely puzzled. Hilary says mad. Bates says wicked. Intoxicated, she explains it, by evil. I don't know. Maybe he takes some kind of dope. They say dope is dangerous—it blurs the distinction between sanity and dottiness to such an extent that nobody can tell. No interest to me. Psychology explains nothing any more. I haven't even any philosophic basis for what I am going to do. Just theology. And I fear that I am a very poor theologian.

"You must try and forgive my stupidity," Saint was saying easily. "Sometimes we cannot see what is under our nose. And I felt sure that the police would quickly

252

identify their target. You wouldn't like a cup of coffee? No; you're certain? As I was saying, it simply never occurred to me and everybody will be finding me very simple-minded."

This, thought Arlette in slow motion, is Neil's son of woeful Assynt. She knew nothing of the personage at all. Save what Van der Valk had told her—that he betrayed the Marquis of Montrose.

"Mr. Saint," she said. "Your life is forfeit."

"I beg your pardon?"

"Your life," she said distinctly, "is in my hands. I have thought carefully. I must give it back to you—I have no choice."

"I am afraid," Saint was saying, with raised eyebrows, "that I do not understand you."

"No. Well, I'll explain. Legal processes, we think, cannot grip you. We don't know. I suppose that the police, and the tribunal, and the Officer of Justice, and all the rest, could give you a lot of trouble. I haven't much interest in all that, I fear. My husband was a professional and knew how to bring people to book. You killed him. I do not know why. Some people think that you are mad. Others say that you are merely wicked. I do not care. You seem to be clever. You seem, too, to be quite confident that human justice cannot touch you. Again, I do not know. If I am to believe what I heard this evening, you are able to pin the responsibility on a boy. Whether you can or not seems to me unimportant. I did not know what to do, so I took the advice of my friends. They wish to kill you."

Saint had assumed an expression of wide-eyed, faintly horrified amazement. Can there really be such lunatics at large, he seemed to be thinking. Arlette, indifferent to the effect she was causing, continued stubbornly.

"Yes, Mr. Saint. A friend of mine has proposed simply killing you, to rid the world of a threat. How? Because one can say one would like to kill someone, and indeed it is very easy, because human life is very cheap, but to carry it out is a more serious matter. I will tell you. My friend has done it before. She is a very decided, single-minded, competent, and efficient person. Once before—long ago—she threw a grenade at a man. It was during the war. A high officer of sorts in the Sicherheitsdienst, here in Amsterdam, in what was then called the Euterpestraat, of evil memory. And now she is prepared to do it again. She is perhaps—no, not mad, but there is a monomania. When you have done a thing like that, you see, Mr. Saint, it marks you for life. You are too young to know that. I am perhaps ten or fifteen years older than you—I was a schoolgirl in France, but I know how such things are done, and how such decisions are taken. This is why I understand this mentality. But we are not at war. You will probably not understand when I say that I could not accept this, because it seemed to me philosophically wrong. To blow you up, Mr. Saint, is perhaps a right and just action; I cannot tell. You planned and carried out a cold-blooded assassination. My husband. I thought about that for a very long time, and I think I went mad myself. But I cannot accept this."

Saint was sitting very still. His smooth intelligent forehead was entirely covered with a fine beading of sweat. Arlette saw this, and was pleased that he was frightened, and ashamed of herself for being pleased.

"You are frightened. Well you may be. I passed you on the stairs here this afternoon and I wanted to kill you. In my house in France, I have two rifles that belonged to my husband. And two pistols. If I had had any of them under my hand, then, I would have killed you. So that I can understand my friend. I can take it seriously. That is why I say to you that your life is forfeit. And also it is the reason why I come to you now, and warn you. Your life does not belong to me. I must give it to you. You must live with what you have done. I see that you do not understand that. You think this is a trick. A trap. That is your mind. You will live your entire life in misery, because you are cowardly and treacherous. My husband, before you killed him, had understood that. He wrote it down. That has led me to you. Now I am going. I have made up my mind. I am going to the police. They have not yet understood you as I have understood you. But when I tell them, they will. I do not know what they can do. I do not care. It is their affair. Or, I should say, yours. You can run away; I am indifferent. You can try to hide behind this boy. He spoke to me, and I know he is not guilty, and I will say so."

She had rehearsed her words so carefully. She had been word-perfect. She was in complete control. Only now did she lose her command, standing now and looking at Saint.

"You have a gun, I think. You can try and kill me." And suddenly in anger she took a step forward toward him. "Try, you little traitor to human existence. Try. Spoiled tree of the rotten apples. I'm going from here to the police. You will perhaps try to stop me. You are free. Do so."

Arlette turned toward the door to go. Standing there quietly in front of the door, leaning against it, was Louis Prinz.

Arlette had never seen him. She did not know who he was. Fright had nothing to do with it. The physiological shock was so great that she gave an enormous, terrifying, tearing great scream. Saint, who had jumped out of his chair in an insane gesture, and whose hands were stretched to catch her throat, fell back against the chair arm as if he were shot.

Louis was holding a revolver. A woman's pistol made about 1910—6.35-millimeter, what the Americans call a .25 caliber. A silver-plated pistol with rococo decorations. The cylinder, instead of being chased, was ornamented with cherubs, like repoussé work on toilet-table accessories of the period—a hand mirror, for example. The narrow part of the stock, above the butt and below the hammer—which itself was erotically modeled, in the shape of a man's penis—was plain. The barrel, modeled in the shape of a concave hexagon, pointed at Saint.

"Stay still," said Louis, "or I'll shoot you." Saint, tallow-colored, stayed still.

"I heard you, Madame. Forgive me for eavesdropping." It was so ridiculous that Arlette began a hysterical laugh, stopped herself, opened her handbag, took out a paper tissue, and wiped her face. She was as sweaty as Saint. The inconsequent automatic gesture brought her back to sanity. The tissue smelt of Roger & Gallet eau de Cologne. Her husband had always used it.

"Madame," began Louis with old-fashioned formality. He was confused. He didn't know who to speak to. "You," he said to Saint. "You. My own sister's son. You. You have blackmailed me for ten years. And I— God forgive me, I was frightened—allowed it. You have tried to blackmail that poor wretched boy. He came to me, God permitting. He told me everything. I had to act. I had this pistol," looking at it as though it would, when the trigger was pressed, shoot out a little fan, as in the Feydeau farce *Un Fil à la patte*. This resemblance struck Louis.

256

"I was going to kill you, just like Madame here was going to kill you. I came in quietly. The boy gave me his keys. You had forgotten to block the locks. I was going to kill you and arrange it to look like a suicide before I told the boy to go to the police. But now I have heard what Madame van der Valk said to you. And I have you now, you ordure. I have a thread, tied to your leg. And you will not escape. I will testify. Stay still, you filth. I will shoot you in the stomach and in the spine, and you will live the rest of your miserable life paralyzed. The gun is here—the boy told me. Cleaned. But in your possession." Louis reached into his pocket, fetched out an enormous white linen handkerchief, and wiped his face, keeping the pistol pointed at Saint.

"Madame," said Louis with his formal politeness. "Will you go, please, and get the police? The bureau is on the Westerstraat. I will keep this—my nephew Leopold—quiet. Tenu en respect." How odd the French words sounded. Arlette, who found herself in a breath again the silly woman being told what to do by a responsible man, did what she was told. At this time of night, since it was too early for drunks, whores, or hippies, the police station was beautifully quiet.

"I am Mevrouw van der Valk. No, that means nothing to you. The wife of Commissaire van der Valk."

"Oh!"

"Who was assassinated."

"Oh!"

"And we have found the assassin. Will you come, please?"

"Mevrouw . . . one moment, please . . . excuse me, please. . . . Brigges!"

An Amsterdam police sergeant has the title of brigadier. He was enormous—bones of a brewery horse. Slab-sided, rock-ribbed. One meter ninety-two.

257

That is six feet five. He would have made a second-row forward for the All Black rugby team. He was chewing orange-flavored gum.

"Mevrouw . . ."

"Sir . . . please put down that gun. And I'll be wanting to know today or tomorrow how you come to be in possession of that offensive weapon. Now . . . you . . ."

Saint, with unexpected speed and agility, made an attack. Feet kicked. A fist landed stingingly under the nose. A hand clawed. The mouth spat and bit.

The brigadier spread his immense boots apart, parried a scratch, brought the bottom of a fist down upon a forehead, picked Saint up by the neck and the crotch, lifted him about a foot, and set him down again with such a clonk that he staggered and sat down.

"You be quiet. Mevrouw, you'll have to come and see the inspector. Mijnheer, you'll give me that firearm, if you please, and you'll please come, too. My," looking at the silver pistol, "that's pornography, that is."

Arlette would have got the giggles but she felt too drained.

"My dear . . . I've been worried: I couldn't think where you might have got to. I feel quite relieved; would you like some cocoa?"

"I'm sorry," said Arlette penitently, "I ought to have thought. Yes, I would rather. I've been to see Saint."

"You didn't!"

"I had to. You see, doing something like that . . . I couldn't let you . . . I had to do it myself. I hope you'll forgive me."

"But, my dear . . . what have you done?"

258

"Nothing much. Told him where I stood. And where he stood. Somebody came in . . . I don't know, but I think he might have tried to kill me."

"Oh, my dear—that's what I was afraid of."

"I went for the police. A large, utterly stolid man— in the end, that's what we needed. We'd all gone quite dotty, you know? A massive great brigadier, who be- haved exactly as though he were separating two scream- ing housewives."

Bates meditated. "Funny. I mean I'd thought I was being sensible. Damn, the milk's boiled over. Like me. Dotty old fool. You're right, of course."

"I mean I started all this. I couldn't let you and the others . . . in wartime, of course, then you had no choice. The police—either frightened or paralyzed. But now—it seemed bad theology. . . ."

"Yes."

"I thought—my husband, I mean; he wouldn't have let either of us get loose. I was ready to kill that man, and I thought, I can't let you. And the police: we all thought them useless, but I mean, it's the best one can do."

"My poor pet. And I was wanting to help you."

"But so you did."

Despite everything, one had to laugh. The de Vries version of theology . . . When they confessed, later, Arlette did laugh.

"I say, Hilary—you're not really going to make a bomb, are you?"

"Oh, don't be stupid. I had to say something, didn't I?"

"I've been thinking all evening," said Dan. "I've about made up my mind. I don't suppose you'll like it, but I'm going to the police."

Hilary astonished him by looking extremely relieved.

"You mean you agree?" asked Dan, not quite believing it.

"But of course."

"I mean one hates to. Against all one's principles, somehow. But I don't see we've any choice."

"I may as well admit," confessed Hilary. "If you hadn't—I would."

"Without telling me?" shocked.

"Oh, I suppose I would have eventually, screwing myself up."

"You think she really threw a bomb, the old dear?"

"Oh, yes. I would have, too—that is to say, I don't know whether I'd have had the courage. She has. Think—get killed on the spot, or get arrested knowing you'd be shot the next day. But one does what one has to. The difference is, we'd sit there hesitating. She wouldn't."

"We'd better not hesitate any longer now."

"Shall we go together?" asked Hilary timidly.

"I wonder if we've been forestalled," said Dan. "Did you notice Arlette?"

"Slipping out like that, all white? Yes, I saw. But it's her right, you know. One couldn't stop her."

"You think she's done something melodramatic?" stopping, worried, outside the police station.

"We can't help that," said Hilary firmly. "Everyone has their own responsibilities."

"I feel an awful fool," said Dan.

"You can't help that, either."

"What the hell am I going to say?"

"You're not waiting for me to tell you, I trust."

Dan looked at what he was fond of calling "his abominable female" without pleasure and walked up the steps. A uniformed policeman, sitting in an agreeable fug behind his switchboard, yawned and pushed the glass shutter back.

"My name is de Vries," said Dan in a mumble. "This is my wife."

"What? Speak up."

"I wish to get as quickly as may be into contact with whoever's in charge here. I have some important and urgent information."

"On what subject?"

"The assassination of Commissaire van der Valk."

"You being funny or what? How many more of you?"

"What do you mean?" furiously, "being funny?"

"Stop fooling about, man," said Hilary in her Prince Consort voice.

"Sir!"

"What is it now?" asked the night-duty inspector crossly.

"Two people with information—they say—about the Van der Valk killing."

The inspector stared, made an effort in front of his subordinate to swallow incredulity, fluster, and harassment, but could not stop a poisoned glance of utter detestation across the room. In one corner were sitting Trix and Willy, wearing expressions of righteous stupidity. In the corner opposite, Louis Prinz and Saint were looking very fatigued. Between them, a large-size uniformed policeman was staring with tranquil indifference at his own boots. At another desk across the room, the big brigadier was tying labels to the trigger guards of a small antique silver-mounted revolver and a 9-millimeter Luger pistol.

"Bring them in, then," crossly, "and wait here with them." He got up and went into the inner office, sat

261

down heavily behind the commissaire's desk, picked up the telephone, and said "Headquarters."

"It is expedient," I said with gloomy pomp, "that a man die for the sake of the people."

"It has to be voluntary, though, doesn't it?" said Arlette.

"I suppose—uh?" I felt thick and muddled. I poured out some whisky, aware I'd had too much already.

"Shooting someone, or hanging them, or guillotining them—it just arouses nausea. And it helps nobody. Whereas Max Kolbe—"

"Who's he?"

"Oh, stop being so dense. Max Kolbe was the Polish priest at Auschwitz who walked out and volunteered when they were taking hostages. They're making a saint out of him."

"We need one."

"They starved him for a fortnight and then got impatient because he wasn't dead yet. So the injection of carbolic acid."

"I remember now," I said, belatedly, as usual. "He laughed."

"Yes," said Arlette, "and it had more effect than a million deaths."

I woke up with a jolt.

"My man," she said calmly, "I saw him lying there on the ground in the rain. And he had a contented look. As though he knew that, after all, it hadn't all been wasted."

Yes.

## ABOUT THE AUTHOR

NICOLAS FREELING was born in London and raised in France and England. After his military service in World War II, he traveled extensively throughout Europe, working as a professional cook in a number of hotels and restaurants. His first book, *Love in Amsterdam,* was published in 1961. Since then, he has written seventeen novels and two non-fiction works. His most recent books have been *Gadget,* a novel of suspense, and the fourth Henri Castang novel, *The Night Lords.* Mr. Freeling was awarded a golden dagger by the Crime Writers in 1963, the Grand Prix de Roman Policier in 1965, and the Edgar Allen Poe Award of the Mystery Writers Association in 1966.

Mr. Freeling lives in France with his wife and their five children.